HURRICANE

PHANTOM QUEEN DIARIES BOOK 9

SHAYNE SILVERS
CAMERON O'CONNELL

CONTENTS

Shayne Silvers & Cameron O'Connell

Hurricane

The Phantom Queen Diaries Book 9

A TempleVerse Series

ISBN 13: **978-1-947709-37-9**

© 2019, Shayne Silvers / Argento Publishing, LLC

info@shaynesilvers.com

SHAYNE AND CAMERON

Shayne Silvers, here.

Cameron O'Connell is one helluva writer, and he's worked tirelessly to merge a story into the Temple Verse that would provide a different and unique *voice*, but a complementary *tone* to my other novels. *SOME* people might say I'm hard to work with. But certainly, Cameron would never...

Hey! Pipe down over there, author monkey! Get back to your writing cave and finish the next Phantom Queen Novel!

Ahem. Now, where was I?

This is book 9 in the Phantom Queen Diaries, which is a series that ties into the existing TempleVerse with Nate Temple and Callie Penrose. This series could also be read independently if one so chose. Then again, you, the reader, will get SO much more out of my existing books (and this series) by reading them all in tandem.

But that's not up to us. It's up to you, the reader.

You tell us...

WHAT'S A GODDESS TO DO?

After being lost at sea and taken prisoner by yet another denizen of the Titan realm, Quinn finds herself cold, wet, miserable, and very much alone. Until a familiar and unexpected face steps back into her life to remind her who she is—and has always—been: a fighter. Following this revelation, Quinn can only acknowledge that some journeys require circuitous routes, even if that means attaining her freedom and rushing—not to the rescue of her besieged allies—but to the mythical island of Aeaea, home to the infamous witch, Circe, where Quinn will be confronted with cryptic visions of the present and a brutal choice: to sacrifice everything she is on the altar of what she could become, or to continue stumbling around in the dark.

No matter her decision, Quinn knows she must see order restored to the Eighth Sea if she hopes to save her friends and allies. But at what price? The answer to that could cost Quinn her very humanity and will reveal stark truths about her role in the war to come. A war her father predicted and, apparently, prepared for. A war which has already begun to claim the lives of those she cares about and will likely claim many more before all is said and done.

But, before she can worry about any of that, Quinn must go to battle against her old friend and nemesis, rescue her besieged friends, and honor her end of a lopsided bargain—a task which will pit Quinn against her wildest nightmares and her darkest dreams with just one person at her side...a certain mouthy wizard from St. Louis—Nate Temple.

The waters get even murkier as Quinn gets caught in a current that draws her closer and closer to the secrets which surround Atlantis, to the gates of the Underworld and the lost souls which lie beyond, and to the mysterious figure of her father, a wizard so powerful he defied time itself.

Some people like to say that when it rains, it pours. But then they must never have met Quinn MacKenna...because in her case it's always hurricane season.

DON'T FORGET! VIP's get early access to all sorts of Temple-Verse goodies, including signed copies, private giveaways, and advance notice of future projects. AND A FREE NOVELLA! Click the image or join here: www.shaynesilvers.com/l/38599

FOLLOW and LIKE:

Shayne's FACEBOOK PAGE

Cameron's FACEBOOK PAGE

We try our best to respond to all messages, so don't hesitate to drop us a line. Not interacting with readers is the biggest travesty that most authors can make. Let us fix that.

The nose-wrinkling odor of rusted iron mingled with the briny aroma of the sea, undercut by the musk of wet leather and the reek of rotting fish, filled my nose. Perpetually wet, my hair lay lank across the nape of my neck like a dead animal, and it was all I could do not to retch all over my boots. Of course, if I did, I knew the fetor would only get worse, adding some congealed icing to the already moldy cake. My mute guards—ethereal women with luminescent skin covered in various patterns of iridescent scales, hair like matted seaweed and soulless, pupilless eyes—had fed me nothing but raw fish for days, now; I'd never thrown up seafood before, but I sincerely doubted regurgitated sashimi would improve the bouquet.

Naturally, it didn't help that the walls of my cell—an aperture so narrow it would barely have fit two of me standing side-by-side—were eternally slick with condensation, the stone sweating even as I huddled on the ground, my knees drawn up, my tailbone aching where it pressed against the unforgiving floor. I'd learned to sleep like that, my head hanging over my folded arms, crunched and freezing. But then, cold had become my new normal; I'd woken up shivering in this hellish place day after day since falling unconscious beneath the waves, uncertain of whether I'd survived, or this was actually some horrific afterlife—the beginning of my eternal punishment.

In order to distract myself from that awful possibility, I dwelled instead on memories of what had happened in those final moments leading up to my captivity, as well as the days which preceded them. Indeed, it seemed I had nothing better to do but play them out again and again in my mind, to experience each recollection anew, re-examining my emotions and sensations like trying to distinguish complex flavors with my tongue.

I felt them reaching for me even now, drawing me away from my oppressive cell with a siren call as tantalizing as what I'd expected to hear when I first sailed through the storm into the Eighth Sea—otherwise known as the Titan realm. I welcomed the diversion; anything to be away from the stink of this putrid place. And so, I dwelt on the weight of Typhon's monstrous gaze, the sheer vastness of his existence, and how it had felt like looking up at a starlit sky, struck by the infinite nature of an apathetic universe. Other faces, other gazes, soon beckoned. The uncertain, crystal blue eyes of James Pan tracking me as I crossed the deck of his ship, his dark hair twisting in the wind. Tiger Lily's fierce, predatory smile, her death mask splashed across her face like a promise. Narcissus, fretfully washing his ink-stained palms with the intensity of a cat licking itself clean. Tinkerbell holding a blade with my blood on it, her pink glow so faint I thought an errant gust might blow it out. Helen of Troy, staring up at the sky beneath the shadows of her cowl, her intentions as obscure and indecipherable as her expression.

From there my mind tackled larger scenes, each surfacing haphazardly as though my brain was a novel being shuffled through and read piecemeal, my emotional states bite-sized and easily consumed. Greeting the Laestrygonians and that first blush of optimism. Being ambushed by naked giants, my heart racing. Sailing the Jolly Roger, feeling ironically adrift. Sailing the Crow Boat, feeling deflated. Staring out at a graveyard of ships, but more concerned by the cloaked figure beside me. Staring up at a stunning temple overlooking a cliff face, awed and curious. Falling from so high up it seemed as if I'd never land, certain of death. Thrown from a boat, too exhausted to feel anything. I dissected each of these and more, though I had to be careful not to stray too far; when I did, occasionally I'd encountered memories that belonged—not to me—but to Neverland. These I shied away from. Perhaps it was their alien nature, or perhaps it was simply that any reminders of Eve and Cathal, who I'd left behind to make this journey, made me more melancholy even than the stark reality of my current circumstances. Some hurts, after all, are borne more easily than others.

Footsteps from farther down the chilly corridor startled me from my reverie, likely belonging to the guard I thought of as Lady Clownfish, judging by the wet slap of her feet against the floor; she had delicately webbed feet that resulted in a distinct thwap when she walked. One of only a few guards, she had a uniquely orange cast to her skin, with pale, winding lines that snaked over the contours of her waifish body. Today she wore a white shift I'd never seen before, though the frown she bestowed on me was all too familiar. The stench I'd come to associate with this place worsened as she drew closer and set a tray in the shape of a giant clam shell on the floor within easy reach. Once, I might have grabbed for her, but I knew not to bother, now; she and her companions moved with the uncanny speed and grace I'd come to associate with otherworldly creatures. Besides, they were cautious, apparently as wary of me as I was of them. Of course, I couldn't blame them; I had tried—and nearly succeeded—to break out of the first cell they'd put me in. Far roomier than my current accommodations, I'd shattered two of its iron bars before I was found and forced at spear-point into this alternate receptacle. In here, unfortunately, I had no leverage—no way to break free, despite my strength. And no privacy, either.

"Here," I croaked, passing over the bowl I'd been given for my waste. In many ways, that had been the most dehumanizing part of this whole thing; freedom doesn't mean a whole lot until you have to relieve yourself in plain view on someone else's schedule. Lady Clownfish wrinkled her nose, but took it away dutifully, leaving me with nothing but the echo of her flopping footsteps and a mound of gutted fish.

And...something else.

I craned my neck, squinting up through the bars of my cage at the faint miasma left behind in her absence. Something lingered out there, perhaps a few feet from where the guard had stood only a moment before. No, not something. Someone. A man—or at the very least it was man-shaped. I rose gingerly, hissing with the discomfort of moving sleeping limbs. I leaned heavily against the bars, pressing my face through the gap as that silhouette became clearer, features and colors materializing out of thin air like a picture coming into focus. When the image finally asserted itself in all its clarity, however, it was all I could do not to jerk back in surprise.

"What the hell are ye doin' here?" I exclaimed.

"Oh, hey," Nate Temple said, rubbing his jawline self-consciously as he studied his surroundings, his expression mildly vexed. "Well, damn. This isn't where I parked my car."

I reached for the wizard instinctively, trying to snatch at his lapel and draw him close, but what my hand met was neither clothes nor skin. Instead, it felt as though my hand collided with a solid wall of air, like holding your palm up to an industrial fan blowing at full strength. I drew back immediately in surprise, fingers tingling as though I'd touched a live wire.

Nate, for his part, seemed mildly amused by my attempt—the way you might react to a child teetering about or a drunk singing shoddy karaoke. But there was something else going on with his expression, something which belied the twinge of a smile playing at the corners of his mouth; there were deeper creases around his eyes, even new folds which hadn't been there before, all of which spoke of exhaustion and disappointment. There was a degree of suffering lurking beneath his haughty facade, far more so than I'd noticed when we last met—the night he broke into my apartment and tussled with a former lover of mine under dubious pretenses. God, how long ago had it been? Months? Years? So much had happened since then that, truthfully, I no longer felt the slightest indignation about any of it. All that righteous rage belonged to someone else, to someone younger and more easily riled. After all, what was the point of holding grudges in times like these?

"Seriously," I asked again, dropping my hand to my side, "what are ye doin' here?"

Nate swiveled his head back and forth, taking in the dank, dark corridor and the empty cells on either side of mine. The wizard frowned, shook his head, and turned his attention back to me. He opened his mouth to speak, stopped, then opened it again. "Hey, wait...I know you," he said, making a snapping motion with his fingers, though oddly enough no sound accompanied the gesture. "You're that Irish woman. Othello's friend. The thief."

Then again, I thought, maybe grudges are what keeps us going when hope isn't taking our calls.

"What the hell d'ye just call me?" I hissed.

"Sorry, that wasn't supposed to be an insult," Nate replied, waving that away with aplomb. "But then, and I do hate to be the one to point this out, but you are behind bars..."

I glared at the man, though I couldn't exactly argue that point. Indeed, I felt a tad conspicuous. Here I was, soaked to the bone, my clothes rotting, my hair a mess, my face bare as the day I was born. I bet I looked pitiful, maybe even pathetic. And there he was, sporting a tailored blazer and tight-fitting shirt that sat dark against a pair of acid washed jeans and brown leather loafers. Indeed, whereas I was certain I looked every bit the guilty prisoner, Nate might as well have been about to head to a risqué nightclub and slip into a VIP booth.

"I didn't steal anythin' to get locked up, ye idget," I said, at last. "And ye still haven't answered me question. How d'ye get in here?" Maybe, I thought, I could use whatever method he'd employed to break in, to break out. Now that I knew I wasn't alone down here, hope began to swell, tantalizing me with possibilities.

"Not sure," Nate replied. "I was trying to find someone, but it looks like I failed. Again."

"Find who?"

"Someone useful." Nate flashed me a tired smile that soothed the bite of that criticism. "Anyway, I better go. Looks like I've got miles to go before I sleep."

The wizard began to blur before I could debate my utility, disappearing much as he had only moments before—his vibrant clothes fading to a dull, monochromatic grey, his features smoothing to a tan, shapeless nothing. But I couldn't let him do that; I had too much to say, too many questions to ask, to let him get away from me that easily. So, when I reached for him this time, I didn't draw back. Instead, I thrust my hand into the center of his chest, clawing into that roaring wind, my fingers feeling as though I'd shoved them into a light socket. I held my hand there for a moment, then jerked back with a yelp, the pain too much to bear.

"What the hell was that?" Nate barked, clutching at his chest. Only this time when I looked at it, his chest was no longer covered, but bare and sunburnt so badly it made me wince in sympathy. And it wasn't only his chest; the clothes he'd been wearing before were gone, replaced by relative rags, his wrists scabbed and bleeding, his shoulders so burnt they were nearly purple. A thin beard littered his face, making him seem much older, if not a tad wilder. Upon closer examination, I noticed a series of sores and tiny cuts abrading his body.

He looked, well, awful.

"What on earth happened to ye?" I asked, holding my own hand close to my chest, cradled, waiting for the throbbing pain to subside.

Nate glanced down, cursed, and closed his eyes. In seconds, his appearance shifted once more. His skin smoothed, the beard fell away, and the clothes mended themselves. When at last he opened his eyes again, I found myself staring at the billionaire playboy I'd always thought him to be—the very same man who'd first appeared outside my cell.

"It took me a while to figure out how to alter my appearance," the wizard confessed, as though that made any sense. "Astral projection isn't all it's cracked up to be, but it works a lot better if you don't pop in on strangers looking like a leper."

"Astral projection?"

"It's how I'm here. Well, sort of here. It's complicated. Let's just say I'm making the best of a bad situation."

"What situation would that be?"

"I got myself in a bit of a bind, that's all."

"Imagine that," I drawled. "Go on."

Nate looked uncertain, his eyes gauging my face, perhaps wondering if I could be trusted. I didn't shy away; whatever was happening with the wizard, I felt I at least had a right to know. In fact, after learning what I had about his parents' involvement in my life, if not my birth, I felt the Temples owed me a great many things—not least of which being an explanation.

"I pissed off a god," the wizard admitted.

I snorted, unfortunately far more familiar with that scenario than I'd have liked. Though I supposed it had been a while in my case since I'd aggravated anyone of note. Here's to staying under the radar, I thought.

"Which one?" I asked.

Nate blinked at me in surprise.

"We can swap stories later," I insisted. "Which god d'ye upset? Wait, wait, let me guess...d'ye break into Hestia's house?"

"The goddess of the hearth. Clever." Nate rolled his eyes. "That was a long time ago. And I didn't break into your place. I just wanted to ask you to get something for me, and you overreacted."

I took a deep breath, resolving to keep a civil tongue no matter how much I wanted to throttle the man. Besides, it wasn't like I could take a swing at him; if Nate really was projecting an astral version of himself, then the best I could do was stick out my tongue and call him names—neither of which would improve our circumstances.

"What was it ye wanted?" I asked, instead.

"Doesn't matter, now. A jewel, I think. A lot has happened since then. More than I care to think about."

I frowned, my gut rumbling with more than mere discomfort. Was it possible he meant Balor's eye? The jewel Ryan stole from me and intended to use to restore Lugh's Spear—if my mother could be believed? Before I could ask about that, however, Nate went on.

"Anyway," he said, "it wasn't Hestia I upset, though you're on the right track. See, I sort of set Prometheus free. And, in the process, ticked off the god who put him there. Since then I've been, you know...hanging around."

I grimaced, realizing which god he'd pissed off at the exact same moment I realized why his wrists had been so damaged, why his skin had looked like an overripe tomato. As ruler of the Olympians, Zeus, who'd been duly offended by Prometheus bestowing the gift of fire to mortals against his express wishes, had punished the Titan by chaining him to a cliff face to have his liver eaten by an eagle every morning for eternity; Titans healed quickly enough for that to be a fresh, enduring form of torture. In terms of cruelty, I could think of almost nothing worse.

"How long have ye been Zeus' prisoner?" I asked.

"I'm not sure, anymore. This is how I escape, how I stay sane. When I'm like this, it doesn't hurt." Nate slid his hand across his chest as if he felt

8

something pleasant; something whole and hale and unbroken. Nothing at all like the whirlwind I'd thrust my hand into.

"And your friends?" I asked. "Aren't they comin' to save ye?"

Nate flashed me that tired smile. "Shouldn't you be worried about yourself?" He gestured to the bars of my cell. "That doesn't look cozy. What did you do to get put in there?"

"It's a long story," I said, after a moment's hesitation; his attempt to change the subject was clunky, but if he didn't want to talk about his problems, so be it. "This is the Titan realm you've wandered into. At least, I t'ink it still is. I was chasin' someone with a grudge against ye, tryin' to stop him before he hurts anyone, and that's when—"

"A grudge against me?" Nate interrupted, eyes wide. "Wait, is that what you said?"

"Aye, and don't ye sound so surprised, like you've never done anythin' to harm anyone in your life," I admonished. "Ye and your friends killed his father, who was a member of the Wild Hunt tryin' to track ye down for the Queens of Fae. And let's not forget your parents stole an hourglass from under his watch, which got him exiled. Frankly, he has good reason to hate ye, all t'ings considered. But when he signed on to work for the Winter Queen to see ye killed, he started crossin' lines, lines he shouldn't have crossed."

Nate seemed floored by the news; he kept shaking his head, one hand pinned to the bridge of his nose as if working to relieve a migraine. "This is ridiculous. I mean, we did fight the Wild Hunt once. But that was ages ago. And my parents...the hourglass..." Nate drifted off. "It wasn't stolen. Or, if it was, I'm sure they had a good reason."

"That's what I'm told," I replied, bitterly, thinking about his parents and what they'd done to Neverland, to me. "Always a good excuse, Calvin and Makayla Temple."

Nate was suddenly pressed against the bars, his eyes a little wild. Indeed, all of him gave off a barely constrained ferocity. It was as if he'd flipped a switch; his hands strained against the iron but made no sound. For a moment, I thought I saw his skin smolder with power as the dim light in the corridor seemed to fill him up like a freshly snapped glow stick.

"What," he said, teeth gnashing, "do you know about my parents?"

"More than you'd t'ink," I replied, huskily. I gripped the furthest two bars and leaned in, careful not to get too close, but unwilling to back down in the

9

face of Nate's animosity. My own impulsive side—once distinct from me but no longer—recognized this alternate persona for what it was. It seemed Temple and I were both predators, though of different breeds and temperaments. Which meant he and I had to be careful of each other, now. "If it weren't for your parents," I continued, "I might never have been born."

"Wait, what does that even mean?" Nate's savage expression faded, giving way to something baffled and a bit lost. The glow of his skin dimmed as the wizard released his grip on the bars and rocked back on his heels, his hands hanging loose at his sides as if he suddenly wasn't sure what to do with them.

But, before I could answer him, before I could even begin to pull at the serendipitous knots that bound us to one another, I heard a shout. Not down the corridor as one might expect, but above us, somehow—as if the ceiling itself was crying out with rage. Nate cursed, glanced back over his shoulder, and finally turned back to me looking like a man about to step out onto the gallows.

"I have to go," he said, though he lingered, staring at me with more interest than he'd ever displayed before. His image waned, flickering. "If you ever get out of here, you little delinquent, come find me."

And, with that, he was gone.

3

I leaned against the rusted metal cage, only mildly annoyed by the copper streaks they left on my tattered clothes, feeling inexplicably exhausted and more than a little frustrated. After all this time, despite all the questions I'd wanted answered, Nate and I had only been able to brush the surface of our bizarre and serendipitous connection. Why had he appeared, now? Was it mere coincidence that we'd both been caught and locked up at the same time, or were we on parallel paths, somehow, our destinies truly intertwined? Where were his friends, I wondered, his supposed allies?

Where were mine?

These questions and many more plagued me in the miserable silence the wizard's departure left behind, leaving me with a bitter taste in my mouth I couldn't ignore. But no, that wasn't Nate's fault, I realized; the bitter flavor worsened with every passing moment until at last I heard the distinct sound of approaching footsteps. I backed away from the bars, aware that something—or more likely someone—was coming. And worst of all, assuming my taste buds were any judge, I doubted I'd care much for whoever it turned out to be.

Seconds later, a face, if a face you could call it, appeared on the other side of the bars: black eyes bulged on either side of a scaled, whiskered snout, and a fin rose like a mohawk between the creature's sloped brow, neatly bisecting its oblong skull. Teeth, misshapen and engorged, ground against each other with a sound not unlike sheets of sandpaper being pressed together. I'll admit it took me a long time to look away from that hoary visage, to focus instead on the creature's firm, muscular upper body, his skin decorated in scales the color of sea foam. The creature wore a white satin sheet about his waist, the hem of which was rimmed in golden beads. Neither the material nor the colors suited him; to me they seemed as incongruous as a shark in a tuxedo.

"Who the hell are ye supposed to be?" I asked, fighting to keep my voice calm and even.

The creature, who looked more and more like a mutant hybrid caught between a man and a catfish, didn't speak. Instead, he produced a key. The key to my cell; I recognized it from when I'd been shoved into this smaller aperture courtesy of Lady Clownfish and her posse. Without so much as a word, the newcomer slid the key into the lock, turned it, and quickly withdrew. The gate swung partially open on creaking hinges. Some people, in that moment, might have hesitated—fearing a trap of some sort. After all, it seemed awfully odd to be released without so much as a word after days of begging to be set free. Indeed, lately I'd become the sort of person who found it hard to act decisively, who often worried her impulsive behaviors might not be in everyone's best interests. And yet, for some reason, my little chat with Nate had my blood up; the billionaire's smart-assed attitude had a tendency to bring out some of my worst traits.

Or some of my best, depending who you asked.

And so—without so much as a thank you—I kicked the gate wide, stepped out, and booted the clam full of fish guts against the wall with all the savagery I possessed. Then, fearing a reprisal or an ambush of some sort, I spun in a quick circle, arms raised in a defensive posture. No matter what they tried, I swore to myself, I'd die before I let anyone put me back in a cell.

Never again.

Except it seemed that wouldn't be necessary; the fishman stood some twenty feet down the narrow hall, not the least bit fazed by my first act as a free woman. Instead, he waved one webbed hand for me to follow before shuffling further down the corridor as though he could care less whether I did so or not. Taken aback by the strange turn of events, I lingered outside my open cell door. What if I were to turn and go the other way, I wondered?

Would he double back and try to stop me? Somehow, I doubted it. I studied the other end of the hallway, searching in vain for the faintest light and the promise of true freedom. But of course, the odds of that were basically nonexistent; if I went that direction, I was more likely to get lost than to escape. Depending on the complexity of these corridors, I might as well have curled back up in my cell.

No, I knew what choice I had to make.

Even if I hated it.

"So, where are we off to?" I called as I caught up to the fishman. But again, there was no answer. Instead, I was left to study his sloped back as he moved, to watch the play of alien muscles across his shoulders, to marvel at the way his head fin drifted back and forth like hair.

Eventually, of course, I grew bored of that and began to take note of my surroundings. Soon, the damp stone gave way to warmer climes, to walls that gleamed and shimmered beneath torchlight. Pearl. They were made of pearl. I reached out to run my fingers along their opulent surface, amazed somehow more by the presence of such valuable material than I was the improbable creature playing tour guide. And he was guiding me; he took multiple turns, choosing one path over another with the assurance of someone who knows precisely where he's going. Frankly, it made me feel better about my decision not to run; I'd have gotten lost for sure, if I had.

Of course, all that vindication was called into question the instant we reached our final destination: a throne room the size of an amphitheater carved entirely out of alexandrite, its stunning purplish hues coated in coral polyps of every color and description, each somehow more brilliant than the last. Sadly, I barely noticed any of it; my attention was drawn immediately to the figure seated on the throne itself—a being so eye-catching, so imposing, that I could do nothing but stare up in awe.

"Welcome, mortal," the fishman whispered, his voice like that of a frog's, if only frogs could speak, "to the throne room of Lord Oceanus. Now, I suggest you bow."

4

*S*poiler alert: I wasn't the bowing type.

"Oceanus?" I echoed, instead. My mind quickly latched onto the fragmented mentions of the Titan whose worshippers had included sailors and fishermen alike before he was shunted aside by Zeus' brother, Poseidon. Having chosen neutrality rather than side with Zeus against his brethren, Oceanus had survived their calamitous war and subsequently carved out a space for himself amongst the mortals as the primordial god of all freshwater, giving him dominion over the sources of many a civilization —for a time.

"Who speaks my name?"

The voice broke through the throne room like the roar of a raging river, somehow both sibilant and ear-splitting. The mouth it belonged to was lipless, snake-like. Indeed, the Titan had several serpentine qualities; his lower half—nothing but a pale silver tail ringed with black stripes—wound the throne in rigid coils. His upper half, however, was like that of the fish-man's: muscular but undeniably anthropomorphic. Bullish horns rose from the Titan's forehead, their sharp tips hovering just below the vaulted ceiling. I watched in mild fascination as Oceanus—like Typhon in so many ways, if only Typhon had been saner and less terrifying—surveyed his throne room, squinting. How we must have appeared to him I had no idea; I was but a speck of dust compared to this giant, ancient being. Of course, even dust can be a nuisance.

"Me name is Quinn MacKenna," I declared, proud that my voice didn't waver. "By what right have ye kept me prisoner here?"

"You shall not speak to—" the fishman began, snatching at my arm.

Unfortunately, I wasn't all that interested in what he had to say.

I was over it. Over being cramped up in a cell. Over being humiliated. Over being cold, and wet, and miserable. And frankly, even had I been in the best of moods, I wasn't about to let some fish-faced bastard tell me what I could and couldn't do. So, before the fishman could finish, I took a quick half step back, latched onto his wrist with my right hand, pressed my left to his elbow and shoved with as much force as I could manage. Which, it turned out, was a bit more than I expected; I heard the bones in the fish-man's arm shatter as I drove him to the floor. His scream was piteous, more an extended croak than a wail. I rose, leaving him there to nurse his wound.

"I'll ask ye again," I said, doing my very best to ignore the creature flopping about on the floor next to me, "by what right have ye kept me prisoner here, Lord Oceanus?"

Maybe it was the title that did it, or maybe it was the violent way I'd dispatched his flunky, but I could immediately tell I'd gotten the Titan's attention. Oceanus drew forward, using his lower half to keep him steady even as he loomed over us, his eyes blazing with anger. "Right?" he bellowed. "You, a mortal responsible for the poison infecting this realm, ask me by what right I call you captive?"

"Poison? What are ye talkin' about?"

"Don't pretend to be ignorant of what you and your fellow mortals are doing to our home," Oceanus roared, flashing fangs that might have impaled an elephant. "I won't tolerate it!" The shout brought a rush of familiar footsteps. Lady Clownfish and her fellow guards, including a few I hadn't seen before, rushed into the throne room brandishing their barbed spears. They took one look at the writhing creature at my feet and leveled those spears at me. I held my hands up but gave them cool eyes; I'd done nothing wrong.

Well, nothing he knew about, anyway.

"I swear on me power," I said, "that I have no idea what you're talkin' about."

That seemed to surprise the Titan; he drifted back in his seat before flicking one gigantic hand. The guards lowered their spears, following the unspoken command, though I strongly suspected they were more than willing to make a shish kabob out of yours truly, should the opportunity present itself.

"There is a stain, a blight, upon the Eighth Sea," Oceanus said. "My people speak of it; they tell me of the invasion of our home. An invasion that coincides with frozen lakes and rivers, of tides that flow thick with the blood of our people, of flesh stolen from Hades himself. Are you truly insisting you have played no part in this campaign? If so, I find the coincidence...unpalatable."

Ryan. He was talking about Ryan, I realized. Had Ryan really done all that—brought war to the Titan realm? After seeing his undead crew for myself, not to mention his butchering of Polyphemus, it seemed not only probable, but likely. But why? What was Ryan's agenda? Was it simply to reach Atlantis, or did he have something else, something bigger, in mind? The fact that I no longer knew bothered me more than I cared to admit.

"I swear I did not. But," I said, forestalling the Titan's reply, "I know who did. Meself and a few others followed him here. We planned to stop him, to take him far from this realm, where he won't be able to hurt anyone else."

Oceanus paused to consider this. His tail flicked, rasping across the floor. At last, he nodded. "Very well, I accept your explanation. You were wise to swear on your power, for nothing else would have sufficed."

"Good, so can—"

"However," the Titan interjected, "I am not inclined to rely on mortals, as a rule. As a pact to guarantee you succeed, or at the very least die trying, I will have a vow from you."

"A what?"

"A vow. This creature you spoke of, the one defiling this realm. I would hear you swear on your power that you will end his campaign against my people. That you will kill him. And I would hear it now."

Another gesture from the Titan, and the barbed spears were leveled once more.

Looked like Quinn was back on the menu.

5

The spear wielding sea creatures advanced slowly, menacingly, jabbing at invisible enemies, gnashing their teeth in anticipation. Some were sharp as shark teeth, others as flat and ordinary as a human's. But each and every one of them seemed more than happy to run me through if I failed to give Oceanus what he wanted.

Of course, all it would take to get them to back off was a simple phrase: a vow binding me to the will of Oceanus and his Titan brethren, a vow which would pit me against Ryan in such a way that our confrontation could have only one outcome. Unfortunately, I couldn't—no, I *wouldn't*—swear it. I supposed I could blame sheer obstinance; I had no desire to be told what to do and too much stubbornness to bow down before the will of some strange primordial being I'd only just met. But deep down, there was a simpler, more rational explanation: I'd done it once before and had immediately regretted it. When I'd agreed to the Winter Queen's terms back in Fae with the fate of two worlds on the line, I'd essentially signed away my rights to confront Nate Temple on my own terms. Maybe that's why I'd avoided him, why I'd passed on Othello's invitations to come to St. Louis, why I'd changed the subject whenever one of our mutual friends brought him up. Only this was different. Whereas Nate may have hurt my people, may even have done some truly awful things in pursuit of power and security, I *knew*

Ryan was out there causing harm. I couldn't avoid him. But that didn't mean I had to kill him, either.

"I refuse."

Oceanus hissed, a forked tongue protruding from his lipless mouth, the end of his tail vibrating like a rattlesnake's. "So, you lied, after all. Very well, mortal. If you wish to die in less pain, I suggest you fall to your knees as your kind once did before us all. My daughters will make it quick."

Oceanus' daughters swarmed towards me, lunging as if the first to bloody me would win a prize. For a moment, I dwelt upon what it would mean to die here, my quest unfulfilled, my crew abandoned to whatever fate had in store for them. A clean, relatively merciful death awaited me if I accepted it; I knew enough about gods to know they spoke the truth as they knew it. All I had to do was fall to my knees and accept the first lethal blow, and it would all be over. I'd no longer be cold, or wet, or aching. I'd no longer be this melancholy wretch standing in a puddle before a being so ancient he could blink and miss my whole lifespan. But, in the back of my mind, a teasing voice spoke, a voice that reminded me of who I was—who I'd always been.

If you ever get out of here, you little delinquent, come find me.

"There's somethin' ye should know before ye go runnin' your mouth, Lord Oceanus," I said, bristling at the notion that I should fall to my knees in any capacity, my fists clenched so hard it felt as though my nails might draw blood. "I'm not exactly mortal."

Lady Clownfish reached me first, but by then it was too late. I'd already called to the shadows with every fiber of my being, to the pockets of darkness huddled among all those coral protrusions and indentations. I'd called to the heat inside me, to the flame I'd kept burning within, fed only by my dwindling hope of ever making it out of my cell alive. Both came to me in ways I couldn't predict, couldn't articulate: green flames rushed over my skin, flickering so brightly I had to shut my eyes even as I saw the shadows surge to snatch away the spears of the guards from their very hands.

But the flames died as quickly as they'd flared, and the shadows retreated so swiftly I wondered whether it had only been my imagination. I slumped, suddenly exhausted, into the startled arms of one of my captors, who quickly dropped me to the floor. Which hurt, though at least it seemed no one was going to stab me. I tried to sit up, groaning, which made it hard to understand what Oceanus said next.

"What was that?" I asked.

"I said you should have told me what you were from the start," Oceanus replied, sounding cross, almost as if I'd pulled a trick on him. "We never would have locked away one of your kind."

"What I am makes no difference," I countered, my thoughts sluggish. "Ye should have dealt with me fairly, no matter what."

"Perhaps. But I would have trusted the word of a witch far more than that of a mortal whose best interests lie with their own kind."

I wasn't sure what to say to that. Had a Titan really just called me a witch? Was that because I'd put on a little pyrotechnic display, or had he just assumed that's what I'd meant when I'd told him I wasn't exactly mortal? Either way, it didn't seem prudent to belabor the point, now. Better Oceanus treat me as a relative equal than someone to be mowed down at the first opportunity.

"Does that mean I'm free to leave?"

"To leave?" Oceanus considered that for a moment. "I do not see why not. Witches have always been allowed to do as they please in this realm. But where will you go?

"I'm goin' after the one I told ye about, the one who's hurtin' this realm and your people."

"I see. Very well, but first you must tell me," Oceanus added, leaning forward eagerly in his chair, "where is your army?"

"Me what?"

"Your army. Your fellow witches. Your followers and servants. Surely you must have some who owe you their lives, or who will aid you in this."

I frowned, wondering if this was all a ploy to discover how big a threat I was, to find out whether anyone would come looking for me. Had he agreed to my release simply to set my mind at ease? But no, if Oceanus wanted me dead, he could have simply ordered it done the moment I collapsed. And besides, what sort of reprisal could concern something as ancient and powerful as him?

"I didn't bring an army," I replied, at last. "I have a crew and a ship. We were promised aid by the Laestrygonians. Once I have it, I plan to reach..." I hesitated, the word "Atlantis" on the tip of my tongue. "I plan to head him off. To set a trap."

But Oceanus was already shaking his head, his horns nearly grazing the ceiling. His tail whipped out, and his daughters left the throne room, each of them gazing back at me as though I were some sort of monster—a hideous and repulsive thing. What had I done to earn that look, I wondered?

"The island of the Laestrygonians," Oceanus began, "is under siege. When I learned of the scourge affecting our realm, I sent my finest scouts to discover what could be done. They have recently returned to report that the mortals and their undead soldiers have invaded the island of the giants, though I do not know why. All I know is that the island is covered in snow, its harbors blockaded by sheets of floating ice. So far, I believe the link the Laestrygonians share with Gaia shelters the island's inhabitants from the worst of it. But this stalemate will not last forever."

I shook my head, unable to comprehend what I was being told. The Laestrygonians were under siege? Having experienced the island's gorgeous weather for myself only a few days prior, I knew it had to be Ryan and his infernal powers at work, but why would he bother? Was it simply because I'd knocked him out, then managed to slip away? Was he really that petty?

"I have to go," I insisted as I rose to my feet, struck by the sudden urgency. "To help."

"Wait." Oceanus held up a hand, his voice remarkably stern. "You must not be foolish. You have no army. No fellow witches. What you face, whatever this power infecting my realm is, I do not think you alone are up to the task. Not as you are now, at any rate."

"As I am, now? What's that supposed to mean?"

"It means I have seen gods rage with enough power to destroy the heavens. I saw Zeus hurl a thunderbolt that blew apart the head of a hundred-handed giant. I witnessed Helios pluck his crown from the heart of the sun when it would have burnt the rest of us to ash. I know something of power. Which means I know a lack of control when I see it. A lack of stamina, too, if I'm not mistaken. And I am never mistaken."

I bit my tongue on that one.

"What's your point?" I asked.

"My point is that there is another possibility."

"Such as?"

"There is an island not far from here upon which dwells someone who can help you awaken the powers you have only meddled with thus far. A witch with powers far greater than your own. She's my granddaughter, and it's possible she will give you the tools you need, if you can strike a bargain with her."

"Wait, d'ye say she's your granddaughter?"

"Yes. Her name is Circe. I believe you may have heard of her."

6

The name of Oceanus' granddaughter, unsurprisingly, rang more bells for me than his own had. A goddess and witch, Circe and her siblings had played major roles in more than a few mythological tales, though her place in Odysseus' story was perhaps the most notable; the witch gave Odysseus and his men succor on her island and even became the Greek's lover for a time. According to Homer, she was a beautiful enchantress who took great pleasure in luring men to her island before transforming them into animals. What she was actually like in the flesh, of course, I could only guess. Having met my fair share of Greeks—including two of the Muses, Narcissus, and Helen of Troy—I could only say for certain that the myths had a contentious relationship with the truth, at best.

"Why would she agree to help me?" I asked.

"Circe can be difficult, but even she would prefer this realm remain as it is. You will simply have to plead your case and pray she agrees to aid you. I expect she'll ask you for something in return, so long as she doesn't turn you into swine, first."

I grimaced at the thought.

Oceanus crooked a finger at the fishman, who'd remained prone on the floor for the duration of our conversation, cradling his shattered arm. I felt a stab of pity as he rose to his feet; the fishman teetered, his bulging eyes rolling as he fought to stay upright. And yet I kept my distance, certain any sympathy I showed would be perceived as a sign of weakness.

"Triton, take this witch to the Cetu," Oceanus commanded, before turning his attention back to me. "Get rid of the menace who plagues us, witch, and soon. Or I will have no choice but to sink the island of the Laestrygonians beneath the waves and drown every last creature who stands upon it."

I shuddered as I pictured the city of the Laestrygonians being swallowed by the sea, its massive temple rotting on the ocean floor. If Oceanus followed through on his threat, it might end Ryan's reign of terror, but it would also spell the end for all my companions—not to mention the Laestrygonians, themselves. But then, there was no if; gods didn't deal in idle threats, they dealt in prophecy and promises. Oceanus' mention of an island beneath the waves, however, prompted a question, one I'd thought to avoid earlier, fearing I'd give too much away. But now, with so much on the line and no guarantee I'd even make it that far, I felt compelled to ask.

"Lord Oceanus," I said, "can ye tell me how to get to Atlantis?"

The Titan snorted.

"You cannot 'get' there. No one can."

"Not even a Titan?" I challenged.

"Especially not us." Oceanus narrowed his eyes, his head cocked so far I seriously wondered whether the weight of his horns would drag him to the ground. "Are you really trying to reach Atlantis?"

"Aye, that's where...where the mortal ye want me to kill is tryin' to go."

Oceanus stared at me for a long time after that. So long in fact that I wondered whether he'd heard me, or if perhaps he'd fallen asleep with his eyes open. Weren't fish able to do that? I wasn't sure. But then, before I could ask, the Titan began to chuckle. Indeed, Oceanus began to laugh outright; great peals of gurgling laughter spilled out his throat while I stood there, more than a little baffled. The Titan waved us away, unable to speak. Triton, as the fishman had been called, waved for me to follow, but I ignored him.

"And what's so funny?" I demanded, instead.

Oceanus dabbed at one eye. "If you ever do reach Atlantis, you will understand. Not that it will matter, by then."

My cheeks burned, but there was no point delaying things further. I knew what I had to do, even if it meant abandoning my friends to their fates

23

for a little while longer. If Oceanus was right, and Circe could help me unlock—or even rein in—my temperamental powers, then it was a necessary detour; I'd seen how powerful Ryan had become and knew I stood little chance against him, especially with my allies under siege. Indeed, as far as I could tell, I had only two choices: I could return to the island of the Laestrygonians and try to outwit the Faeling, or I could beg for Circe's help and try to amass an arsenal of my own. Unfortunately, considering I barely recognized the thing Ryan had become and had only the faintest idea what he wanted, any plan I cooked up would be a shot in the dark, at best.

So, Circe it was.

"Is there anythin' you'd like me to tell your granddaughter when I see her?" I asked.

"Yes," Oceanus replied, voice still thick with mirth. "Tell her what you told me, about Atlantis. She always did appreciate irony, especially the morbid kind."

I opened my mouth to respond, but Triton was already ducking into one of the branching corridors, which meant I had to hurry not to get left behind. And so I left the Titan's throne room, forced to jog behind my guide as he moved gracefully through the corridors, surging from one hallway to the next like a fish angling downstream along unseen currents despite cradling his injured arm.

"Wait up!" I called, still uncomfortable with the idea of getting lost in these murky hallways. Triton slowed to a crawl so quickly I accidentally collided with the bastard, the impact of which jarred us both.

"I am sorry, witch," Triton groaned, his voice laced with pain. "I thought you were pressed for time.

"Please, call me Quinn," I insisted. "And it's not your fault. Just go at a normal pace, alright?"

Triton nodded and resumed walking, this time at a reasonable clip. I, meanwhile, stepped into the fishman's shadow, trying to place his name. Triton. There was something familiar about it, something faintly...nostalgic. It was only after several minutes, however, that it came to me.

"Wait, I know ye! You're a god!" I exclaimed. "Triton, you're a son of Poseidon, aren't ye?"

Triton ducked as though I'd struck him across the back of the head, a keening sound emerging from the back of his throat. "I am as you say," he replied.

"But...what happened to ye?" I asked, unable to reconcile this ugly, awkward creature and the well-proportioned merman who Disney later popularized as a certain redhead's overbearing father. "Where's your conch? Your trident?"

"Gone. Long ago."

"How?"

Triton kept on walking for a while before he spoke again, seemingly mulling over the details of what happened to him, or perhaps deciding whether or not it was worth discussing; the fishman didn't strike me as the chatty type. "It is a punishment," he confessed, at last.

"What for?"

"For siding with my goddaughter in a war she did not win."

"Your goddaughter?"

"Yes. Her name was Athena."

I stopped in the middle of the hallway, struck by the name and all the baggage that came with it. Athena, Zeus' daughter—in so far as a whole ass goddess being pulled from one's mind could be called offspring—was a mythical figure known for waging and winning wars, for her strategic brilliance and cunning mind. It was she, according to Homer, who'd aided Odysseus time and time again as he sought to return home to Ithaca. Indeed, her blessing was so coveted that the Greeks had named their capital city after her. And, oh yeah, there was this key little aside worth mentioning: to the best of my knowledge, Nate Temple had killed her.

"Who punished ye?" I asked once I caught back up.

"Lord Oceanus. He warned me not to leave. He said I would suffer if I chose to return to the mortal realm and fight, and he was right."

"So, what, he turned ye into this? For disobeyin' him?"

"No, this happened before."

"I don't understand."

"Magic. The magic of a Tiny God and his apprentice. They caught me spying for Athena and tried to capture me. I got away, but at a cost."

Comprehension dawned on me as I studied the sea god's unwieldy frame. I wasn't sure what a Tiny God was, although it sounded vaguely familiar, but I could see what had happened to Triton clearly enough; he'd been inverted, given the head of a fish and the body of a man as opposed to the upper body of a man and the lower body of a fish. It was an unfortunate combination, though frankly I doubted the tail would have done it for me, either—bit gender neutral, if you asked me.

"Oceanus refused to change ye back."

"Yes."

That one word carried more sadness in it than I knew what to do with. Unfortunately, cheering up gloomy sea gods wasn't on my resume. Maybe I could tell him a joke, take his mind off his sorry condition and the fact that I'd shattered his arm? There was one about a priest, a sailor, and a seahorse that might have done the trick…

"So—"

"We are here," Triton said as we slipped down another hallway, cutting me off before I could relay my sympathies...or screw up a punchline. "When you see her, do not be afraid."

7

*H*ere—it turned out—was a cavernous space with a glass ceiling, neatly bisected by a channel of glossy, undisturbed water. Although a tad disturbed by Triton's cryptic warning, I was simply too glad to be seeing something other than a stone ceiling overhead to fret; I stared up in anticipation at what I assumed was the night sky. Only what lay beyond the glass was too dark to make out at first, so I was forced to squint, to search in vain for those unfamiliar constellations I'd noted the one and only night I'd spent on the island of the Laestrygonians. That's when something on my periphery caught my eye, drawing my gaze to the left. A fin as long as I was tall, tapered and cerulean, brushed against the glass. The tailfin which followed—several times as large and forked—did the same before being swallowed by the gloom. I stared after it for a long moment, unable to comprehend what I'd seen.

"Wait...are we underwater?" I asked several seconds later, dumbfounded by the possibility that we'd been traipsing about in submarined hallways this entire time.

"This is Lord Oceanus' home," Triton replied, as if that should have been obvious—which, in hindsight, I supposed it was. "Ah," he continued, "here she comes."

I craned my neck to see what Triton was referring to and caught a glimpse of a shadow above our heads—the silhouette of the same fins and tail I'd spotted earlier, but this time angled in a dive. She—whatever she was —quickly disappeared from sight behind the cavern walls. I opened my mouth, prepared to ask Triton perhaps a dozen pertinent questions, when I felt the floor shudder beneath our feet.

"Clumsy of her," Triton noted, wincing from the jostling of his wounded arm.

I, meanwhile, fell back to the nearest wall, pressing myself against its cragged surface. Terrified by the thought of what would happen if that glass ceiling came down, or if this section of the tunnel sprung a leak, I had to force myself to breathe. A sheen of sweat prickled my brow. Oddly enough, I'd never really had a fear of drowning until today, but it seemed between plummeting from the sky onto the open sea and being cast into the frothing waves of the Eighth Sea with a head wound, I wasn't eager to try my luck a third time. Or, as my good friend Othello might say:

Fool me once, shame on you.

Fool me twice, shame on me.

Fool me three times...and they'll never find the body.

If Triton noticed me hugging the wall, however, he gave no sign of it. Instead, he walked gingerly to the edge of the channel, peering over the edge as if waiting for something to emerge. Drawn by my own curiosity, I shuffled until I could see the water's surface clearly. It had begun to churn. Something was rising from below, I realized, like a submarine climbing from untold depths. I moved closer. Was this the creature Oceanus had referred to? The Cetu? I joined Triton at the edge, leaning over to catch a glimpse of whatever was coming, my breath held in anticipation.

Which is all that saved me from what happened next.

A geyser of briny sea water erupted as the creature surfaced, washing over me in a violent cascade that damn near sent me sprawling backwards. I sputtered, trying to clear my eyes, reminded of the time Dez—my aunt and guardian as a child—took me to a waterpark for a church event she'd helped organize. There, I'd been forced to stand on a bridge with the other children as a roller coaster full of adults hurtled down a slope to crash into the pool of water coursing beneath our feet, soaking those of us in what they'd jocularly dubbed "the splash zone". To say I'd never entirely forgiven organized religion for that experience would be an understatement.

"What the hell was that?" I sputtered as I parted my drenched, mangled locks and threw them angrily over one shoulder. I was once again thoroughly drenched from head to toe, and what little warmth I'd regained from my time in the throne room seemed to have fled entirely.

But Triton wasn't listening to me. Instead, the god pressed his hand against the smooth, muscled side of what appeared to be a humpback whale; in open air, the creature had a cobalt cast to its skin, its belly white and riveted. It was also astoundingly large, running the full length of the channel as if the waterway had been created solely for that purpose. In hindsight, it probably had been. Together, Triton and I approached the majestic creature's head, though I was careful to keep my distance; I wasn't interested in becoming yet another victim of Darwinism.

"This is the Cetu," Triton intoned as we walked, still tracing his good hand along the creature's flank. "She once served my father, but was lost after he sent her to devour an upstart mortal princess. We found out later that she was attacked by a mortal prince fated to steal the Golden Fleece." Triton motioned to a section of the Cetu's back that I hadn't noticed before, but didn't elaborate further on the tale, leaving me to note the scars which littered her flesh. Ragged and pale against her dark skin, I felt I could trace every sword slash, every gouge. "Oceanus nursed her back to health," he continued, "and she has served him ever since."

"This is all very interestin'," I admitted, "but what are we doin' here, exactly? What's she got to do with me, I mean?"

Triton didn't respond. Instead, the god continued walking until at last we reached the sea monster's head. I froze, startled to find—not the head and throat of a whale as I'd been expecting—but that of an enormous grey-hound. Long-snouted and speckled, with thin, pinkish ears, the face that sat partially submerged was both completely incongruous and shockingly proportional. I began to say something to that effect when her eye—a brown pupil large enough to reflect the whole room—found me, and I was suddenly overcome by a surge of recognition.

"She—" Triton began.

"I saw her," I insisted, cutting off whatever Triton had been about to say. "When I was drownin'. She was there, in the water."

"Yes. She saved you, brought you to us, and told us what happened in the strait."

I could only gape at the sea monster. Imagine that, saved by a whale with a dog's face after narrowly avoiding the whirlpool that was Charybdis and tangling with the mash-up monster that was Scylla. What the hell was wrong with the Greeks? Why couldn't any of their nightmares include monsters with knobby hands and a bum leg or missing teeth and bad breath? Still, I had to admit I was grateful; I made a little curtsying motion with an imaginary dress, dipping my head in the process. Water dripped from my hair to the floor in a muddy puddle.

"T'ank ye for savin' me."

The brown orb darted away. If I hadn't known better, I'd have said the Cetu was embarrassed. Regardless, I was still left with the question of what was supposed to happen, now. I turned to Triton, but the god was already showcasing the sea monster with his good arm, gazing at me expectantly.

"Are you ready to go?" Triton asked.

I flicked my eyes from Triton to the Cetu and back again. Surely he couldn't mean...but one look at his ill-favored face, and I knew that was exactly what he'd meant.

"Ye want me to ride her? Seriously?"

"Not ride," Triton replied, sounding affronted. "But yes, she will take you. The Cetu swims faster than any boat sails, and she knows the way to Circe's island."

"I'll pass."

"Pass?" The sea god cocked his head.

"I decline."

"But you have no choice."

"Excuse me?"

Triton made as if to shrug, but the pain of doing so was too much; he gritted those engorged teeth of his, grinding them together so hard I thought they might chip, or even shatter. Feeling sympathetic despite his attitude, I crossed the distance between us and placed my hand on his good shoulder.

"Listen, I appreciate Lord Oceanus' help, but there has to be another way." Triton made to speak, but I held a hand up to forestall him. "And please know, I never meant to break your arm. It was cruel of me, and I'd take it back if I could."

I felt my knees buckle the instant the words left my mouth. In fact, I probably would have collapsed to the floor had it not been for Triton's hand at the small of my waist, ensuring I stayed upright. Blinking rapidly, my breathing suddenly shallow, I turned to study the arm that hand belonged to. It was whole. Healthy, even.

Except it shouldn't have been.

Triton let out a croak of surprise as he helped me regain my footing. This close, his scent was cloying, as bad as the raw fish I'd been served day after day. I stepped away, fighting my gag reflex. But Triton didn't notice; he was too busy swinging his arm in loose circles, admiring the limb as though he'd just bought it.

"You healed my arm," he said, clearly shocked.

"Can't all witches do that?" I asked, playing coy. Honestly, I had no idea how I'd done it—or if I even had. Aside from my momentary fainting spell, I hadn't felt anything worthwhile. No rush of power. No green flames or writhing shadows. What the hell was happening to me, now?

"Healing mortal flesh, perhaps. But to speed the recovery of a god's..." Triton trailed off, perhaps momentarily exhausted by how many words he'd spoken in a row. "No, it is not common."

Huh. Good to know, I guessed. Still, I wasn't exactly thrilled to find out I had a new ability to wrestle with. If anything, I was getting a little pissed; my legs felt like jelly, the fish stench lingered no matter how far away from Triton I stood, and moving in my sopping wet clothes was quickly becoming an exercise in excruciating discomfort. What I wanted, more than anything, was to leave this miserable place, to see sunlight, to be warm and dry and far from the rank odor of seafood. I glanced back at the Cetu, uncertain of my accommodations but suddenly more than willing to take that risk if it meant getting the hell away from here.

"Triton?"

"Yes?"

"Tell me more about the Cetu."

8

I found out shortly thereafter that Triton's comment regarding the method of transportation hadn't been an idle one; riding the Cetu really wasn't what he had in mind, after all. Instead, it seemed my travel itinerary included a brief layover...inside the sea monster's mouth.

Or so Triton would have had me believe.

"Ye can't be serious," I said for perhaps the third time as Triton gestured once again to the gaping jaws of the Cetu, whose lolling, absurdly long tongue reached out to form a fleshy pink bridge between the stone where we stood and the yawning interior of her impressive maw—if only I would step onto it.

"I am always serious. How do you think she brought you here to begin with?"

Honestly, until now I hadn't thought about it. The sea monster had carried me in her freaking mouth? No wonder I'd felt so icky all over ever since I'd woken up in my cell; the notion that there'd been saliva mixed in with all that salt water I'd spent days covered in was enough to make me physically ill.

"There has to be another way," I insisted.

"The only other path to the surface would mean using the hatches—"

"Let's do that! I t'ink that's a fine—"

"Except the water pressure would kill you instantly," Triton continued, speaking over me. "And, even if it didn't, you'd suffocate and drown long before you reached the surface."

"I'm not exactly fragile, in case ye hadn't noticed," I muttered. "Don't make me break your other arm to prove it."

"Witch or not, you would not survive. There is a reason some gods rule the seas while others rule the skies. We are not all created equal." Triton sighed, though it sounded more to me like the creepy sound made by the drowned girl from *The Ring*. "Inside the Cetu's mouth, you will be sheltered from the pressure, you will travel swiftly, and you will be able to breathe."

"That's what I'm afraid of," I joked, wrinkling my nose at the thought of spending any amount of time confined to a mouth of any description.

"She will not eat you. Not intentionally."

"Oh, that's reassurin'. And what d'ye have to say about all this?" I called to the sea monster herself, leaning as far as I could to meet one of those humongous brown orbs, trying to gauge the Cetu's feelings on the subject of having a foreign object hitch a ride on her tongue. But the sea monster's doe-eyed expression gave me nothing. If anything, she seemed impatient to be on her way. So, it was up to me.

Frankly, if it were solely a matter of trust, none of this would've been a problem; if Oceanus wanted me dead, there were far less elaborate ways to do it than this. No, the issue was how much of this could end up outside my control; say the Cetu got lost and dropped me at the wrong island, or she got mauled by some monster even bigger than she was, or she forgot all about me and decided to swallow on reflex...whatever the scenario, I wouldn't be able to do a damn thing about it.

"You're sure this is safe?"

"It is the best option," Triton replied.

"That wasn't what I asked," I muttered as I closed my eyes and pictured the faces of my crew of misfits, of my friends back in Boston, of everyone I'd thought about while I sat huddled in my miserable cell, hardly able to hope I'd see daylight again, let alone reunite with them. If making that dream a reality meant riding on the tongue of some ancient Greek monster for a couple hours, then what was I waiting for?

"If you agree to do this, there is—" Triton began.

"It's fine," I interjected. I let out a long breath I hadn't realized I'd been holding and stepped onto the tongue before I could talk myself out of it, my eyes still pinched shut. For a moment, nothing happened. Aside from the slightly spongy surface, I might have been standing on anything. Until—that is—the Cetu slid her tongue back into her mouth.

I yelped and opened my eyes just in time to see the room swim past. Despite my superior reflexes, I could barely keep my feet and was forced to lean hard in the opposite direction to avoid flying off the tip of her tongue. Wind gusted from above, whipping my knotted mass of hair across my face, and then, suddenly, there was nothing but darkness.

Water lapped at my feet; I could feel it invading the tops of my boots, soaking my ankles and feet. The air, hot and stale, stank. It seemed I was finally inside the sea monster's mouth, secure behind rows and rows of jagged teeth. Of course, it should come as no surprise that I felt anything but safe.

"I swear, if ye eat me, I'll burn ye from the inside if it's the last t'ing I do!" I yelled, praying the Cetu could hear me. Not that it mattered; I doubted the threat of a little spice was going to ruin her appetite, assuming she called my bluff.

For a long moment after that, I heard nothing. Then, breaking through the silence like a distant foghorn, what might have been Triton's voice. I thought he sounded panicked for some reason, his shouts rapid, though unintelligible. I waded towards the sound of his voice, straining to hear, my arms outstretched. The cries grew louder. What was going on out there? At last, I managed to reach the slick side of one massive tooth, to press myself against it, fighting to hear beyond the almost oppressive stillness.

"Find something to hold onto, or else—" Triton was saying.

But that was as far as he got before the Cetu submerged, and I found out what he'd been trying to warn me about before I'd stepped onto the sea monster's tongue: gravity. Not that his advice would have done much good; I had nothing to hold onto. I flew violently upwards as the sea monster dropped, colliding with the roof of her mouth with enough force to drive the breath from my lungs. The water I'd had to wade through only moments before followed, splashing over me in a fetid wash that very nearly got in my mouth. I squirmed, but the pressure of her descent kept me pinned firmly in place until, after what seemed an eternity, she bottomed out, and I was flung back down to land face first on a soft, rubbery surface. Her tongue, I realized with a groan. More liquid crashed over me, this time coming down like rain.

Double gross.

"I'm goin' to die in here," I moaned, my body already aching from careening this way and that inside the maw of a sea monster whose every sudden move seemed to redefine the laws of gravity. But then, I thought, maybe I was being pessimistic. Maybe that had been the worst of it, and I'd end up spending the remainder of this little journey relaxing on this surprisingly comfortable tongue, twiddling my thumbs out of sheer boredom. Or hell, maybe a handsome flight attendant was already halfway up the Cetu's esophagus with my bag of peanuts and an overpoured cocktail.

A girl could dream.

9

The light of the midday sun, when it finally shone down upon me in all its glory, seared my retinas. I winced and flung both arms up to shield myself from its brutal glare, blinking through tears. A draft of clean, salt-laden air blew through the Cetu's parted maw, brushing my cheek like a caress. After spending what seemed an eternity in the mouth of a sea monster, it was all I could do not to cry from relief; I'd spent nearly every second of the trip tense and expectant, blind in the darkness, both praying for and dreading the parting of the sea monster's maw. I wasn't sure how much time had passed, but my nerves had fried long ago, leaving me twitchy and hypersensitive.

Still, I felt compelled to step out into that light, to feel its heat against my skin. I took several steps forward, my eyes adjusting incrementally. From this direction, the Cetu's open mouth reminded me of Polyphemus' cave; the sea monster's teeth were little more than silhouettes against the clear blue sky, looming like stalactites. Had we made it to Circe's island, at last? Eager to find out, I picked up my pace. I'd nearly made it to the edge, in fact, the sound of lapping waves was fresh in my ears, when the ground gave way beneath my feet.

I was immediately flung forward, launched into the air with a flick of the sea monster's tongue. I screamed in surprise, only to swallow a mouthful of saltwater as I hit the sea and sank beneath the waves. I came up spluttering, cursing, but more or less unhurt. The Cetu, I saw, floated perhaps a few dozen feet away. I caught a brief glimpse of her unreadable expression before she plunged beneath the surface, creating a massive swell that I had to duck under to avoid.

Guess I'd overstayed my welcome.

"Goodbye to ye, too!" I spat once I'd kicked to the surface. I treaded water, turning in a slow circle, until at last I saw it: an island paradise. Lush and densely forested, Circe's island—or at least what I presumed to be Circe's island—was far more accessible than those I'd seen thus far in the Titan realm; long and mostly flat, there were no imposing bluffs promising an arduous climb, no shattered ships littering its coves, no sense of foreboding choking the very air. In fact, from where I swam, the island seemed almost too perfect, too picturesque.

But then there was only one way to find out if it was, in fact, a paradise...or a trap.

The swim to the beach wasn't exactly pleasant with all my clothes weighing me down, but I wasn't complaining; despite being thrown around inside the Cetu's mouth, it felt good to stretch my limbs, to impose my will on something—even if that something was only the sea. Once on the beach, however, I got a better sense of just how ragged I really was. My body ached, my sopping wet clothes clung to me, my jacket was torn to bits, one pant leg was shredded at the knee, and I'd lost my boots. I felt like a castaway, washed up on shore. What would Circe think when she saw me, I wondered? Would the goddess even hear me out, or would she simply snap her fingers and turn me into the sewer rat I undoubtedly resembled?

Sadly, the only way to definitively answer that question was to track down the witch. I scanned the horizon, searching for signs of habitation—anything to suggest a goddess called this place her home. But I saw nothing of the sort. No smoke rising above the treetops, no deforestation, nothing. It looked like I'd have to move further inland, though I quickly decided to avoid the trees until I had a better grasp of my surroundings; the island wasn't absurdly large, but wild forests were notoriously easy to get lost in and—depending on your choice of fairy tale—devoured in.

I strode across the beach, my feet sinking deep into the sand, relishing in the sensation of sunlight beating down upon my exposed skin. To say I'd missed daylight was an understatement of epic proportions; during my tenure in Oceanus' cells, I'd begun to worry I'd never feel it again. I closed my eyes, delighting in the sound of the surf, the mantle of warmth across my back and shoulders, the press of fine sand between my toes. I was so immersed, in fact, that I didn't realize I had company.

"Who are you, and what are you doing on my island?"

I whirled, eyes wide, towards the speaker. A frizzy-haired blonde woman stood at the edge of the forest to my left dressed in a pair of loose trousers and a bulky button-up shirt tied at her waist that revealed a slim, tan waistline. No, not a woman, I amended. She'd called this her island, which meant this was likely Circe, herself. Except...there was something decidedly ordinary about her, something that defied everything I'd come to expect from a goddess. Whereas the divine beings I'd met in the past had come across as lighter than air, their skin flawless, their mannerisms graceful and vaguely sensual, Circe stood awkwardly with one hand resting on her cocked hip while the other shaded a face flecked with the faintest signs of age.

"Me name is Quinn MacKenna," I replied, then hesitated, wondering how I should answer her question. Despite the hours spent in the Cetu's mouth, I hadn't really had time to draft my appeal. To be honest, I hadn't even thought to come up with one. "Your grandfather sent me," I said at last, praying familial obligation alone might be enough. "He thought ye might be interested in helpin' me."

"Oceanus said that?" Circe cast an appraising eye over me. "And I don't suppose you could go back and tell him he was mistaken?"

"I...well, no." I jerked a thumb over one shoulder. "This was sort of a one way trip."

Just saying that out loud made me realize how precarious my position was at the moment. What if Circe chased me off? For that matter, how was I going to get back to my crew from here—wherever here was? Once again, I'd asked too few questions and had failed to think far enough ahead. Damn it. But then, very much to my surprise, Circe agreed.

"Come along, then. But hurry, I've got a show starting soon."

"A show?"

This time, however, Circe didn't respond. Instead, she turned on her heel and slipped between the trees. Fortunately, for all her talk about having somewhere to be, the witch moved at a leisurely pace, making it easy to catch up. I tried to venture several questions as we went, but Circe continued to ignore them, leaving me with little to do but study the witch as we traipsed through the sun-dappled forest. Occasionally, she'd branch off the path to snatch up a flower or pocket a leaf, and it was during one of those detours that I got my best look at the goddess who'd once wooed Odysseus.

Circe's features were surprisingly asymmetrical, her chin a tad longer than most, her nose thin and aquiline, and yet there was a roughness to her that drew the eye, that defied conventional beauty in favor of competence; she'd thrown her hair back in an unpretentious messy bun riddled with leaves and twigs and even patches of spider webbing. All in all, she struck me as more geologist than goddess.

"How much farther is it?" I asked after perhaps ten solid minutes of marching through the woods, stops included. At this point, my bare feet were covered in a sheen of sand and dirt, my clothes damp but dryer than they'd been in days. What I needed was a long bath and a new wardrobe.

"Further," Circe replied, at last. "And not very. I thought you might like to stretch your legs after being cramped up in Oceanus' dungeons."

"How d'ye know I was—"

Circe held up a hand to silence me, her whole body suddenly tense. We both froze, listening. After perhaps a solid minute of utter stillness, she let out a breath and continued walking. "You never know who's listening," she said, cryptically. "Best to wait."

"I'm tired of waitin'. I want ye to tell me how ye knew about the dungeons. Please," I added, fighting to keep my voice low and to prevent my frustration from showing.

"I saw it."

"Saw it?"

"Yes."

"And could ye elaborate on that?"

"I could, but I won't. You'll understand soon enough. Until then, prove to me that you can be a little patient." Circe flicked her eyes to me, and I realized she had gold flecks in them—dozens of tiny shards that obscured her pupils. The gaze itself, unfortunately, wasn't a friendly one; my incessant questions seemed to have irked her, for some reason.

"Could ye at least tell me what ye meant when ye said 'show' earlier?" I asked, unable to shake the feeling that I was being led into a trap of some sort—that the show had something to do with me.

"I was talking about his execution," Circe explained. "It's scheduled for today."

"Wait, what? Whose execution?"

"Nate Temple's, of course."

$\mathcal{W}$e reached the edge of the forest before I could demand answers from Circe, my mind swirling with half-formed questions and wild, half-cocked theories. How the hell could Circe know what was happening to Nate, wherever he was? And how did she know him? It seemed entirely possible this was all some sort of test—a cruel attempt to gauge my reaction. But then, that meant she knew Nate and I shared a connection, of sorts. Afraid to give anything away, I clamped my mouth shut, determined to glean what answers I could using good old-fashioned observation. What lay on the other side of the tree line, however, was too distracting to ignore; the sprawling compound we'd stumbled upon, which could only have belonged to Circe, contradicted everything I'd have expected from the seemingly unassuming goddess.

"What is this place?" I asked.

"This is my home," she replied, simply. If Circe was impressed by the palatial villa with its gurgling fountains and lush gardens—a villa which could have adorned the cover of any Tuscan brochure—she didn't sound it. If anything, it was as if she hoped to trivialize the place, to dismiss its beauty, though for the life of me I couldn't understand why; her home was stunning.

Indeed, the instant I stepped foot onto the meticulously manicured lawn —immediately surrounded by myriad floral scents and the charming songs of chirping birds—I felt more at ease than I had in months, maybe even years. I felt lighter, somehow. No, that wasn't it, I decided. Not lighter. I felt tranquil. That's what it was—an unassailable sense that everything was right in the world, if only I would stop fighting it.

"You really live here?" I asked, nearly breathless from the sudden and insidious euphoria. My thoughts wandered freely while I waited for Circe's answer, completely unanchored. Had I truly thought to grill the goddess and find out what she knew about Nate and I—by force, if necessary? It seemed so silly, now; Nate was a wizard with powers that put him on par with the gods. He could take care of himself, couldn't he? It certainly wasn't my problem if he'd gone and gotten himself tangled up with the Olympians.

"This is the heart of Aeaea," Circe replied, studying me with those beautiful, gold-flecked eyes of hers. "And yes, it is my home, as well as the seat of my power. No one will overhear us here. Or trouble us, for that matter. Now, come." Circe picked up her pace as she strode past, gesturing for me to follow. Together, we cut through her gardens, weaving to avoid rows of verdant shrubbery, slipping between trees bearing exotic fruit at a frantic clip. "Mind yourself," Circe called back over one shoulder. "Especially your feet."

I frowned and glanced down to find vines snaking towards my naked ankles. I danced away, narrowly avoiding them, only to feel a nearby tree limb claw at one shoulder, its leaves pinned to my flesh as though I were magnetically charged. Thankfully, Circe was immediately there; the witch took my hand and drew me away from the tree's clutches, leading me out of the garden.

"Why do they do that?" I asked, oddly more confused than disturbed by the experience.

"I raised them that way. I'm not fond of intruders. Especially spies." Circe flung one hand in the general direction of a pen full of dirty, sunbathing pigs as if they were somehow responsible. One porker perked its face up and made a disgruntled noise as we passed, its beady eyes tracking us with uncommon intelligence. "Some thought to get a good look at my pools. They failed. Others sought me out, hoping I'd grant them a favor. They were wrong."

"D'ye say 'pools'?" I asked, oblivious to her implication.

Circe didn't bother explaining. Instead, she slipped between the tapered columns that held up the east wing of her villa, angling for a navy blue door covered in marble murals depicting what looked like acts of heroism: svelte figures facing off against monsters and rescuing damsels. The witch yanked the door open before I could take a closer look and hurriedly padded through, taking little notice of the gorgeous fountain that lay on the other side, nor the vibrant tiles which formed a lovely mosaic beneath our feet. Circe circled the fountain and headed directly for an atrium, the floor of which was littered with an array of bathing pools, each varying greatly in size and overall shape. I made to follow but hesitated just outside the threshold, struck by an abrupt sense of foreboding. A sudden wave of panic, hot and oppressive, beat against the fog that clouded my mind.

"Where are we?"

Circe hardly spared me a glance before hurrying to the edge of one pool —a shallow, triangular bath with a sunburst at its tip. She knelt and brushed her fingers across its still surface. Ripples quickly spread, followed immediately by the rasp of a man's heavy, labored breathing. From where I stood, I couldn't quite make out what I was looking at. A man, I thought, naked from the waist up, kneeling on an alabaster floor, his head hung so low I couldn't see his face through his mane of hair. Beyond that, the sky, maybe? Light blazed across the man's back, hot and bright enough I had trouble focusing on it without seeing spots. Circe, meanwhile, stared down at the pool for only a few seconds before cocking her head, quizzically.

"What day is it?" she asked, absentmindedly.

"What day?" I repeated, surprised. I held up both hands and shrugged, completely at a loss as far as that question was concerned. The last time I'd consulted a calendar was the morning Scathach dragged me from my apartment to the shores of Scotland. Since then I'd travelled to the Otherworld, to the Fae realm, and now to the Eighth Sea. "I have no freakin' idea."

Circe pursed her lips. "No, I suppose you wouldn't." She sighed, then swiped at the water's surface a second time, and the man's ragged breathing cut out. "Looks like I was a bit premature. Zeus must be dragging this out, for some reason."

"Wait, ye can't mean that Nate—"

"That was him, yes. And it seems he's still alive, for now. In any case, I wouldn't worry about it. You have plenty to worry about, already, without concerning yourself with the Catalyst."

"What's that supposed to mean?" Another surge of panic cut through the haze that clouded my mind, bringing me back—if only a little. I clenched my fists, digging my fingernails into the skin of my palms; pain helped chase away the tranquility.

"Come here, and I'll explain."

I shook my head without meaning to, backing away from the kneeling goddess as though she had threatened me rather than extended an invitation. "I'm fine where I am," I replied, wary of a potential trap. "It...I don't t'ink this place is for me."

"No, it isn't." Circe rose, brushing her knees clean despite the immaculate floor. "I'll admit I'm glad to hear you say that. I was worried you might feel somewhat...proprietary, where my pools were concerned."

"Why would I? It's not like they're mine."

"Not exactly, no. But I believe you are familiar with the original design." Circe showcased the atrium with one arm, putting her pools on display as though they explained everything. When I gave her a blank look in response, she shrugged. "I'm not a fan of windows. Windows can be broken, or left open."

"I don't understand..." I began. But then, I *did* understand. That tight-chested feeling I'd had earlier—not panic, after all, but painful recognition; the atrium reminded me of my mother's cosmic hallway and of the windows she'd used to reveal the flow of time. From them, she could peer into the past, the present, and even—presumably—the future. "Are ye like her, then?" I asked, unable to hide the quaver in my voice at the thought of the spectral figure who'd watched over me for most of my life before her vigil ended. "A goddess of prophecy?"

"Not at all. It's true my father could sometimes scry into the future, but my talents lay elsewhere. Magic, spells, potions, the sorts of things gods would never deign to meddle with. Later, they gave me, and those who trafficked in such trifles, a name: Witches." Circe crossed the room to kneel beside a crescent-shaped pool. She brushed her hand across it and beckoned me to come close. "These pools were not meant to look into the future, nor do they show the past. Only the now."

More than a little hesitant, I inched towards the goddess, wary of any sudden moves on her part. The moment I stepped over the threshold, however, I felt that peculiar sense of tranquility dissipate completely, dispersed by whatever power lay dormant within the atrium itself. Suddenly crestfallen and more than a little cranky, I'd only just opened my mouth to accuse the witch of casting a spell on me when another voice interrupted.

"What are you looking at?"

The voice came from the pool. Thinking only to glance down at it for a moment, I shuffled closer. But what I saw was too damn odd to look away from. A silver-veined skeleton wrapped in a maroon hood scarf with smoke curling from its eye sockets stood framed in the half-moon pool, his chrome bones glinting beneath flickering candlelight. I gaped at the strange apparition, then turned to Circe, baffled. But then, a woman's voice answered.

"Something I was told not to."

Callie Penrose. I recognized the Kansas City native's voice immediately, though for some reason she sounded somewhat older, perhaps a tad rawer than she had when we'd spoken last. Maybe the sound was distorted, I thought. Except, when the pool's view shifted and Callie came into focus, I realized she didn't only sound older—she looked it, too. Decked out in what appeared to be all white special ops gear, the pale-haired woman I'd forged a brief but memorable friendship with stood in what seemed to be a library, cradling a book which emitted its own light.

"Where in Hades did she find that?" Circe hissed, clearly discomfited.

"Can I see?" the skeleton asked, clearly oblivious to our presence.

"Sure. Here, look at this and tell me what you—" Callie began, turning the book towards her companion and, coincidentally, towards us.

Circe made a choked sound and swiped at the pool's surface, cutting off whatever she called these strange transmissions of hers. The waters went still in seconds, and the witch rose with a groan, a faint sheen of sweat across her brow. She wiped it away with her sleeve and shook her head. "It's a miracle none of you have blown up the world, yet," she said, leveling a pointed look at yours truly.

"And what's that supposed to mean?"

"It means—"

"Wait," I interjected, swiping at the air with both hands. What I needed, I decided, were answers to questions that actually mattered; I couldn't keep getting distracted every time Circe hit me with some new bit of information or I'd never leave her damn island. "Was that really Nate? What d'ye mean he's goin' to be executed? And Callie? Where is she? What was it she was readin'?"

"Something she should not have been," Circe replied. "I was hoping to catch her alone. But it seems my timing was off...again." The witch hesitated for a moment before continuing, as though she'd just had a thought. "Anyway, it's best we take this conversation elsewhere."

"Hold on a minute, what about all me other questions?"

"I'll give you one. One question."

"Oh aye, then what?"

"Is that your one question?"

I bit off what I was going to say next and glared at the witch, considering her offer. I could inquire about Nate's fate, about Callie's current preoccupation with some mystical book, about the improbable existence of a silver-plated skeleton, about the atrium and its resemblance to my mother's cosmic hallway...or I could ask the one question I should have prioritized the instant Circe met me on the beach.

"How d'ye know I was comin'?" I held up a hand before she could speak. "I mean, how d'ye know who I am, at all?"

"Isn't it obvious?" Circe replied, cocking one eyebrow as she jerked a thumb over her shoulder. "I've been watching you for some time now, Morrigan's daughter. And I think it's time someone sorted out the mess you've become."

"Excuse me?"

"You're not excused."

"If ye have a problem with me, I suggest ye spit it out," I growled, hackles rising. "Preferably before I bust your mouth open and drown ye in your own pools."

"Well, you've got your fighting spirit back, at least." Circe gave me a bland, considering look. "But that's about all you've figured out, it seems. The rest of you remains a tangled ball of knotted power." The witch traced the curve of my body with her hand as though she could feel the heat radiating off my skin. "Tell me, Quinn MacKenna, would you like to find out what you really are?"

Before I could even begin unpacking that bizzare statement, however, Circe flashed me a wry expression, spun, and headed for a hallway that branched away from the atrium. I stared after the witch, feeling decidedly out of my depth. What the hell was going on here?

"If so," Circe called back over her shoulder, "follow me. If not, you have twenty-four hours to get off my island before I turn you into a fish and toss you into the sea."

*I*n the end, I followed the witch. It wasn't the threat so much as the notion that I might have wasted precious time by coming here, which prompted the decision. I figured that once she'd had her say, I might be able to ask for the assistance I'd originally hoped to gain. What I needed was to better understand my powers, to grasp their limitations as well as their advantages. If Circe could help me unlock them, great. But if she couldn't, or wouldn't, then I'd made a grave error in judgment.

"I know *who* I am, thank ye very much," I mumbled as I followed Circe through the villa's west wing, irked by her assumption. Unfortunately, I realized my assertion wasn't entirely true the moment I said it; I knew who I *wanted* to be. A loyal, steadfast friend, a fierce and relentless enemy, and—perhaps above all—someone capable of protecting the people I cared about. Whether I was that person yet or not, unfortunately, was still in the air.

Along with a ridiculous number of other things.

"I didn't say who," Circe retorted as she turned into another annex, her voice trailing after her. "I said what. You need to pay closer attention."

"And what is that supposed to—"

"Hurry up and get in here and we'll talk."

"A please wouldn't kill ye," I muttered under my breath as I stepped into a room which seemed like a cross between a high school chemistry class and a spiritual wellness boutique; precious metal decanters and cylinders stood next to wooden bowls filled with all manner of bizarre items: locust husks, teeth, bone fragments, locks of hair, piles of fur, and more. Planters hung from the ceiling, each laden with bizarre and unique flora. Circe took a tin cup from a nearby table, sniffed its contents, and handed it to me as I entered.

"Drink this and tell me what it tastes like."

"I'm sorry, what?" I eyed the dubious concoction, letting my incredulity show as I swirled the liquid within. I pursed my lips, then passed it back to the witch. "Ye first, Jim Jones."

Circe shrugged, accepted the cup, took a drink, and returned it to my open hand in the time it would have taken me to say "drink the Kool-Aid." She swallowed and made a get-on-with-it motion with her finger. I grimaced, wishing I'd set up better parameters before agreeing to drink—like pouring some of the liquid on a plant to see whether or not it would wither and die. Looked like I'd failed Disney Princess Survival Tactics 101.

Again.

"What's in it?" I asked.

"Herbs, mostly."

"Herbs like what? Hemlock? Nightshade? Oleander?" I racked my brain for other notorious poisons, but that pretty much exhausted my knowledge.

"Why would I want to poison you?" Circe asked, cocking an eyebrow.

"Why wouldn't ye want to poison me?" I countered.

Circe retrieved the cup with a sigh and replaced it on the table, then fetched two chairs from the other side of the room. She slid one across to me before plopping down on hers. "Sit down," she insisted. "I can see we won't get anywhere until you feel safe."

I scowled, irritated by the way she'd phrased that—as if I were the one being unreasonable in this situation simply because I was skeptical of her intentions and reluctant to drink some strange, witchy homebrew. Still, I did as she asked and took a seat. When she didn't immediately begin, however, I started fussing over what was left of my clothing; at this rate, by the time I returned to the island of the Laestrygonians they'd have no choice but to assume I'd converted to their nudist ideology.

"I want something from you," Circe said, at last. "Something only you can get for me." The witch held up a hand, cutting off what I was about to say. "Before we get into all that, let me be clear. I know who you are, and I know why you're here. I've been watching you and your acquaintances for some time now. It should go without saying that does not mean I like or care about you. I like very few people, and the rest I turn into whatever creature I think suits them best. On the other hand, I do have a vested interest in seeing you succeed, which is why I'm offering my assistance." Circe lowered her hand. "You may speak, now."

"What d'ye mean when ye say 'succeed'?" I asked, struck more by her use of the term under the circumstances than the fact that she'd been spying on me for reasons I couldn't yet grasp. Besides, no matter how tempted I was to call the immortal voyeur out, I strongly doubted there'd be anything to gain by it. Circe didn't strike me as the remorseful type.

"I mean, succeed by saving your friends, or whatever they are to you, before that monstrous creature recruits them and the Laestrygonians to his cause."

"His cause? Ye mean Ryan?"

"We can discuss that later. First, let's talk about why you're here."

I waited in silence for half a minute, anticipating further commentary, but the witch sat peacefully in her chair, one eyebrow cocked in expectation.

"Well?" Circe prompted.

"I thought ye said ye knew why I was here?"

"I do."

"Then why—"

"Me knowing why you've come and you knowing are two very different things. Tell me why you think you're here."

"I'm here because…" I began, then frowned, wondering whether my initial response was the wrong one, somehow. I cleared my throat and chose my words carefully. "I'm here because I need to learn how to control me powers."

"If that's true, you've made quite the mistake by coming here."

"Excuse me?"

"You cannot control something you don't have."

"What's that supposed to mean?"

"It means I can't help you. Not if control is your goal. I mean look at you, you're a wreck."

I glanced down at my shabby appearance and stiffened, prepared to defend myself. But I could tell almost immediately that she hadn't meant to insult my raggedness; she was staring directly at me, but her gaze itself was unfocused, which meant whatever she was judging lay beneath the surface. Of course, that just made me angrier.

"Listen, I'm gettin' tired of the runaround, not to mention the insults," I admitted, frustration bubbling up in my tone. "If you won't help me, say so, and be done with it. I have t'ings to do."

"On the contrary, I plan to help you." Circe flashed me a cryptic smile. "But first you have to understand that what plagues you is not a lack of control. Control implies understanding your limits. Except you, Quinn MacKenna, haven't the faintest idea what your limits are. And how could you? You don't know what you are, yet, let alone what you're capable of."

"Ye keep sayin' that like I should know the answer to your little riddle, but if you've been watchin' me at all ye should realize it's not that simple." I dug my nails into the wood of my chair, my forearms tight with tension. "Just because ye tune in from time to time doesn't mean ye know the first t'ing about me."

"Oh, but I do. What's more, I sympathize."

"Right. And I'm the Easter Bunny's candy supplier."

"You don't believe me. Very well, let's begin at the beginning, shall we?" Circe began ticking off her fingers as she went on, her expression oddly amused. "Originally, your very presence nullified power, though that was later attributed to the geas your mother put on you. When you traveled to Fae, however, you inadvertently tapped into your bloodline and began exhibiting inhuman traits and characteristics common to their race. The geas began to wear down, your father's dormant power manifested, and you began fiddling with time. Then, when the geas broke at last, you began siphoning magic from any and all nearby sources to fill the void left by your mother's power. As of this moment, you've gifted away your father's power, but have gained at least some of what you were meant to inherit as Morrigan's daughter. Does that about cover it all?"

I gaped at the witch. To say I was floored by Circe's monologue would have been a colossal understatement; she'd managed to succinctly describe every painful, peculiar transition I'd had to endure since I first learned what a Freak was. What's more, she'd brought into sharp perspective just how much shit I'd gone through in such a short timespan. Each transition, after all, had been accompanied by a crisis of one sort or another—each catastrophic event seemingly more dire than the last until, well...here I was.

"Well?" Circe prompted.

"There was another t'ing," I replied after a moment's hesitation. Though it seemed minor compared to the others, I felt it was important to mention my experience with Triton in the depths of Oceanus' underwater kingdom in case it had some bearing on Circe's take.

The witch looked at me, expectantly.

"I healed the broken arm of a god."

"Oh? And which god would that be?"

"Triton. I'm not sure how I did it, or if it's part of me new abilities, but I touched his shoulder, told him I wished he'd never been hurt, and the arm mended itself."

"Hmm. Were you the one who broke his arm in the first place?"

"Well, aye, but—"

"Then you didn't heal him," Circe interjected. "You simply fixed something you broke in the first place. It's the least someone like you should be able to do."

"Look, ye asked, so I told ye. There's no need to get nasty," I countered. "And what's that supposed to mean, 'someone like me'?"

"Don't be obtuse. I meant someone with your gifts. With your potential." Circe sighed, then fluttered her hand in midair as if fighting off an errant fly. "Everything I've listed, all these...mutations of yours, they've left you tangled and useless, like an untended rose bush."

"Call me useless again," I growled. "I dare ye."

"I believe your mother had a plan for you," Circe replied, oblivious to my threat. "Your father, too. Both were forward thinkers. And yet, here we are. You, relatively powerless to save the few people you care about. A conflicted creature coming to grips with her own shortcomings. But then of course there's me, one of the very few goddesses capable of remedying the situation."

"Remedyin' how?" I asked through gritted teeth, mere moments away from getting up and saying the hell with it. Sure, it would mean pitting myself against Ryan, Frankenstein, and their undead crew without knowing the extent of my powers, but I was beginning to think I'd be better off without Circe and her vague pronouncements—not to mention her scathing snubs.

"Here, I'll show you." Circe rose from her chair, retrieved a thin vial from a chest made from what I could only assume was pure, polished silver judging by its luster, and resumed her seat. She held the vial pinched between her fingers, tipping its cerulean contents from side to side.

"What's that? Wait, let me guess, somethin' else you'd like me to toss back without question?"

Circe frowned for a moment as if I'd lost her, then flicked her gaze to the tin cup and snorted in amusement. "That was my attempt at a pumpkin spice latte. Every time I tune into the mortal realm, it's all I hear about. I was hoping you could tell me if I'd gotten it right or not." The witch waved the vial in front of my face. "This, on the other hand, is something else altogether."

"Don't keep me in suspense," I replied, petulantly, my cheeks flushed at the notion that I'd suspected Circe of trying to poison me with a pumpkin spice concoction. That, and I'd passed on something which might have contained the greatest, most potent ingredient known in all the realms: caffeine. Seriously, I wondered, what mythical, man-eating monster would a girl have to slay to get a cup of coffee around here?

"What I hold is an elixir," Circe explained, snapping me from my private musings. "A potion originally designed to kill a god."

"Oh? And which god would that be?" I asked, mocking her earlier tone.

"Any god. All gods. This potion strips us of our divinity, for a short time. Long enough to win a race or a contest of wits. Possibly long enough to carve out a heart, if someone was feeling ambitious."

"That sounds...potent." I eyed the vial, dubious at best. "I'm surprised somethin' like that exists."

"It's quite powerful, yes. But the elixir must be willingly consumed, or it will have no more effect than a sip of water. That tends to offset the likelihood of death by dismemberment."

"How'd ye come by it?"

"That's none of your concern. What should matter to you is how it can help us."

"Oh? And how is a god-killin' potion supposed to help us, exactly?"

"Before I explain, I'd like to hear your answer."

"Me answer to what?"

"To the only question worth asking." Circe leaned back casually in her chair. "What are you?"

"This again?" I sighed and mimicked the witch, drawing my chair's front legs off the ground as I wobbled backwards, considering the question.

"It's not that complicated," Circe assured me. "You simply have to admit that you're no longer mortal, and that you were never entirely human. In fact, let's ignore lineage, altogether. Once we remove all that, what's left?"

I opened my mouth, then shut it. What *was* left? If I wasn't mortal, that meant I was immortal. If I wasn't human, that meant I was inhuman. But I wasn't a Freak because Freaks were of the mortal realm. Was I Fae, then? No, I realized. Sure, the Fae and I shared a common ancestral bond, but after my time in the Otherworld I knew I was something else, something stranger, something more powerful—a being who stood out even among the worthiest of heroes and the wildest of creatures. A word rippled across my mind, one that had been alluded to but never explicitly applied to me, specifically—a title I wasn't sure I wanted to accept.

"A goddess," I muttered. "That's what's left."

"Was that really so hard?"

12

*C*irce and I sat on stone benches on a veranda that overlooked her garden of horrors, the sun dipping beneath the tree line. The faint sense of euphoria I'd experienced earlier had returned, but Circe assured me it wouldn't have as much influence now as before. According to the witch, the spell was meant to lure any unwelcome trespassers into a false sense of security. That I'd managed to fend it off was a testament to my moody nature—or so Circe claimed. At the moment, I couldn't disagree; after everything I'd been through over the past few days, I'd lost what little decorum I possessed.

"So, what is it ye want? In exchange for your help, I mean."

"There's an island to the north. On it, a flower blooms. A golden flower I need to cast a particular spell. Once I've helped you and you've dealt with the besieged Laestrygonians, I'd ask that you retrieve your ship and sail there. Bring me one of those flowers, and our bargain will be fulfilled."

"Why can't ye get it, yourself?"

"I'm not allowed to leave my home, nor would I wish to. Besides, you'd owe me, either way. This way you get what you need, and I get something I want."

"Let's say I believe ye. Why send me? Why not someone else who owes ye? You've been here for who knows how long...surely I'm not your first and only visitor. Or the first person to owe ye a favor."

"No one else could be trusted. Only an immortal can retrieve the flower without consequence, and none of those who live here will deal with me. They distrust witches. I like to think it's learned behavior." Circe tapped the top of the vial with one short fingernail, a slight smile tugging at her lips. "We tend to make better friends than enemies."

I pretended to study the sky while I considered the witch's proposal. I could tell she was keeping things from me, but couldn't put my finger on any one specific omission. Something about the island, perhaps, or what spell she meant to cast using the flower once she got it? The bit about consequences had certainly stuck out. Unfortunately, it didn't matter whether the witch was holding her cards to her chest or not; if making a deal with Circe could give me a puncher's chance to save my crew and stop Ryan before he did any more damage, I was more than willing to risk it.

"Alright, say I agree, hypothetically. What would that do to me?" I gestured to the vial, squirming uncomfortably on my bench at the notion of tossing back some god-killing formula. "If I'm some alleged goddess, won't it make me vulnerable?"

"You're already vulnerable," Circe replied, eyeing me up and down. "I mean, look at you."

"I will cut ye."

"Think of it like a...pruning," Circe went on, ignoring my threat altogether. "Once you take this—provided you agree to my conditions—all those knots that bind your true power will untangle. Then, and only then, will you be able to flourish." Circe leaned forward, her gold-flecked eyes flashing with a surprising amount of zeal. "What your mother did to protect you was undoubtedly necessary, but what you've become as a result is neither woman nor Fae, neither goddess nor mortal. What I am offering is a true transformation, but only if you are brave enough to leave everything else behind."

Brave enough. The words drifted between us like a dare casually tossed out between two old friends. But we weren't friends, and there was nothing casual about Circe's offer. The notion that I'd be forced to relinquish everything I'd gained up to this point and exchange it for some other unknown power threshold wasn't all that appealing; having temperamental abilities and having them stripped away in their entirety weren't remotely the same thing. Sadly, this wasn't about what I wanted. It was about what I needed—

what I had to be willing to risk to say I'd done everything I could to protect the people I cared for.

I held out my hand.

"Swear on your power," Circe said as she dangled the vial above my open palm. "Swear you will find the flower and bring it to me."

"Once I've saved me crew and stopped Ryan," I amended, studying the witch's face for any signs of deceit, any trace that she planned to betray me. She simply nodded, her expression unreadable. I sighed. "Alright. I swear on me power that I will get your flower and return it once I've done what I have to do to save me friends."

Circe hesitated, clearly skeptical of how I'd chosen to phrase my promise. I didn't blame her. I'd purposefully altered the terms of our agreement, giving myself the slightest bit of wiggle room should things go sideways. I'd suffered my fair share of setbacks lately thanks in large part to making promises I either couldn't keep, or had kept at great personal cost. Fortunately, something told me Circe wanted to make this deal as badly as I did; no matter what she claimed, that flower clearly meant a lot to her—which meant I had her over a proverbial barrel.

She dropped the vial into my palm.

"So, I just drink it?" I asked.

"Yes."

"All of it? In one go?"

"Yes, in one go."

I pulled the stopper, eyed the liquid, and studied Circe with my peripheral vision. She watched me expectantly but appeared otherwise reposed. I wasn't sure what I expected to find her doing...rubbing her hands together and cackling like the crone who passed Snow White the apple, maybe? I grimaced and downed the vial's contents in one long gulp, like tossing back an Irish Car Bomb before it curdled.

It tasted like plums.

"Huh…" I turned the empty container over in my hand, licking my lips. "That wasn't so…"

Exhaustion hit me like a tidal wave, zapping me of the energy it took to sit upright. I toppled, falling to the grass with an audible thunk, finding it difficult to overcome the impossibly slow churning of my thoughts. A pair of naked feet approached, dirt-stained, the ankles covered by trousers rolled at the hem. Circe's feet. My eyelids were so heavy that I had to fight to keep them open as the witch knelt beside me, her torso barely visible. I tried to form words. Poison, I wanted to say—to scream at the top of my lungs. I wanted to demand why she'd betrayed me but could barely gather enough energy to breathe.

Circe's face drifted into view as my vision tunneled, her expression somehow both neutral and faintly sad—like a doctor about to deliver a fatal prognosis. She reached out, brushing away a strand of hair that had fallen across my face. Then she patted my freaking head.

"Welcome back to mortality, Quinn MacKenna. Come and find me when this wears off and we'll get you some new clothes." Circe rose and disappeared, leaving me alone in the grass, staring out at a beautifully manicured lawn until my vision blackened and I careened into unconsciousness.

13

I woke up at the crack of dawn the next morning to the shock of ice cold water splashing over me, the sensation not unlike being jabbed by a thousand needles at once. I squealed, rolling for cover and using the blanket I'd been given the night before as a shield. Unfortunately, both it and the bed I'd slept on were already soaked, which made for a rather pathetic defense. Thankfully, it seemed I wasn't under attack, after all.

I was just being tortured.

"Time to get started," Circe said, casually tossing the pail she'd used to douse me, its cacophonous clang nearly as abrasive as the bath had been. "You should have recovered enough, by now."

Despite Circe's assurance, I felt hypersensitive, my skin raw, my senses overworked; the light in the room made my eyes ache, and the sound of Circe's voice was like nails grinding down a chalkboard. Continued side effects of the potion, perhaps. Or maybe this was the harbinger of some burgeoning power? Circe had confessed something like this might happen the night before, after I'd limped into the atrium like a flu victim and collapsed a second time. She'd insisted I might begin to experience a different reality than what I'd become used to—sort of like when I'd developed my inhuman reflexes and superhuman strength. Maybe this was the beginning of some sort of heightened awareness, like enhanced hearing, or eyes that could see for miles in any direction, or a nose that could track evildoers to their lairs by the scent of their deodorant...but God, I freaking hoped not. I had enough to deal with without becoming the poster goddess for Obsessive Compulsive Disorder.

"It's not even mornin', yet," I complained, shading my eyes from the pale light of dawn streaming through an open window. Now that I was awake, I recalled more details from the previous night: Circe helping me change out of my clothes, showing me to this room, and tucking me in with more kindness than I'd thought she possessed. And then, of course, there were the dreams: inverted visions of the past, of vanquished foes standing triumphant over the bodies of my friends, of former allies engaging in increasingly devastating betrayals—each seen through my own eyes, my hands grasping at nothing, my arms and legs bound, making it impossible to move—flashed in front of my eyes. I shielded my eyes completely as I rose to my feet and traded in my doused nightshirt for the tank top and trousers I'd been given, doing my best to ignore the fact that I wasn't alone. By the time I was done, I'd mostly forgotten the nightmares, though my arms remained pebbled with gooseflesh.

"You said you were pressed for time," Circe replied once I was dressed. "If you truly want to discover what manner of goddess you were meant to become before the turn of the century, we'll need to challenge you. Which means I suggest you get used to being inconvenienced."

"What if I'm supposed to be a lazy goddess?" I asked, yawning hard into a closed fist. "A goddess of sleep, or naps. Shouldn't we figure that out, first? Just to be sure."

As though I'd said something particularly offensive, Circe pursed her lips and snapped her fingers. Two men appeared in the doorway on the other side of the room. Both were tall, hairy, and faintly bestial; covered in dried mud, they stood slumped over, their shifty eyes flitting about my sleeping quarters like there'd be a *feng shui* pop quiz later. When neither Circe nor I spoke, they shuffled into the room, noses twitching.

"Who are they?" I asked.

"They are your first test. Greek wrestlers, Olympic contenders. They washed up on shore, long ago. Drunkards, the both of them." Circe cast one disapproving look at the two men that sent both ducking. "Now, boys, I'd like you to subdue this woman."

I cocked an eyebrow and had only just thought to ask what the hell was going on when I realized Circe was pointing at yours truly. Which meant, sadly, I didn't have enough time to shout, let alone demand answers; the two wrestlers launched themselves at me between one breath and the next, moving with the easy grace of trained fighters. The taller of the two, his skin several shades darker than his companion's, reached me first. Thinking me easily caught, the darker man drew me to his chest as if to crush me to him.

Unfortunately for the brute, there was nothing easy about me.

Using his momentum against him, I slammed the heel of my palm against his sternum. The impact jarred my shoulder, setting my nerves on fire, but it had the desired effect: the wrestler released me, clutching at his chest with a cry of pain. Sadly, it seemed his buddy had better instincts; the shorter man came at me low, tying up my legs as he lifted me into the air and twisted. We fell together with him on top, and he drove his shoulder into my core with practiced ease. I grunted, unable to breathe as he slid up the line of my body, mounting my hips in a motion that might have been sexual were it not for the awkward placement of his anatomy; he rode my waist, pinning my forearms with his hands. I bucked, but he didn't budge. Sensing that he held the upper hand so long as he could stay mounted above me, I drew his forearm close by yanking my arm towards my face, my muscles screaming in agony, and latched my mouth over his skin. I bit so hard I tasted blood, could feel his flesh breaking between my teeth. He squealed, releasing my arm to pry my mouth from him. For a moment, I thought I might be able to roll free, but then the darker man joined in, locking both my arms between his hands and pulling them high over my head until my shoulders threatened to pop from their sockets. I screamed, thrashing, until it felt my whole body would be torn to pieces.

"Enough!"

The hands holding my arms fled, and the weight across my belly disappeared. I scrambled away, panting, my every instinct prepared to lash out the moment someone touched me. My vision narrowed until I could hardly see anything, the sound of my harried breathing pulsing in my own ears. I'd kill them all if they came near me again. Every single one of them. Anyone who dared touch me.

"Well, you certainly have spirit. But you're not a martial goddess, that much is clear." Circe sat on the edge of my cot, legs crossed, staring at me with her gold-flecked eyes. "Are you hungry?"

I spat a strange man's blood onto the floor between us, then wiped my chin clean with the tank top she'd given me. It took me longer than I'd have liked to get my breathing under control, especially once I realized this had only been a test, after all. A sick, psychotic test.

"Go fuck yourself."

"I'll take that as a no. Come outside when you've had time to collect yourself, then. We have at least five more tests today. I'd hate to waste any more time than is necessary."

Circe rose, beckoned to her two men, and left. The darker man glared back at me with anger riding his face, still clutching at his chest. I'd probably shattered his breastbone. I hoped I had. The shorter of the two, however, looked at me with a measure of respect that bordered on awe; he held his hand clamped over his wounded forearm, blood spilling from between his knuckles to drip on the marble floor. Both men quickly left me on my own, my heart still hammering in my chest, all my quips sitting like ashes in my mouth.

14

*J*knelt in a glade, the noon day sun high overhead, sweating profusely as I drew back the bowstring and sighted my target. The stag was massive, his flanks decorated with the scars of a dozen forest battles with critters I could only imagine—boars and bears and whatever else called this island paradise home. My shoulder burned with the effort, but I managed to stay steady, to track his easy gait the way Scathach had shown me when we'd trained with the bow—her preferred weapon. I hadn't exactly shown aptitude with the instrument of death during our sessions together, not like I could claim with my guns, but I did alright given ideal conditions.

Sadly, these were nothing of the sort.

"You've drawn a bow before," Circe whispered, her lips mere inches from the ear that wasn't being brushed by a bowstring. The witch sat back on her haunches, leaning against a tree trunk, studying me as intently as I tracked my prey.

"Aye."

I inhaled deeply, trying to ignore everything my brain was telling me about how implausible this was; the stag was so far away it would have taken a miracle to hit it, let alone claim its life with a heartshot. A miracle...or an act of a goddess. Circe was clearly betting on the latter; she'd insisted on these conditions before we even began. Which meant this was the second of her tests—a feat fit for a goddess of the hunt.

It'd taken me nearly half the morning to recover from what the witch had done, though to her credit she hadn't rushed me. In hindsight, it was clear that she'd been in control the whole time, that I'd been in no real danger...and yet what little trust she'd earned in the wake of my arrival had been extinguished the instant she sent those wrestlers after me. Since then, I'd decided there would be no more light-hearted exchanges, no more banter. I'd find my aspect, save my friends, get her stupid flower, and leave her to her wretched island paradise, never to return again.

Assuming she did nothing else to piss me off.

I let my breath out slowly, waiting until my lungs were completely empty before releasing my grip on the string. All that tension vanished in an instant as the arrow launched into the air, soaring towards the stag. The magnificent beast froze in mid-step, his ears cocked in our general direction, and I watched with bated breath as the fletching of my arrow grazed one of his horns before disappearing into the trees beyond. The stag, startled, galloped away with a cry of alarm that sent birds flying into the skies above our heads.

"Did you miss on purpose?" Circe asked.

"What?"

"On purpose. Intentionally. I know how it affects some of you modern women," she added. "Hunting defenseless animals, I mean."

"No," I said, teeth gritted. "I didn't miss on purpose." Frankly, the idea hadn't even crossed my mind; after this morning's traumatic start, I simply wanted to discover my abilities and be done with it all. Hell, even my reasons for agreeing to this in the first place, my desire to save my crew and stop Ryan, seemed less pressing than they had the day before. Frankly, everything did.

Being assaulted has a way of doing that to you.

"Well," Circe said, shrugging as though that one word was enough. "Come, then. I have several more tests to put you through before the day is out."

"Hold on," I said, gripping the bow so tightly it creaked from the strain. "How many more?"

"As many as it takes to figure out where your power lies."

"But we already know where me power lies."

"Do we?"

"Well...we know it's got somethin' to do with shadows and flames. Isn't that enough to go on? A place to start, at least?" I waggled my hand in the general direction the stag had flown, letting my frustration show. "I mean, this just feels like a waste of time."

"Tell me where you'd prefer to begin, then."

"What?"

"Your aspect. Tell me what you think it is, and we'll start there."

I opened my mouth, then closed it. Frankly, I had never given it much thought. My abilities had often come and gone so swiftly that—until now—I'd never even considered they might stem from a source of some kind. Before returning to Neverland, I'd assumed it had something to do with time, or perhaps prophecy. But now I wasn't so sure.

"Do you even know how many aspects there are?"

"Of course I do," I replied petulantly, though I sounded uncertain even to myself. "There are gods of war, of light, of love. Of music. Of death. All sorts, really."

"Precisely. Once, all manner of gods lorded over humanity. Each had unique characteristics, unique traits. Those who hunted could take a stag down with a single shot with their eyes closed, for example, while those who reveled in bloodshed could tear two mortals apart with their bare hands without breaking a sweat." Circe rose, pinning me with her cool, dispassionate gaze. "Now that we've completed the second test, I can at least say what you are not. It's not ideal, but unless you have a better idea, it's all we have."

I bowed my head to hide my expression, letting my hair fall across my face; I didn't want Circe to see my reddened cheeks. For some reason, I was reminded of Scathach and her scathing wit; both she and the witch had a way of making me feel naive when I least expected it. I passed the bow to the goddess.

"Fine. What's next?"

"Next, we head back to the villa. We'll need to hurry, though. We only have until sunset."

"Why until sunset?"

"Because I have errands to run while my father sleeps." Circe gestured to the sky overhead, visible between the trees, before jerking her chin towards the villa. "Let's go."

I fell into step behind the witch, only dimly recalling Circe's paternity; I couldn't remember her mother's name, but I knew Helios—the Titan whose chariot carried the sun across the sky—was her father, according to the myths. I scowled, disturbed almost as much by the notion that a Titan could track what we were up to as I was by the idea of the sun being anything other than a celestial body anchored in the heavens.

"Does he really spy on ye?"

"When it suits him. We aren't what you'd call close. None of us are. It's the destiny of a god, I'm afraid, to be eternally alone. The price we pay, you might say."

"Ye sure it isn't just because ye push people away?" I challenged, bitterly.

"That's precisely why. Those who stand too close to the fire are destined to get burned, and we gods are fire incarnate. You will see that for yourself, someday, I'm sure." Circe spared me a glance. "Though I hope not, for your sake."

"What's the next test?" I asked, eager to change the subject.

"You are no Artemis. No Ares. Perhaps you will follow Athena's path as a tactician. For that, I have just the test. But first, let's see if you have anything in common with the sky gods.

"And how are we goin' to figure that out?"

"Easy. We just have to see if you can fly."

15

*A*t the cost of severely grazed knees and palms, I found out I could not, in fact, fly. Also, after nearly drowning in the sea, that I couldn't breathe underwater. Indeed, we'd concluded I couldn't break boulders with my bare hands no matter how hard I bashed my knuckles into the rock, I couldn't predict the future even if that meant guessing which potion was most likely to make me sick, I couldn't weave a tapestry even with a savant guiding my every move, and I couldn't transform one object into another at will even if that meant turning a chucked stone into a feather before it hit me. Circe's tests had come one right after the other in brutal succession, each one breaking me in unique, and often visible, ways. The blood stains I'd left behind were of particular interest to the witch; she routinely peered at their crimson contents, appraising the color and consistency as though both were of utmost importance, going so far as to prick my finger with a needle without so much as a doctor's "you'll feel a slight pinch" before she struck.

"Athena's test, then," Circe said at last as she wove between her treacherous flower beds, her trees lunging for me at every opportunity. I dodged them as nimbly as I could; every motion was accompanied by a fresh wave of agony. My knees and shoulders had taken the worst beating; I could hardly stand upright after so many fruitless jumps, dives, and erroneous guesses. Which is why I was obscenely glad to find two chairs and a table waiting for us when we entered the atrium.

What I was less excited to find was another man waiting for me at said table. Unlike those who'd attacked me at Circe's behest that morning, this one was older, dressed immaculately in silk robes that reminded me of those worn by Roman senators in Shakespearean plays. He was also black. Not merely tan as the others had been, but as dark as the mahogany chair he sat upon, his iron-streaked hair and beard thickly curled and freshly oiled. The man rose as we entered, bowing his head, eyes downcast in obvious reverence.

"Goddess."

"No need for that, Barca," Circe replied. "I've brought you a present. Let me know how she does." Circe flicked her hand, turned on her heel, and gave me one brief nod before turning to leave the way we'd come. I stared after her, fuming at her abrupt departure. What the hell was she playing at? Who was this strange man, and what was he supposed to be gauging?

"Where are ye goin'?" I demanded.

"I'm tired of watching you fail," the witch called back. "Good luck."

"Ye can't be—"

"I'm afraid you'll have to come closer, my dear," the old man said, beckoning. "My eyes aren't what they used to be. My mind, either, but don't tell her." Barca, or whatever his name was, flashed me a wry smile and a wink. At first, I bristled, thinking he was flirting. But it quickly became clear that wasn't his intention; he resumed his seat, indicating the other chair with a parting of his hands. "Please, join me. I get so little pleasure playing against myself."

I frowned but eventually wandered further into the atrium, struck by his polite mannerisms and his easy conversation. In that regard, his company exceeded Circe's by leaps and bounds; the crazy witch had spent the entire rock throwing exercise whistling the tune to *The Andy Griffith Show*. Once I stepped closer, however, and saw what the old man was referring to—a ratty red box with *Yahtzee* splashed across its faded surface sat square in the middle of the table—I wasn't sure whether either of them were entirely sane.

"I don't get it," I confessed.

"What does 'get it' mean?"

"It means I'm confused. What is this?" I waved a hand at the board game as I took a seat across from the old man, eyes narrowed in suspicion.

"Oh! I was told this was a popular game among mortals, forgive me." Barca retrieved the box and removed the lid, fumbling at its contents. "The goal is to roll six dice in a variety of patterns to get the highest point total possible. The trick, of course, is to make the best choices possible according to the sheet. To play the odds, essentially."

I found myself staring into the old man's earnest eyes, trying to figure out whether or not he was messing with me. It seemed he wasn't; he passed me a score sheet with a wide smile, his gnarled, knobby fingers moving swiftly as he pulled out the necessary pieces and tossed all six dice into a plastic cup.

"Ye can't be serious," I said, shaking my head. "Yahtzee isn't a strategy game. It's all about luck."

"Oh, no." Barca was already shaking his head, chuckling. "This game may revolve around luck, but I promise you it requires significant, albeit subtle, tactical skill."

"Prove it."

The old man jostled the plastic cup, his smile widening until it threatened to bisect his face, his eyes bright and eager. "Oh, I intend to. Shall we roll to see who goes first?"

16

*W*e played ten games, and I lost every single one of them. Most were by margins so wide it was all I could do not to yank the old bastard across the table and search him for loaded dice. But deep down, I knew I'd have found nothing of the sort. He'd simply beaten me, one round after the other, by rolling and choosing his points with uncanny precision. I'd nearly had him once, thanks to several strokes of good luck, including a robust roll featuring five 6s, an early Yahtzee, and a healthy Chance. And yet, somehow, I'd still lost.

"Eleven out of twenty-one," I muttered, though I didn't mean it. Even I knew when to quit. Besides, the sun was setting, and I could feel my eyelids trying to close despite myself. My head felt heavy, my thoughts sluggish. Indeed, I barely managed to look up when Circe reappeared. She'd changed into a darker set of clothes, but appeared otherwise the same as when I'd first seen her—practical and tough as nails. Sadly, I realized I no longer appreciated those traits in her; her practicality was too emotionally distant, her tough exterior abrasive and unyielding.

"So, how'd she do?"

"She played well." Barca shrugged, offering me a gentle smile to soften the blow we both knew was coming. "Nothing special transpired, however. She has no talent for strategy beyond what you'd expect from a clever person. No consistent knack that I could see, either."

"So not a goddess of luck, either." Circe sighed as she rebound her nest of hair, pinning it back and away from her face. "I suppose that was always a long shot. She'd have done significantly better at the other tests, if that were the case."

"If I may say so, goddess..."

"Yes, Barca?"

"I think you may have overtaxed her."

I frowned, realizing the old man was referring to me. I opened my eyes to find the two of them looking at me. Had I drifted off? I pushed away from the table and made to stand, only to stumble and nearly trip over my chair. A dark, wrinkled hand cupped my elbow. I tracked up that arm to the shoulder and eventually to the old man's face.

"Ye played really well," I said. "But I still t'ink ye got lucky."

"Yes. But I only relied on luck when I had no other choice. That's what set us apart."

"What, ye t'ink a goddess would have beat ye, is that it?"

"Depends on the goddess, lady."

"Athena?" I said, picking a name at random simply because I'd heard it recently.

Circe twitched.

"Perhaps," Barca replied. "We'd likely have split the wins, if I had to bet on it."

The witch made a disgusted noise. "Athena would have let you win, Barca, only to bring ruin down upon your head as soon as the stakes were greatest. The scope of her games dwarfed even your campaigns."

The old man shrugged off her dismissive tone, though I could tell she'd struck a nerve; he straightened imperceptibly, his patient smile giving way to an impish grin. "It's a shame she wasn't around to aid the Romans, then, or perhaps I would have lost."

"Don't forget whose hospitality you count on, Hannibal." Circe shot the man a withering glare. "Pride is a dangerous thing."

The old man bowed.

"D'ye just call him Hannibal?" I asked, trying to place the name. God, I was tired. Still, I felt I should have known it. Something about elephants...or putting lotion on its skin...no, that couldn't be right. Maybe I'd remember in the morning. Definitely after I'd gotten some rest.

"Our guest is tired, indeed," Circe said, speaking past me as though I didn't exist. "Escort her to her room, but then come find me. I need your advice about something."

"As you command, goddess."

The old man offered up his arm graciously, and I—too exhausted to think of anything I'd rather do than be led to bed—took it. I cast Circe one last, searching look, but the witch was too busy studying the open window and the dwindling light to notice. Somehow, in that moment, I thought she looked more tired than I did.

Or maybe I was just delirious and seeing things.

17

I'd barely managed to throw a blanket over myself before the siren song of sleep dragged me under. Ordinarily, I'd have forced myself to stay awake, to weigh in on the day's trials, and reflect on what I'd put myself through in the name of ascension. There were realities, after all, that I had to accept: my aspect belonged to neither sea nor sky, I was as frail as I had ever been in my life, and I was luckless—not that the last surprised me in the least. Sadly, I couldn't be bothered. Circe had pushed me too hard, too fast. So much so that even the old man with his dice had noticed. But why? I knew she wanted her flower, and yet there was something else to this frantic pace which spoke of desperation.

Unfortunately, there was no time to dwell on that now. Tomorrow was a new day, and I needed rest. So, rather than fight it, I succumbed, praying for a dreamless sleep—anything but the nightmares that had haunted me the night before. Mercifully, it seemed my prayers were answered; my troubled mind stilled as the sun finally dipped below the horizon line.

I slept soundly.

Until, that is, the sound of footsteps padding across the floor of my room woke me. I surged upward, swiveling towards the source of the noise to find a torchlit figure looming just inside the doorway. I opened my mouth to scream for help, but the figure's raised palms—held out in a universal gesture of "I mean no harm"—made me hesitate.

"What d'ye want?" I snarled, whipping off my blanket with such force I thought I heard it tear. I held it up to cover myself, aware suddenly of the slim nightshirt I'd changed back into, of my bare feet on the marble floor. Feeling vulnerable and exposed, I wrapped the blanket across my shoulders and slid off the bed into a crouch. "Why are ye here?"

The figure lowered its hands, taking the torch with both hands and drawing it close. Beneath that amber glow, I realized I recognized the man. It was the wrestler I'd bitten, the smaller of the two men who'd attacked and eventually pinned me. His eyes were clearer than they'd been when I last saw him—more human, less bestial. He'd washed and shaved, trading in his loincloth for a silk sheet wrapped artfully across his narrow waist.

"I have come as the goddess commands," he replied, his accent thickly Greek, but intelligible.

"Which goddess? Circe?"

He responded with a curt but emphatic nod.

"What is she askin' ye to do this time?" I asked, my fists clenched around either end of my makeshift shawl. "I can promise ye, one on one you'll find me a lot more dangerous."

But the wrestler was already shaking his head, his face racked with guilt and...something else. Something which flushed his cheeks. "The goddess says you needed my help," he said, then cleared his throat. "She says you must be tested, and that I am to be the recipient of your power."

"What the hell is that supposed to mean?"

The wrestler shuffled awkwardly from one foot to the other, clearly not comfortable answering my question. As he moved, I thought I caught the faintest whiff of roses and elderberry. Perfume? No, oil. It was all over his skin, I realized, accentuating the tight curves and bulging swells of his body. With a sudden burst of insight, the precise nature of the test Circe had concocted for me became clear.

"Ah. So, you're what, supposed to take me in the middle of the night?" I spat in distaste, unable to conceal my disgust.

"The goddess says that it would be you who took me," the wrestler countered, his tone wretched. "That I would be consumed by our passion. That I would burn to ashes in your arms."

"She said..." I hesitated, struck by what the Greek was describing. Did he really think I was going to screw him until he died, like I was some sort of succubus? No way, I decided; no one would willingly accept that fate. "Why on earth would ye agree to come, if that were true?"

"To die in service to the goddess is all I wish." The wrestler shook his head from side to side, the torchlight catching his profile from each direction. "My companion and I once tried to harm the goddess. For that we must pay, for eternity. Unless you can give me what she will not, I will be bound to serve her. Forever."

"And what is it she won't give ye?"

"Death. My death."

"Death," I echoed, glaring at the man, hating everything about what was happening, not the least of which included being woken up to something this ridiculous; I may have been many things, but a goddess of love and desire certainly wasn't one of them. "Seriously? If ye want to die so badly, why not climb on the roof and jump off. Or run off into the forest. Pretty sure there's a bear or two who would have ye."

"We are forbidden to take our own lives, or to leave the grounds. But to die in the arms of one such as you...that would be a blessing I do not deserve."

Despite the flattery, I felt a rogue wave of rage well up inside me at the mere idea of the wrestler's hands on me; the notion of his touch was, especially after this morning's assault, repugnant in the extreme. I stalked forward, letting that anger show. I put all my built up frustration into my walk, into the rigid set of my shoulders. I let the wrestler see the violence I represented, let him sense the deepest, darkest impulses which lurked within.

He froze like a startled rabbit, his breath rattling in his breast as I reached for him, as I planted my palm against the center of his oiled chest. In that moment, with his heart pattering against my hand, he seemed nothing more than a tiny speck of light—a flickering candle flame I could reach out and extinguish with but a thought. Subconsciously, I wanted nothing more than to blow it out, to feel his body go cold and still beneath my fingertips.

"Goddess..." he whispered.

I flicked my gaze to meet his and saw in his pitch black pupils a reflection of myself that startled me from my dark thoughts. I danced away so swiftly that the wrestler fell to his knees, barely maintaining his grip on the torch from which—inexplicably—green flames now burned. I held up my hands, staring at my glowing flesh, an emerald gleam radiating from the veins that bridged my knuckles and flowed down my bare arms.

The wrestler—apparently seeing this for himself—fell to the floor in a subservient position, and the torchlight sputtered out. And yet, I could sense him, perhaps even more so than I had before; I could feel the light he represented, was even drawn to it. I stalked towards the man and found I could read his thoughts—after a fashion. Strong among his own kind, but weak to his addiction, he'd done something unforgivable. He'd deigned to think himself stronger than a goddess, to believe he could take what wasn't offered, and all because he'd been too drunk to recognize his foolishness, his heresy. Such suffering...I could practically taste it.

I held out a hand, drawing the pitiful man to his feet, and led him through the doorway. Together, we stole quietly through the villa, though I was quite certain no one was awake; Circe, I sensed, was not even here. The wrestler made no noise, not even as we stepped out beneath the stars, my skin burning with so much power I felt like a beacon on the shore meant to guide lost ships. Or, in my case, lost men; as a reward for his unquestioning obedience, I turned to the wretch and laid a hand on his shoulder, letting him see in my eyes how much I knew—how much I understood.

Tears rolled down his cheeks.

"Will you save me, goddess?"

Save him. Such a curious way to phrase it. But, from a mortal perspective, I supposed that was entirely how it might appear. After all, what was all this power for if not to grant such wishes? I honored him with my most beatific smile, let him drink in the sight of me, and watched him draw his last breath. Such a lovely, broken thing he was. I snuffed him out in an instant, feeling only the slightest bit lightheaded as the poor, frail creature crumpled to the grass.

I took a moment to steady myself before bending to lay a chaste kiss upon his clammy forehead, but I could not afford to linger long; I had wrongs to right before the night was through. There were others, after all— so many others—who needed saving.

18

I was waiting up for Circe when she returned home only a few minutes before dawn. I'd chosen to rest beside the pool that had once born Nate Temple's ravaged face. It was a curious pattern, this pool. I recognized it, though faintly, like a half-remembered tune the lyrics of which had long ago faded from memory. I resolved to ask Circe about it, once she'd calmed down.

If she calmed down, I amended.

"What are you doing in here?" the witch demanded, disturbed to find me soaking my legs in her precious pool. But then, how else was I supposed to get all the muck and blood off them?

"I was waitin' up for ye," I replied. "Where d'ye run off to?"

"That's none of your business."

I shrugged, not the least bit concerned with the goddesses' reply; if she wanted to play coy, that was her prerogative. I wasn't that sort, fortunately. Which is why, when Circe asked me what I was up to, I told her the truth. The whole truth, and nothing but.

The witch ran out of the room with a shouted curse, moving clumsily for a goddess; she lacked the easy grace that came to the rest of us. But then, I'd suspected her of lacking the finer traits. It wasn't her fault; we were all made for a purpose, even if that purpose no longer existed. Sadly, her screams were equally unrefined. They assaulted my ears, shrill and unpleasant.

"What have you done?" Circe shrieked as she strode back into the room, her trousers stained with the mud and shit I'd been forced to clean off. Her hands, however, were stained with a redder, fresher substance.

"What ye were doin' to those poor creatures was monstrously unkind," I explained as I slipped my legs out of the pool and rose to my feet, brown water running down my calves in rivulets to puddle at my feet. I scowled, realizing it was far too dark for this sort of conversation. I flung out one hand, igniting the torches around us with the barest flex of power. Green flames cast an eerie pall over the atrium, though it did wonders for Circe's face; she looked quite fetching in green, even if she appeared to have swallowed something unappetizing.

"Your aspect..." Circe began, then hesitated, eyes going wide. "You're a goddess of death."

"Nonsense," I replied. "We're all goddesses of death. And of life. Some lives we take, some we spare. Even mortals are capable of that much. Try again."

Circe clamped her mouth shut, fuming. Unfortunately, I'd expected this sort of reaction; she'd spent most her life collecting her menagerie of mortal pets, her poor pigs, and I'd released them all into the wild. Well, all but the few who'd chosen to die rather than live out their remaining years as wild beasts. She really was a cruel creature, this daughter of Helios. But then, what else should I have expected from a goddess who'd traded her divinity for raw power?

"I'll give ye a hint," I supplied as I waved a hand in a loose circle, letting the shadows trail behind my fingers like tendrils of flowing cloth. It was but a parlor trick compared to what I'd discovered I could do in the intervening hours, but it was enough; understanding shone in Circe's gold-flecked eyes.

"A goddess of night," she said. "Of darkness. Like your mother."

"At your service." I curtsied, creating a gown out of shadows that bunched between my fingers. "Though I don't mean that literally, obviously."

"What happened to Milo?"

"To whom?"

"The wrestler, the one I sent to you." Circe scanned the atrium as if the mortal might pop out at any moment. "Did he not come?

"Oh, aye, he found me. I'm surprised ye didn't see him." I pressed a finger to my lips, tapping them thoughtfully. "I suppose I should have done somethin' with his body, but I wasn't sure whether he'd have preferred a proper burial, or cremation. I seem to recall somethin' about coins on the eyes?" I snapped my fingers and one of the torches went out. "Don't ye worry, I'll take care of it."

"You killed him?" Circe looked stricken.

"Isn't that why ye sent him to me? As a sacrificial lamb?" I chuckled to see her troubled expression. "I suppose it didn't work the way ye thought it would, but the end result was the same. Don't beat yourself up about it, he was glad to die, and I was quick about it. With him, and the rest, as well."

Circe flinched and fled the room.

"Was it somethin' I said?" I mused aloud.

The witch appeared only a few short heartbeats later clutching a wand as long as her forearm. She brandished it like a sword but spoke to me as though she were trying to mollify a child. "Quinn, it seems you've attained a great deal of power. More than I would have thought possible in such a short—"

"Really?" I interjected. "It never occurred to ye that I might be somethin' ye couldn't predict? Even with all these pools at your disposal, despite everythin' ye thought ye knew about me?" I laughed, amused right down to my toes. "How novel this must be for ye, then."

"It's too fast," Circe insisted as she crept further into the atrium, still waving her wand about. "You need time to adjust to the power, to control it, to remember how it feels to be human. To think like they do. If you don't, you'll be lost."

"Oh, Circe...if this is what it means to be lost, why would I ever wish to be found?"

I lifted both arms and let my power fill me up, let that emerald light burn beneath my skin, let her see what she would be up against if she tried to take me on here and now; even in the heart of her domain, I knew I could break her spirit. I knew I could defeat her, that I could rule here. After all, she'd seen only the barest glimpse of my power; the night itself was mine to command, and there was more to darkness and flames than the shadows they cast.

"Time to say good—"

Only the second half of the word faltered on my tongue, because it was no longer true; the night was finished, and so was I. I collapsed to my knees beside the pool, panting, sweat prickling across my brow even as I fought not to retch. The green flames went out in an instant, replaced almost immediately by the pale blush of dawn. I fought to look up but couldn't; my head was too heavy, my body uncooperative. I wasn't merely tired, but frozen, as though every muscle had seized up all at once—like a cramp that had taken over my entire body.

"What...the hell...is happenin'...to me?" I wheezed, managing to finish my question just before my legs gave out and I tumbled into the disgusting pool. Water and other, far less welcome liquids splashed across my face and filled my mouth, my nose. I wanted to come up for air but couldn't; my arms and legs refused to move. But then Circe was suddenly there, drawing me forcefully to the surface. With more effort than it should have taken the goddess, she lugged me to the pool's edge and threw me over with a grunt. In seconds, I felt her collapse beside me, panting at least as hard as I was. I tried to turn my head and look at the witch, but it was no use. All I could make out was her discarded wand beside my head and the light of day filling the nearest window. From outside came the sound of chirping birds.

"Circe, what..." I began.

"Shh. That's enough talking, for now. Just rest."

Rest, yeah.

Rest sounded good.

$\mathcal{M}$y jaw hung open in disbelief as I listened to Circe's explanation of what I'd done, which was sadly about all the movement I could afford at the moment; the rest of me was barely functioning. I tried to respond, only to have another spasm run its course, forcing me to clamp my mouth shut and hiss through the pain. It seemed the aftereffects of the previous day's grueling schedule, getting no sleep, and relishing my newfound godhood had worn me out in the extreme.

"You awoke the power prematurely," Circe went on, ignoring my tortured groan. "And what's more, it appears I was wrong."

"Wrong, how?"

"I thought to compare you to my cousins, to the Olympians. But I can see now that I was wrong. The truth is that you are something very different from us. Your current, pathetic state is proof of that."

"Are ye sayin' I'm not a goddess, after all?" I chuckled bitterly at the notion, then clutched at my aching stomach as a sudden wave of nausea crested. "All this for nothin', eh?"

"On the contrary, there is no doubt that is what you are. But what changed?" Circe cocked her head, studying me. "I sensed your power. I saw the blood of a god flowing through your veins. But now, all I sense is a frail, mortal creature."

"Gee, t'anks."

"I believe the fact that your power deserted you just as the sun rose is no coincidence. That you are indeed a goddess of night. But only *at* night."

It took me a moment to process what the witch was saying; memories of the previous night were fuzzy and haphazard, more like half-remembered dreams than true recollections. Visions of the wrestler, Milo, falling limp to the ground with his life force faint on my tongue, of the wild pigs I'd slain with jagged blades pulled from night itself, of confronting Circe with the certainty that I would drink her power down like a cup of hot chocolate. Of course, there were other visions, too. Ecstatic displays of power I could only begin to describe. I raised my arm, searching in vain for the tell-tale glow that had run beneath the skin only an hour before.

"So, that makes me what, defective? Half a goddess?" I shook my head in disgust. "This was pointless. Worse than pointless."

"Are you ever going to stop whining?"

I glared at the witch.

"I realize you're mortal now," Circe continued, "but that's hardly an excuse to bitch and moan. You are not defective. There are simply roles each of us must play," Circe leaned forward, clutching her wand and sporting a black shoulder bag I hadn't noticed before. "Rules we gods abide by, whether we like them or not."

"Aye? And what rules would those be?"

"I'm telling you, so shut up and listen before I turn you into something without a mouth," she replied.

I pursed my lips together.

"Better. First, a brief lesson. All goddesses can be divided into specific categories." Circe held up three fingers, then began ticking them down. "Maiden, Mother, and Matron. Some goddesses are able to progress from one to the next, from girl to wife to crone, while others are locked eternally in the form which most suits them."

I nodded in agreement, not at all surprised by that bit of trivia; age and experience often went hand in hand, and so it went with authority. Zeus couldn't be portrayed as a child and rule any more than Aphrodite could be past her prime and embody desire.

"But there are three other categories that are often disregarded," Circe continued, her fingers ticking back up. "We know them as virgins, warriors, and lovers. The identity of every single one of us hinges on these roles. At first, I assumed you were a warrior goddess, that your powers would awaken under duress, that you would rise to the challenge."

"Is that why ye had the men—"

"I wasn't finished."

"Fine," I growled. "Please, continue."

"When that failed, I tried a new tack. I gave you tasks which appealed to the virgin gods. Hunting, weaving. Gardening would have been today. But it seems you were neither virgin nor warrior."

"Could have told ye about the virgin bit."

"Yes, well, when I sent Milo I'll admit I was skeptical. You never struck me as a goddess of desire."

"What a lovely t'ing to say," I muttered.

"How many lovers have you had?"

"That's none of your business."

"Very few, I expect. And yet, it appears you awakened your powers as a lover would."

"Oh, come on. We didn't...I mean, I didn't..."

"I don't mean sexually," Circe insisted, a faint smile tugging at the corner of her lips. "Not all goddesses are like Aphrodite. Some are like Demeter, whose entire existence hinges upon her relationship with her daughter, Persephone. So much so that, when Demeter lost her to Hades, she changed the very fabric of reality to create the seasons you know today. Or so the story would have you mortals believe, anyway."

"But I didn't love Milo."

"No, you didn't. But tell me, when your power came, what did you do with it?"

"I...it's hard to remember."

"Think."

I scowled but did as the witch asked. Closing my eyes, I delved into the murky haze that was my memory. I searched for what I'd felt with Milo kneeling before me until, at last, I latched onto something real. I opened my eyes.

"His sufferin', I wanted to end it."

"As I suspected. Love takes many forms, Quinn MacKenna. What keeps you from letting anyone in, from all things casual, is the very trait which defines your aspect. Despite your callous exterior, you are exceptionally attuned to pain. You responded to his in a way you never would have responded to your own. That was my mistake."

"And this?" I asked, eager to change the subject before it got any more uncomfortable than it already was. "My sudden mortality?"

"A rule," Circe replied. "Balance."

"Meanin' what?"

"Meaning the power that laid dormant in you was far greater than I would have thought possible. There are very few gods who claim night alone as their aspect. Not the moon, or sleep, or death, but night. Of my own family, only Erebus, Nyx, and Hades can claim true dominion over it. But you should know that the three I mentioned rarely ever walked the mortal plane. Erebus and Nyx were primordial deities feared by Zeus himself, and Hades was relegated to ruling the Underworld so that the Storm Lord alone held sway over the skies rather than share power."

"Listen, I appreciate the mythology lesson. I do. But still don't understand what that has to do with how shitty I feel," I confessed.

"I believe this is the cosmos exerting its will. That you have been given a great gift at the expense of a powerful curse. Goddess by night, mortal by day."

"So you're sayin' this is, what, some sort of perpetual hangover? That tonight I'll be juiced up all over again?"

"I believe so."

"Great." I shook my head, wincing. "I don't suppose the 'great gift' comes with a freakin' receipt?"

"No. And there's more bad news."

"What now?"

"Before that, we have to figure out how to teach you to control your impulses, or you and I are likely going to try and kill each other." Circe gave me a frank look. "And by that I mean I'm going to have to bury you by this time tomorrow morning."

"Seriously?" I grunted, fighting off the shiver that ran up my spine at her appraisal of the situation. "You know, your bedside manner could really use some work."

"Oh, and you owe me two dozen pigs. I expect you to find and return them all before you leave this island."

"Gonna be hard to do if I'm dead," I quipped, chuckling.

Circe didn't so much as crack a smile.

20

The whisk of Circe's bare feet among the finely cut grass as she walked circles around me was all I could hear besides the gurgle of the nearby fountain and the occasional chirping of birds. My eyes were shut, per her instructions, and I sat cross legged with my arms held loosely in my lap, effectively doing my best impression of skinny Buddha. Mercifully, the spasms had finally stopped, leaving me drained but functional. The consequences that came with lack of sleep, however, lingered; I struggled not to nod off even as Circe explained for perhaps the dozenth time what I was supposed to—and had not yet been able to—do.

"I believe you'll find your ascended self somewhere within. Look deep. Call to her. She's locked away, perhaps, but just because you've been stripped of your power for the day doesn't mean she's gone. Once you find her, let her out."

I considered calling the witch out for sounding like a new age hippie tripping on some extremely potent acid, but Circe had made it clear any movement would only hinder the search for my "ascended self." She'd swatted me twice already—once for fidgeting, the other for scratching my nose. Thing was, I'd experienced altered states of consciousness before, so I couldn't exactly mock her approach. But then, that was also the reason I'd yet to give soul-searching a real shot; previous experience had led me to believe that "letting her out" wasn't such a good idea.

In Fae, I'd accessed something known as my Wild Side—a facet of my personality bent on risk-taking and violence who'd been inexplicably tied to the effect the realm had on newcomers. In the Otherworld, on the other hand, I'd drunk the proverbial Kool-Aid and become Ceara—a fiercely loving, vaguely maternal creature who represented the person I might have been under very different circumstances. Though I'd recently come to terms with both, the resulting identity crisis had left me with more hang ups than a teenage girl escorted to prom by her father.

Unfortunately for me, I had a feeling the witch was right. I'd experienced memory loss like this before, after all, under similar circumstances. Why wouldn't I undergo yet another schism after attaining the power Circe had promised? I had to admit it was possible all my power stemmed from some form of self-realization; I'd survived fusing with both my Wild Side and Ceara by accepting they were simply unacknowledged parts of me.

Which I supposed begged the question: what else had I suppressed?

"And what makes ye so sure there'll be anythin' to find?" I asked, moving my lips as little as possible so as to avoid another slap.

"We gods are proud creatures, by nature. We live to influence, to exert our will on the universe. Our very existence is tied to power, which makes us bold, but also foolish." Circe continued pacing, though I could have sworn I heard a match being struck. "Many mortals crave that power. Politicians and warlords, cult leaders and tyrants. But power like ours comes from within, not without. Which means it could never belong to a human being."

"And that's an answer to me question, how?"

"Take you, for example," Circe went on, as if I hadn't spoken. "As a mortal woman, you are proud, but you're also afraid. Afraid of becoming someone's victim. Afraid of being taken advantage of. So, you mask that fear by acting tough, by cracking jokes and picking fights you aren't sure you'll win just to prove how invincible you are."

"That's not—"

"The goddess I met a few hours ago, on the other hand, was not afraid. She was eager. She was proud and vain and more than a little arrogant. She may have had your voice and your face, but she possessed none of your fear. Which is all that saves someone as volatile and headstrong as you from becoming cruel. But then that's because her power came from within."

Uncertain whether to say thank you or cuss the witch out, I kept my mouth shut and reflected on what she was telling me. On the surface, Circe's premise seemed straightforward enough: gods derived power from what they themselves could accomplish, whereas mortals did so through influence. There were philosophical arguments to be made there, but I wasn't interested in debating theory. I wanted to know what Circe hoped to achieve here.

"So, ye believe ye were talkin' to someone else because, what, I wasn't scared enough?"

"Pretty much. As I said before, I don't see any reason why you shouldn't be able to channel your ascended self as you once did your Wild Side. In fact, it seems almost as if you've been preparing for this moment." Circe's steps faltered before quickly resuming. "Anyway, you have to concentrate if you want this to work."

"And if I don't want it to work?"

"Then night will fall, she will come, and I will be left to reason with her alone...using any means at my disposal."

"Ye really t'ink she'd try and fight ye?"

"She won't be able to help herself. She perceives weakness in me, and gods do not abide weakness. As a rule, they like to know where they stand, especially amongst themselves."

"Weakness? Ye?" I asked, scoffing at the notion. "I take it she's not as perceptive as she t'inks."

"Strength is a relative thing," Circe replied, cryptically. "And I'd rather not have to test the theory, regardless."

Something about her tone made me want to open my eyes, but I didn't. Instead, I wondered whether I was wrong to assume the witch had it in her to beat me, after all. Was the goddess weaker than she let on, or was I simply that much stronger? Unsurprisingly, I realized I was as eager to avoid finding out as she was. Which meant I had no choice but to do as she asked.

"Fine...remind me again what ye want me to do?"

"You have to first recall what you felt, what you saw, when the power coursed through you."

I scowled but did as Circe suggested; I envisioned the moment I looked down to find my veins glowing green beneath my pale skin, the moment I realized I could move about in the dark as though it were a well lit room, the instant I tasted Milo's pulse and recognized him as something inferior. So frail, so easily dispatched. But that was all mortals were, really: sacks of flesh and bone destined to die and be swallowed up by the earth.

Nothing at all like me.

I opened my eyes just as Circe finished another rotation. She held a smoking bundle of twigs bound by white ribbon, its honeyed fragrance rich in the air. Somehow, I hadn't noticed it before. A spell, perhaps? Something to make me more pliable? The witch caught my gaze and froze, her mouth turned down in suspicion.

"Quinn?"

"That's me," I replied, amused.

"Strange. You go by the same name she does?"

"She? What an odd t'ing to say."

"Then tell me this, do—"

"No, how about ye tell *me* somethin', Circe. Like why on earth anyone would give up their gods-given divinity?" I gestured vaguely at her person, unsure which flaw to point out first. There were so many, after all: her slight limp, the arthritis in her calloused hands, the small scar above her right eye. "Or, do I have it wrong? Was it taken from ye?"

"No. It was the price I paid."

"Oh? And d'ye get a good deal?"

"Depends who you ask," the witch replied, her tone utterly deadpan.

"I imagine so," I said, grinning. I had to admit I was charmed by the dour daughter of Helios; she'd recovered from our earlier confrontation and seemed in much better spirits. "So, what d'ye receive in exchange? Love? Fame? Some much needed alone time on an island paradise?"

Circe shook her head.

"Then what?"

"Anonymity," the witch replied. "I was tired of the politics. I saw what my family did to Odysseus when fate and fortune refused to let him return home again and again. What they did to Calypso when she was forced to send him back into the world. All I traded in was my influence. The sway I might have held over mankind." Circe shrugged, as if to say that mattered little to her.

"Hmm..." I pressed a finger to my lips in thought. "Nope. I call bullshit."

"Excuse me?"

"Oh, please, we both know ye could have hidden yourself away without sacrificin' your divinity. I t'ink you'd rather I not know the truth. That I'd judge ye." I flashed her a smile and winked. "Of course, you'd be right. I absolutely would. After all, why would anyone give this up?" I reached out for the fountain's shadow, planning to bend it to my will and let it weave between my fingers like a silk ribbon. But nothing happened. I frowned and tried again, only this time I called for a shadow in the shape of a javelin—a long, slender scrap of night.

"That won't be possible," Circe said.

"What is this?" I asked, holding my hands up in front of my face. The blood that ran beneath was faintly blue—the blood of a mortal, not a god's. "What have ye done to me?"

"Quinn," Circe said, dropping to her knees in front of me, her expression panicked. "Quinn, I need you to come back. Something's not right. Shut it down."

I tried to rise to my feet, but it hurt far too much; I screamed as agony rippled through my body. My poor, aching body. What had the witch done to me? Had she cast some sort of spell to render me mortal, to kill me? I lunged for her, snatching at her wrists, hoping to pull her to the ground beside me. But of course she stood and danced away before I could; even without the spark of her divinity, the witch remained far greater than any mere mortal.

"I was wrong, Quinn," Circe whispered, her face pale. "She's you."

"What are ye talkin' about? What have ye done to me, witch?!"

Circe shook her head.

"I only wish I knew."

21

*W*hen I finally returned to my senses, I found myself trussed up on the bed I'd been given feeling somehow even more broken than I had before. A single glance at my body told me why: bruises littered my forearms, and my chest bore strange abrasions that pulsed with heat. My mouth was dry and similarly stinging, my lips chapped so badly it hurt to lick them. It felt like I'd been in a bar fight...or a freaking cage match to the death that had been called off at the last second. After realizing I was able to move my head at least, I craned my neck to find Circe staring out the window with her back towards me. I spotted Barca a moment later. The elderly gentleman sat in a rocking chair in the corner of the room, studying a chess set carved from what appeared to be obsidian and bone. Judging from the shards of light splashed across the room from the west, it had to be after midday, which meant at least an hour had passed since I sat outside with the witch.

Barca noticed me, first. His iron wool eyebrows shot up in surprise but were followed almost immediately by a slight uplift of lips—a gentle smile that helped make the fact I couldn't move a little less terrifying. The man slid a piece a little darker than he was diagonally across the board, made a small notation on a slip of paper, and rose.

"Glad to see you're awake, lady."

"Knight to E7."

Barca cocked an eyebrow.

"I've just always wanted to say that," I admitted.

"Ah." The old man glanced down at his board, nudged one of the smaller pieces into the gap, and gave me a thumbs up. When I asked if I'd put him in check, however, he gave me a wry look. "Oh, no. In fact, that decreased the odds of winning by ten percent, give or take."

"Good t'ing I'm playin' black, then, huh?"

"What do you remember?" Circe interjected, though I noted she made no effort to turn and face me.

"Not much." I thought about it, then attempted a shrug that only exacerbated the ache in my shoulder. "We were talkin', right? Then I tried to do somethin'...except it didn't work. Everythin' got fuzzy after that. Did we...fight?"

"Fight?" Circe half turned to me, one eyebrow arched. "Not exactly."

"Then what..."

"You weren't interested in our help," Barca chimed in. "Fortunately, we were able to restrain you. Eventually."

"Eventually, indeed." Circe sighed and faced me, displaying a swollen cheek and jagged marks across her forehead. I glanced down at my bound wrists and noted the blood beneath my fingernails with more than a little apprehension.

"Did I do that?"

"In a manner of speaking, yes. But then it was my fault for asking you to channel that part of yourself in the first place. I made a mistake, believing she was distinct from you. That you and I could reason with her. But she isn't, and we can't."

"Wait, why not?" I asked as I pulled against the twisted bed sheets which bound my wrists. "What was the point of all this if not to get this power of mine under control?"

"That's the problem. I'm not so sure it's your power, after all, which means control is the least of our concerns. It seems you're the same person. As in she's you and you are her."

"Well, sure. But then what makes her any different from me Wild Side? Or Ceara? They were me, also, and I was able to find a balance with them."

"Circe and I have been giving that some thought," Barca replied as he wandered over to my bedside. After receiving a nod from the witch, the old man began undoing the knots which bound my aching wrists, his nimble fingers prying the fabric loose until I could at least move my arms.

"Your Wild Side was a sleeping part of your mind, awoken by the Fae realm," Circe explained while he worked. "Your Otherworld self, similarly, took over once you consumed their food and water. Both manifested themselves only after you came into contact with a foreign element, which suggests you never would have encountered them had you stayed put in the mortal realm."

"We believe it's likely that the presence within you is internal in nature, not external," Barca added as he worked to free my legs. "It seems when you drank the potion, you rid yourself not only of your former power, but also any residue that remained from your mother's geas. In doing so, we think both of you were freed. Which would ordinarily be a cause for celebration, except..."

"Except what?"

"Except it appears she shares your sense of self and exists independently from you."

"How is that possible?" I flexed my hands, hissing as blood rushed into my extremities. "I mean, she has to know there's two of us, right?"

Circe and Barca shared a look over my head that was anything but reassuring.

"Right?" I asked, again.

"We think it's possible she does not," Barca replied after a moment's hesitation. "In fact, it seems she believes she's the only one. Which would make you...well..."

"Would make me what, damnit?"

"Quinn, calm down," Circe said as she abandoned the window for my bedside looking like a doctor about to deliver a fatal prognosis. "When your mother removed her power and put the geas on you, I assumed it was to keep you safe from anyone who might be looking for you. Or to give you a relatively normal childhood, maybe. No matter the logic behind it, I was certain she meant to protect you."

"What d'ye mean ye *were* sure?"

"Now, I believe it's possible it wasn't you she was trying to protect. It was everyone else."

"And what the hell is that supposed to mean?" I asked as I kicked myself free, the sheets falling to the floor in a pile. I rose, wobbly, and ignored the

91

outstretched hand of the shorter, older man. I felt woozy and sick to my stomach, perhaps even feverish, as I backed away from the two of them. And yet I sensed, somehow, that what Circe was implying had some merit, even if I didn't want to hear why.

"It means," Circe replied, "that I just spent the better part of the afternoon trying to explain to a goddess why she was trapped in the body of a mortal. It means, Quinn, that it's entirely possible she isn't the stranger, here. Perhaps she's the one who belongs."

2 2

I took refuge in the atrium, far from Circe's prying eyes and Barca's sad, sympathetic smile. The three of us had spent the past half hour talking in circles before I'd finally gotten fed up and left. In the end, Circe's read on the situation—that I was the vagrant squatting inside the body of a goddess—had proven too difficult to entertain. No matter what she said, this was my body. I was the one who'd broken it down and built it back up, who knew the origin of every scar it bore, who'd seen it both caressed and cut. And yet, the longer she and Barca talked, the more counterarguments they made, the less I could say in my defense—not so different from what I'd imagine it was like to argue one's own sanity to a room full of psychiatrists.

"Isn't it obvious? I know because it's me in here," I recalled declaring as I beat my chest. "It's always been me. This body is mine."

"Yes, of course it *is* your body," Barca had replied. "But for the sake of argument, let's consider what might have happened had your mother passed on the power when you were born. What if she'd never cast the geas? Isn't it at least possible that the goddess within is who you would have become? Who you were meant to be, perhaps?"

"Who I was *meant* to be?"

I'd wanted to sock the old bastard in his jaw. To deny any and every outlandish claim they made. Trouble was, I'd often felt like a stranger in my own skin. Ever since I was a little girl, I'd struggled with awkwardness, not to mention an overall lack of coordination. My aunt used to insist my growth spurts were to blame for both, and that one day I'd be able to juggle a soccer ball or jump rope like everyone else. When I complained about her inexact timetable, she took me to my very first martial arts class. There, I finally felt as if I'd gotten a handle on it all.

Until, that is, I discovered I was capable of more—that I could do things everyone else couldn't. Shortly after my eighteenth birthday, I found I could defy and outwit magical creatures using my unique field of influence, a field that seemed to radiate off my very skin. Unable to determine what I'd done to deserve a body that repelled magic as well as monsters, I became the clumsy girl all over again. Only this time I never regained a sense of normalcy. Instead, I went from one power to the next, rolling with every metaphorical punch—even when that meant retraining my entire body to keep from tearing doors off hinges and conditioning my mind to keep my most violent impulses at bay. And now they were trying to say that all that effort was for nothing? That I shouldn't have bothered? Fat fucking chance.

"Are you in here moping?"

Circe stood in the doorway, little more than a silhouette from this distance. The wounds across her face had healed during our argument—the perks of being a goddess, I supposed. Still, I wasn't eager to chat; it was the witch who'd broached the topic of my mother's original intent, citing the possibility that it had all gone awry, somehow. That perhaps it was my destiny to relinquish control to the goddess within.

"What now?" I asked. "Ye want to pass me the knife so I can slit me wrists? Or would ye rather slip the noose around me neck, yourself?"

"Please. Don't be so dramatic."

"Go screw yourself."

"Look, I apologize for what I said earlier. It was just a theory. Conjecture. I didn't mean—"

"To question whether or not I have the right to exist? Gee, t'anks, but no. Ye aren't forgiven."

"Do you know why I bleed like a mortal?"

"I—wait, what?"

"My face," Circe said, sliding her fingertips gingerly across her forehead. "You saw the marks, didn't you? The scratches?"

"Aye, but what's that got to do—"

"It's my weakness, you see. We talked about it earlier, if you'll recall. The reason why you'd have no choice but to challenge me, why a mere mortal was able to wound me. It's because I traded away my godhood for something I deemed far more worthwhile. In doing so, I became a lesser creature. A demi-god, at best." The witch took a tentative step forward, then hesitated. "May I come in?"

"It's your villa, do what ye want."

"Actually, my father had this place built. I've renovated it since then, obviously." Circe showcased the atrium. "It took centuries to make this my home. But then that's the thing about immortality...you're rarely ever in a hurry."

"So, you're still immortal, then?"

"No, thank the gods. I age as mortals do, though far more slowly." Catching my perplexed look, Circe chuckled. "In my opinion, eternal youth is highly overrated. There are mysteries you can only unravel by experiencing them for yourself. Aging is part of what it means to be alive. Besides, it teaches humility. Something gods could use a great deal more of."

"What d'ye trade your divinity for, really? No lies this time," I added.

"I'll do you one better. I'll show you." Circe waved me over. "I call this the Pool of Witches. It was the first. Initially, I used it to keep an eye on my siblings. Then, as the knowledge and abilities we cultivated became more widespread, I used it to keep tabs on the world. Look."

I joined the witch to stand before a crude pool in the shape of a pentagram—a five-pointed star. The water within appeared lighter, its basin filled with a golden, mercurial liquid that seemed to snake back and forth like an eel. I stared down into its depths, tracking that metallic presence, and felt oddly disturbed.

"What is that?"

"That is the blood of a goddess," Circe replied. "I spilled more here than I did with the rest. But I was young, then. The process improved with time and experience."

"Wait, that's your blood?"

"Do you know why I was exiled, Quinn?"

"I...well, not exactly," I admitted.

"They said I murdered my betrothed. He was a prince of Colchis, destined to become king with me at his side. But that was a lie. A convenient one, it turned out, since my brother was the one who had him killed. A dispute over some man or woman. I no longer recall the details."

"Why would they blame ye for it?"

"Because it was the simplest way to be rid of me, short of taking my life. You see, in my own way, I am as talented a witch as they come. But my magic is a subtle thing. It's meant to reshape, to refine. It never inspired fear or loyalty. As a result, I was never given the respect I felt I deserved. Even my marriage to that prince was merely a means to an end. An opportunity to increase my father's standing in the mortal world. But I wasn't satisfied. So, I sought out new power. I consulted with foreign powers, with beings who stood diametrically opposed to my own family. For that, I was exiled."

"Foreign powers like whom?"

"Like the one who showed me how to create this place." Circe cast her gaze around the room, though it seemed to me that she was seeing something else. "A goddess whose prophetic power dwarfed anything I'd ever seen."

It took me longer than I would have liked to admit to realize who the witch was referring to, but by the time I did, Circe had already taken my hand in hers. I thought to pull away but decided against it; I needed answers, not space.

"So, that's why ye kept an eye on me. Ye knew her, didn't ye? Morrigan?"

"Your mother, yes. Though that's not why I kept an eye on you." Circe flicked her eyes to two other pools in quick succession. "Let's just say I've been aware of certain...events brewing. At first, I was content merely to watch. But when fate brought you to me, of all people, I felt compelled to intervene."

This time I did pull away.

"I'm sick and tired of hearin' that shit. Fate didn't bring me here. Your grandfather's pet sea monster did. Why didn't ye tell me all this from the beginnin'? Why hide the fact that ye knew her?"

"I wasn't hiding anything. You saw my pools. I told you who inspired them. You simply never asked the follow-up question, and I'm not the type to volunteer information."

"Oh? And what aren't ye volunteerin', now?" I gestured to the pentagram at our feet. "What's this have to do with me?"

"Touch the water, and you'll see exactly what it has to do with you."

Angry and frustrated and wishing I could do worse, I bent down, cupped my hand, and flung the pool water up at the witch like a child throwing a tantrum. It splashed over her shirt and across her face, but the witch hardly reacted; she calmly wiped her face clean with her sleeve before turning her attention to the pool's surface. For some reason that pissed me off even more.

"What the hell d'ye want from me?" I demanded.

Circe merely pointed.

At first, I couldn't quite understand what I was seeing. It was a hospital bed, that much was clear. A man, once densely muscled but no longer, lay with a tube down his throat and IVs attached to his body, an EKG machine beeping just out of sight. I could hear it, along with the faintest whirring sound and the briefest snippets of hushed conversations. But it was the man's face, what little of it was visible beyond the medical apparatus, that I felt compelled to study. There was something familiar about his broad brow, his wide cheekbones, his cleft chin—something I found inexplicably attractive.

The man's name, when it finally came to me, sent my mind reeling: Maximiliano. I made to kneel, to drive my hand into that water and reach for the brujo—the name his people used to describe a male witch—I'd all but forgotten about after so long apart. But Circe was suddenly there, snatching my wrist and drawing me away with a strength that far surpassed my own. I fought her, yanking free, but it was enough to bring me back to the situation at hand.

"What kind of sick joke is this? Why are ye showin' Max like that?" I demanded.

"Don't be ridiculous." Circe cocked her head to study the bed-ridden brujo. "You should know by now that I'm not really the joking type. Besides, this witch's fate is nothing to laugh about."

"But...what happened to him?"

"You happened to him, Quinn."

"Excuse me?"

"Max, as you call him, fell into a coma the moment you left your realm for the Otherworld." Circe sighed, shaking her head. "That was a surprise, I'll admit. I lost track of you for a while after that. Some realms are impossible to peer into, even for me."

"What are ye talkin' about?"

"This is what I traded my godhood for," Circe replied, throwing her arms wide. "Your mother showed me that true power could only be obtained from a position of strength, and that information was the key to holding the high ground. From here, I can see what's happening across several realms, in several places at once, if I so choose."

"I don't care about that," I hissed. "I was talkin' about Max. Ye said he went into a coma when I left? How did that happen? Did he get hit by a car, or have a stroke, or what?"

"Of course not. It didn't happen *after* you left. It happened *because* you left. You were his life source. His life is tied to yours, didn't you realize that?"

"That's absurd," I spluttered. "How could..."

But then I was struck by a thought—by memories. I saw Max, his body painted in blazing tattoos, standing at the far end of an underground hallway. I saw him broken and bleeding on a hospital bed not unlike this one, his life force fading before my very eyes. I saw him pulling away from our first and last kiss, his skin on fire while my lips throbbed.

"I often wonder what it must be like for you all, not being able to see the big picture," Circe said, sounding faintly amused. "When you brought Max back from the brink of death, you bound him to you using powers you shouldn't have possessed. Powers you clearly didn't understand."

"Why show me this?"

"What?"

"This." I shook my head so rapidly my hair slapped both my shoulders in quick succession. "Why show me this, now? What point are ye tryin' to make?"

"Aren't you the least bit interested in hearing how you can save him?"

"I'm prioritizin'." Though it took a great deal of effort, I studiously ignored the man in the pool and gave Circe my fullest attention, letting her see just how fed up I was with this conversation. Truthfully, I would've given just about anything to find out how to save Max, but the brujo wasn't the only one out there who needed my help; I could only clean up one mess at a time. "Tell me the truth. The whole truth. What d'ye hope to gain from all this? And don't tell me it's some silly flower."

"You're right," Circe admitted as she bent down and dipped her fingers into the pool, appearing to brush Max's cheek in the process. The water grew dark once more. "The flower is important, and I still require it, but that's not why I decided to help you."

I waited, refusing to interrupt until she'd explained herself in full.

"Have you ever heard of something called the Catalyst?"

I fought to keep my face blank, but must not have recovered quickly enough; Circe took a step back and began meandering about the atrium, angling towards a pool I recognized as the one I'd seen Nate in. I trailed the witch, my guard up just in case my inadvertent admission had changed things significantly between us.

"At first, I paid little attention to the rumors," Circe called back. "There are so many dire prophecies out there, after all. Some have even been millenia in the making. And yet, time flows on. Or it did..." The witch glanced at me over her shoulder. "The truth is, I took an interest in you before I knew who your mother was. You see, I've watched many an era pass by from this very room. I know the answers to questions that academics have been asking for centuries, to questions they haven't even thought of, yet. I've been a fly on the wall during the fall of empires, the sole witness to torrid affairs and hired assassinations and so much more. But then something happened. I found there were places I couldn't see. Beings I couldn't track."

"Ye mean me?"

"Yes. Until you shook off your geas, you left a noticeable void wherever you went, like the shadow of a thumb obscuring a photograph. But you weren't the first. There were two others I couldn't locate, couldn't spy on at will." Circe stopped at the lip of Nate's pool, then looked pointedly at Callie's. "I had to ask myself, why you three? I became a little obsessed with the answer. That's how I discovered who Nate was. Callie's role in this remains a mystery, especially as their relationship deteriorates. Yours, however, I believe I finally understand."

"Do tell," I quipped.

"You're the one meant to stop him."

"Stop Nate? From what?"

"From tearing it all down."

"Not so fast," I replied, scowling. "What makes ye t'ink he's tearin' anythin' down?"

"It's already begun. Athena is dead. Olympus is up in arms. With Thor dead and Loki freed, the Norse gods are in tumult. New Horsemen have been chosen. The realms are closer than they've been since the Old Gods exiled themselves." Circe waved a hand idly towards the pool at her feet. "And now Prometheus walks free while the Catalyst answers to Zeus."

"And ye t'ink that's all Nate's fault?" I asked, dubiously.

"If it isn't, then someone really ought to protect him...from himself."

That sent a shiver up my spine.

"Whatever blocked my visions of you three was eventually dispelled," Circe went on to say, "but the more I studied you, the sooner I realized there was truth to the rumor. Nate Temple is the Catalyst. And only someone with the power of a god, but none of the restrictions, can oppose him."

"I've heard that phrase before..."

"Yes, from Morgan le Fey. I happened to be listening in. You were meant to return and learn from her before you were sent to the Otherworld."

"That's right. She was a witch. One who knew me father." My gaze was inexorably drawn to the pentagram we'd left behind, a suspicion tickling the back of my mind. "Were ye in contact with her?"

"No, nothing like that. I can't reach out to anyone, here. Any who wishes to communicate with me must come here. Those are the terms of my exile."

"That's why ye built these pools, isn't it?" I asked, flushed from my sudden insight. I also felt a stab of pity for the witch despite everything she'd kept from me—intentionally or not. "It wasn't power. Ye *wanted* people to come. To seek ye out."

"At first, yes," the witch admitted. "I hoped my family might visit, if only to discover what I knew. In time, I realized I preferred being alone. That watching time pass from the outside gave me more pleasure than being subject to it."

"So, hold on..." I struggled to organize my cluttered thoughts. "Ye wanted to help me discover me power because ye believe I'm the only one who can protect Nate from himself?"

"Something like that, yes. But I realized after you stormed out that, if I truly believed that, my theory had to be wrong. Your mother would never have trusted one of us with that task. The whims of a goddess are too superficial, too narrow-minded. Which means you have to be the one in charge for this to work. Fortunately, another possibility occurred to me, to us, after you left. One that makes a great deal of sense, especially given what you've been through."

"Oh? And what would that be?"

"Do you remember when I mentioned how similar this whole affair is to you interacting with your Wild Side, and how odd that was?"

"Vaguely."

"Well, I have a theory that explains not only that, but also why you've been manifesting so many powers. Why you became someone else in the Otherworld. All of it."

"Go on," I replied, still reeling from the series of revelations I'd been handed on a silver platter since Circe stepped into the room. I found myself staring down at Nate's pool, tracking its peculiar shape, wondering whether or not it had anything to do with the wizard, himself.

"First, can you recall how your Wild Side got your attention? It's important."

"She sort of took advantage of the moment," I replied after giving it some thought. "If I was in a fight or in danger, she tried to take control."

"And your Otherworld self?"

"Ceara? She and I weren't separate for very long." I shook my head, then shrugged. "It was the same, though, I guess. Except she reacted whenever I was feelin' vulnerable. Emotionally, I mean."

"That's what I suspected. Alright, one more question. Hypothetically, how do you think you'd take control?"

"Come again?"

"Well, your Wild Side was supposedly drawn to violence. Ceara, it seems, to drama. So, if you were to assert yourself, which—"

"Hold on a minute. You've got them all wrong."

"What?"

"Me Wild Side and Ceara weren't drawn to either of those t'ings. In fact, I'm pretty sure they were both tryin' to protect me, in their own way. One from physical threats, the other from the emotional ones. That's what motivated them. What motivates me, if I'm bein' honest."

When Circe didn't immediately respond, I turned to find the witch looking at me with the same manic gleam in her eyes she'd had when we talked in her creepy laboratory only a couple days before; she drifted uncomfortably close, gazing at me as though I'd just proposed—or at the very least given her the list of ingredients that go into a scrumptious pumpkin spice latte.

"What is it?"

"Our answer. I think we have it." The witch held out a hand, flashing the first genuine smile I could recall seeing; she was actually rather beautiful, especially now that the swelling had died down and the scars had vanished. I studied her outstretched hand, noting the callouses that ridged her fingers and palms.

"And where are we goin', exactly?" I asked, skeptically.

"To see a man about a boat," Circe replied. "You have a date with your crew, after all, and we wouldn't want you to miss it."

23

*W*aves lapped against the boat Circe had alluded to, far enough out that I could push it out to sea by myself when the time came. Afternoon light glimmered along the water's surface, dusk but a few short hours away by our estimation. Gulls dropped from the sky to roam the beach, pecking idly along the sand. All in all, it was an idyllic scene full of natural beauty, ruined only by the presence of the three of us huddled together; Circe and Barca had come to see me off.

"It should work," Circe insisted for perhaps the fifth time in as many minutes. "It's a simple plan, so long as you time it right."

"Which is what makes it anythin' but simple," I noted, smirking. I faced the witch wearing a refurbished outfit, courtesy of Circe's remarkable weaving skills; she'd stitched my ragged jeans and patched my leather coat and top with dark hides, leaving me feeling a bit like a makeshift scarecrow meant to scare away potential suitors rather than crows. But at least I was a cozy scarecrow.

"If something goes wrong," Barca chimed in, "remember to at least try to—"

"I won't forget, don't ye worry." I turned to grip the old man's arm and gave it a squeeze, surprised to find it lean with grisly muscle.

"Here. A parting gift." Barca reached into the robes of his senatorial garb and withdrew what looked like a blade made from pure silver; it gleamed as he passed it over. The handle of the knife, I noticed, was made from carved bone and shaped like the curled trunk of an elephant.

"That's right. Hannibal," I said, only just recalling the name Circe had bestowed upon him the evening before. Recognition sent a shock through me as I studied the blade's intricate design, accompanied by flashes of insight. "As in—"

"The Carthaginian? Mortal enemy of Rome? The Father of Strategy?" The old man flashed me a wink and a knowing grin. "Once, perhaps. Times change, even in places like this."

"T'anks for this." I pressed the knife to my chest. "And for your advice. But mostly for your kindness."

"It was my pleasure," Barca replied as he handed me a plain black leather sheath to go with the blade. The elderly gentleman looked as if he wanted to say something else, something important...but ended up shaking his head, instead. "Be safe, lady."

"No promises," I said, playfully. I faced the witch after sheathing the blade. I slipped it into the inner lining of my jacket, patted it, and met those gold-flecked eyes for what felt like the last time. "Ye realize I never hunted down your pigs."

"They'll be here when you get back."

We stared at each other as if daring the other to blink, aware that "when" might very well mean "if." As in, *if* I made it to the island of the Laestrygonians, *if* I managed to free both the giants and my crew from Ryan's occupation, and *if* I survived to tell the tale. Saying any of that aloud, of course, would have been a waste of time; neither of us needed a reminder of what was at stake should I fail.

"T'anks for all your help." I smirked, then added, "Such as it was."

"I did what I could with what I had to work with," Circe replied, sounding nonplussed.

I briefly considered hugging the witch, then thought better of it; I wasn't sure she wouldn't turn me into something without arms. Besides, our relationship wasn't exactly built on intimacy of any kind, and if I was sure about one thing it was that neither of us were the touchy-feely type.

"About Max..." I began, sounding guilty even to myself. Frankly, the brujo's fate had been on my mind the whole time the three of us had spent concocting our plan—which was more of a gamble, really. The fact that he wasn't my number one priority, especially knowing I was inadvertently responsible for what had happened to him, ate at me more than I'd have cared to admit.

"We'll discuss it when you return with my flower."

For some reason, that made me feel better; I could put off worrying about Max until I did as Circe asked, or died trying. In the meantime, I could focus on the tasks at hand. Like staying alive long enough to stop a genocide. Compartmentalization...gotta love it.

"Look for me at dawn on the fifth day," I said, gravely, before marching down the beach towards the boat.

"What was that?" Barca called.

"She's bastardizing a quote from one of those moving pictures I told you about," I heard Circe reply, her tone not even the slightest bit amused. "Ignore her."

I offered the critic and her companion a brief wave, stripped off my boots at the edge of the water, rolled up my pant legs, and waded into the surf. Pushing the boat out to sea took some effort but was shockingly easy compared to climbing in at the last moment; I nearly flipped the boat and ended up wet from the waist down in the process, my precautions more or less in vain. Indeed, the effort took more out of me than I would have liked to admit; I'd staved off sleep deprivation and general fatigue thanks to an herb Circe procured for me, but it had done nothing for the aches and pains.

Mercifully, I had at least an hour to dry off and relax, seeing as how I wasn't expected to row the boat; after laying out our plan and addressing possible contingencies, Circe had gone to work casting a variety of spells on the vessel, including one I'd accidentally cast myself on a different boat not so long ago—albeit with a great deal more effort and significantly less control. I tapped the prow with my exposed foot.

"Giddy up," I commanded. The vessel responded immediately, lurching forward with all the power of a motorboat. I settled back to wait, languishing in the feel of the salt-laden air against my skin, my hair blowing wildly in the wind. It'd be a tangled nest by the time I arrived, but looking like Bowie in *Labyrinth* was the least of my concerns.

I glanced over my shoulder, scanning the horizon for Circe's island paradise—the landmass appeared little bigger than my thumb from this distance. Despite our cordial farewells, the sight of it left me with mixed feelings. The witch had done as she promised: I'd received my birthright and attained the power of a god. But the trials I'd faced, not to mention the messy result, made me wonder whether I'd made a mistake when I'd acquiesced to Oceanus' suggestion. Would I have stood a better chance relying solely on my superhuman reflexes and Scathach's training, even if that meant forsaking my mother's power? Sadly, there was no way to be sure. Still, Circe hadn't lied to me back there; she'd done what she could for me, and I certainly couldn't accuse her of taking half-measures.

In the end, I turned back with a sigh of acceptance. We'd placed our bets, which meant I'd discover the outcome once we tested the theory upon which our plan hinged. Until then, there was nothing I could do but cross my fingers and wait for the dice throw. That, I supposed, and pray my luck was a tad extraordinary, after all. And if not, well...let's just say karma owed me one...or two.

Or ten.

"It is you!" a voice cried from the starboard side.

I sat up with a start, one hand pressed to my thumping heart, the other reaching for the knife Barca had given me as a parting gift. I withdrew the blade and pointed it in the general direction of the speaker, only to find a horribly familiar face surging alongside my boat.

"Triton!" I exclaimed in surprise. The god churned forward like an underwater locomotive, his head and neck just above the waves, his arms tight to his sides while his lower body—a tail where once there had been legs—kicked like crazy.

"I am glad to see you," Triton replied, sounding remarkably relieved. "Does this mean you passed the witch's tests and mastered your power?"

"Aye, though I'm not sure 'mastered' is the word I'd use. 'Passed', either, for that matter. Survived, maybe. Barely." I returned my knife to its sheath and moved eagerly to the edge of the boat. Triton, meanwhile, rose further out of the water, his muscular chest dripping with condensation, carried by a wave which rose high enough to put him at eye level with me. "What are ye doin' here?"

"I have been awaiting you, on Lord Oceanus' orders. He had me go first to the cannibals, to give them hope and tell them of your arrival."

"They aren't cannibals anymore, ye know."

"Only for the last three hundred years or so," Triton replied, waving that away.

"Bet you'd get it right if they were pescatarian," I muttered. "But anyway, how were they? D'ye speak to me crew? D'ye tell 'em I was alive?"

"I did."

"And?"

"He seemed...relieved."

"He?" I asked, frowning. "Don't ye mean 'them'?"

"I spoke only to a young mortal, little more than a boy."

"Are ye sure? What about Tiger Lily? Or Helen of Troy?"

"Had I spoken to the face that launched a thousand ships, I believe I would have remembered. Besides, last I heard she and her husband were producing some island reality television show off the coast of Madagascar."

"Wait, d'ye say Helen of Troy and her husband were doin' *what*? Where'd ye hear that?"

"From one of Athena's generals. Helen and Menelaus refused to take part in another of the goddess' wars. It seemed they held quite the grudge against the gods after the fall of Troy. Anyway, the boy said the rest of your crew were either sick, or missing."

"I don't believe it." I shook my head, disturbed by the notion that the Helen I'd sailed with had either left her husband to find us—something that had a track record of going very, very poorly—or the hooded creature I'd met had lied to me from the beginning. The former was bad, but the latter truly bothered me; if it were true, then that meant Narcissus and King Oberon had either been similarly fooled, or they'd been in on the deception. Unfortunately, I couldn't solve any of those mysteries from here. Besides, there were more pressing concerns to consider—like whether there was anyone left to save. "How about the Laestrygonians? Are they still under attack? D'ye speak to their Queen?"

"Their Queen is dead. Her daughter rules in her stead."

"Adonia is dead!" I exclaimed. "How?"

"She was struck down by the Frozen One's magic on the very first day. Her daughter was able to repel him and his undead soldiers with the Gaia's blessing, but lately it seems the Great Mother's influence is waning. The Frozen One grows bolder every day, seeking a way to breach the city's defenses. I believe he will strike again tonight, as he has most nights since he took the island."

Dumbstruck by Triton's revelation, it was all I could do not to have a panic attack right then and there. Discovering Queen Adonia—the strong, noble giantess I'd dealt with not so long ago—had fallen and left Ismene behind to take command was about as far from excellent news as it could get. Frankly, I couldn't imagine easy-going Ismene leading the charge against Ryan and his zombies; the last time I'd seen her, she'd stood on the shore in her birthday suit blowing kisses in our general direction, probably stoned out of her gourd—not exactly Queen Boudica material.

More like Queen Boudican't, if I was being honest.

"Wait, d'ye say tonight?" I flashed the god my most menacing smile, glad at least for that teensy bit of good news. "Perfect. Lead the way."

24

We came upon the island of the giant vegetarians as the sun brushed against the horizon, casting a bloody, ominous pall over the entire landmass. Not that it needed help in that regard. Even from this far out, it was clear Ryan and his horde of undead sailors had taken control; a thick bed of snow coated everything in sight but the tip of a distant cliff while glaciers bobbed about the bay like discarded teeth. From what I could tell, it seemed Telepylus, the city of the Laestrygonians, alone had survived the winter the Frozen One had brought with him.

With a series of touches, I redirected Circe's bespelled boat, dodging icebergs as I angled towards the shore that sat beneath the cliff. From there, I hoped to be greeted by the Laestrygonian fleet and escorted up the hidden footpath that led into the city. Sadly, it didn't look like that was going to happen; Triton, who'd charged ahead to warn those guarding the beach that I was coming, doubled back just as I spotted the smoke rising into the sky.

"They struck from below!" Triton called, gesturing to the blazing remains of the Laestrygonians' ships.

"Ryan must have figured out there was a way up into the city," I said, cursing inwardly. "I've got to hurry. Go warn Oceanus! Tell him what's happened, then go to Circe and tell her..." I hesitated, eyeing the setting sun. "Tell her I arrived safely, but that t'ings didn't go accordin' to plan. She'll know what that means."

Unfortunately, so did I; we hadn't anticipated me having to fight immediately upon arrival, which meant the odds of our plan succeeding were even lower than they'd been before. I fidgeted, slipping the knife in and out of its sheath while I tried to think of a plan. Triton, meanwhile, kept pace with my ship.

"Will you be able to stop them?" he asked, his tone betraying a concern that surprised me.

"I'll do what I can," I replied, knowing deep down that my best might not be good enough. "Go, now. Return in the mornin'. By then you'll have your answer."

Triton studied me with his bulging eyes, jerked his misshapen chin once, and peeled off the way we'd come, churning water as he went. I watched him go, then turned my attention to steering my boat through the treacherous waters. As I closed in, I caught sight of the battle being waged: Laestrygonian forces, armored in what seemed to be thick armor made from tree bark, fought eerie, undead sailors dressed in shades of blue along the path that snaked up the side of the cliff. The zombies were clearly undersized and outnumbered but hardly outmatched; the moment one fell, another took its place, only for the fallen to rise and fight again. So far, it seemed very few had been hacked into enough pieces to turn the tide—the only surefire way I knew to defeat them.

Clearing the last of the icebergs, I adjusted course and prepared to jump off the boat and onto the beach the instant I passed the burning wreckage. Smoke, thick and billowing, clung to me like a jilted lover as I zoomed by; I held one arm over my mouth and nose, my eyes stinging. The beach, once lovely and pristine but for the footprints of giants, had been stained black with charred refuse and littered with the bodies of slain Laestrygonians—those responsible for guarding the port, if I had to guess.

I leapt off the boat before it could run aground and sprinted up the beach, my legs leaden with the effort. Here, the sounds of fighting could be heard above the roar of flames; farther up the cliff, blades rang out as giants bellowed and screamed. I drew my paltry knife, slipped the sheath back into the lining of my jacket, and charged up the path. Before I knew it, adrenaline was thrumming throughout my entire body, chasing away any lingering fatigue.

I turned a blind corner and spotted the first undead crew member I'd seen up close since I'd fled Polyphemus' island. Missing a hand and clearly wounded, the sailor had its back turned to me as it limped up the path. Moving without thinking, I shoved the hoary bastard from behind. It sprawled awkwardly to the dirt. I fell to my knees, made four incisions with my dainty silver blade, and danced away. The zombie tried to climb to its feet, only to tumble sideways to the ground as the popliteus tendons behind its knees snapped like overstretched bubble gum, followed by the aptly-named Achilles. Not that the abomination gave up there; the damned thing began to crawl towards the sounds of battle, dragging its limp legs along like sacks of trash.

"Fuckin' zombies," I swore as I stood over the sailor and drove my blade into its brain. The thing froze, then swiveled its head all the way around so it could stare up at me with its oversized, bloodshot eyes. It opened its mouth as if to speak, and I saw the tip of my blade protruding from the roof of its mouth. Disgusted and more than a little disheartened, I withdrew the knife and stepped away. An inspection of the blade revealed very little blood and gore, though a repulsive odor—acrid and so potent it made me want to spit—drifted up from the metal itself. Formaldehyde. I'd have recognized it anywhere after briefly sharing a flat with a licensed funeral director in New York City; the odor was throat-grabbing, like having someone shove a chunk of concrete down your throat. I gagged and turned away only to find the zombie creeping towards me on his elbows one miserable inch at a time.

Well, so much for the "destroy the brain" approach.

"Great, just great," I muttered. With a quick juke to the left, I cut around the zombie and resumed my march up the path, determined to find the primary battleground and lend a hand however I could; if even a few of the undead made it into the city proper, I doubted the citizens of Telepylus would stand a chance against Ryan's frontal assault. Instead, however, I encountered a smaller skirmish taking place along a precarious leg of the path between two Laestrygonians and a handful of zombies. No, I amended, spotting one of the figures I'd assumed was a zombie until I noticed his face.

His exceptionally familiar, wonderfully welcome face.

"James!" I shouted as I rushed to join the fray. The undead sailors had pushed James and the giants back, leaving them with little choice but to defend themselves or fall to their deaths among the rocky shoals below. James, armed with a rapier, danced under the massive arms of his companions, fending off any attempts to cut the giants at the knees. Despite the soundness of the strategy, it was a losing battle, and it seemed they all knew it; the Laestrygonians—covered in flesh wounds, their armor splintered and cracked—moved so slowly to defend themselves that even I could have forced them over the edge.

"Quinn!" James swung at a lunging sailor, catching it across the shoulder. But the undead bastard took the blow like it was nothing and closed in, reaching for the young man even though it might easily have impaled him on the end of its blade.

Not that I was going to let either of those things happen.

I hit the four sailors like a battering ram, essentially wedging myself between them. Those closest to the edge stumbled, their arms pinwheeling in uncertain circles. Taking advantage of their shambliness, I planted my foot and lashed out with a donkey kick, firing my heel into the nearest zombie's chest with all the strength I could muster. Which was—despite my mortal limitations—enough to send my victim and its companion tumbling over the edge.

Neither made a sound as they fell backwards into the sea—a fact I found oddly dissatisfying. After all, if you're going to go through the effort of kicking someone off a cliff, you want them to scream on the way down. Or maybe that was just me. Fortunately, I had plenty to distract me; I whirled, thinking to take on at least one of the other two sailors, only to find the Laestrygonians tossing their assailants head over heels into the drink with thunderous curses.

Of course, that didn't mean I was out of harm's way just yet; James, screaming my name like a Mel Gibson battle cry, practically tackled me to the ground in his excitement. Tears of what I hoped was joy left uneven marks down his blackened cheeks.

"Really, Captain? I leave ye alone for a few days," I said as I righted the two of us, grinning like a madwoman, "and look what you've done to the place."

"I was so glad to hear you survived," James replied earnestly, his voice breaking with emotion. The young man clapped my shoulder, his expression dampening as the sounds of the fight above drifted down to us—an unwelcome reminder that our reunion would have to be short lived. "Sorry about the welcome party."

"Never did like surprises," I joked. "Where are the others? Not up there, I hope?"

"No, absolutely not. Tiger Lily and Tink are in the city, being cared for by the Vegiants." James, who must have caught my look, snorted. "Queen Ismene liked the name. I guess it stuck."

"Of course she did," I muttered. "What's wrong with Tiger Lily and Tinkerbell?"

"They're sick, Quinn. Really sick."

In my imagination, I saw Tinkerbell tossing up glitter all over my palms, her pink face so pale it might have passed for human. Had she gotten worse than that, somehow? How much worse? And Tiger Lily, her face tight from trying not to betray how much pain she was in...for her to miss a fight like this, however, she'd have to be bedridden, or worse. I shook my head, desperately wishing I'd left them behind in Fae.

"That's all me fault," I admitted. "I'm sorry, James. I'll get 'em back home as soon as I can, I promise. But wait, what about the Greeks? Where are they?"

A strange look crossed James' face—an expression I'd never seen splashed across it. Hate. Loathing. Something so strong and so fierce it made the hairs on the back of my neck stand straight up to see it. I reached for him, but the Neverlander drew away.

"What is it?" I asked.

"I have no idea where they are. But, if I had to walk the plank, I'd guess they were wherever the Frozen One is."

"They were captured?!"

"Captured?" James snorted. "Not unless their minds were taken from them. They weren't taken, Quinn. They defected." The young man showcased the beach and its dead below, now little more than dark specks spread across a scorched shoreline. Horror and malice waged a war behind his eyes, his jaw bulging as he gritted his teeth to keep from screaming. "And, what's more, I'm betting we have them to thank for this."

*T*ogether, James and I hurried towards the battle raging above, trailing far behind the two Laestrygonians he'd fought alongside, while the Neverlander filled me in on everything that had happened since I was lost at sea. Apparently, after the boat sped off towards this very island, Obelius had threatened to jump overboard to find me, regardless of the risks. It'd been Narcissus, ironically, who'd been the voice of reason and talked him out of it.

"Narcissus argued that Obelius, if he were captured by the Frozen One, would be used as a bargaining chip, or worse, tortured for information and discarded," James explained. "His fellow giants agreed, and we fled, hating ourselves. Well, except for the Greek, of course."

"Naturally," I replied, puffing from the exertion of running uphill.

"Are you alright? You seem out of breath."

"I'm fine," I lied. "What happened then?"

"We sailed back here and told the Queen, gods rest her soul, what happened on the Cyclops' island. She was surprisingly empathetic, but mostly glad to hear Polyphemus had perished. She even offered to throw a party in your honor."

"I hope ye took her up on that," I joked.

"We thought about it, but with Tink and Tiger Lily sick, I decided it best to retrieve the *Jolly Roger* and try to find a way home. Helen agreed. She even said she knew a way out." James spat to one side in disgust. "I believed her, until the Frozen One came and she abandoned us."

"When did this happen?"

"Shortly after he landed. The Frozen One sent his undead ahead, and they must have caught up to Queen Adonia as she returned to the city from helping us get our ship off the beach."

"And where were ye lot, then?"

"We were sailing the *Jolly Roger* along the coastline, planning to leave. We'd said our goodbyes. I had the helm." James shook his head in frustration. "Helen wanted to abandon the Vegiants. I refused. We argued, but eventually I turned us about and we came to their aid. By then, Queen Ismene had already taken command."

"Is she any good at it?" I asked, unable to contain my curiosity.

"Wouldn't know. Haven't met many queens. But her power, or the 'will of the Great Mother' as she calls it? That's nothing to mess with. The undead found that out the hard way. She buried the first wave to reach the city, and has kept the Frozen One's snowstorms at bay for over a week. But the tide was against us, and we knew it." James locked eyes with me. "Their gardens began to freeze over, which meant less food. There's been talk of returning to the old ways out of necessity, and now this."

"Wait, what about Helen and Narcissus?"

"We sailed here, returned to the city, and fought alongside the Vegiants. But, midway through the battle, Helen got cornered by one of the undead. She used that face trick of hers, probably to get away, I don't know."

I nodded, knowing the "trick" James was referring to; Helen had the ability to attract people against all reason. As a fallback plan, I couldn't fault it. Few people who want to have you are inclined to kill you first. And the ones who don't mind either way, well...yuck.

"Only it didn't work like she thought it would. The undead didn't come for her, it stopped. Just stopped. Then it spoke."

"They can talk? Seriously?"

"I don't think so. The voice came out of the thing's throat, but it was like it belonged to someone else. A man, if I had to guess. Anyway, it insisted Helen join its master. Except it didn't say master, at first. It called its master Captain."

"Are ye sure that's what it said? Captain?"

"Yes." James balled his hands into fists as he jogged, his ruddy complexion growing darker by the second. "She took one look at me, then snatched Narcissus by the arm and ran through the enemy lines. They parted for her like nothing I've ever seen."

"That prophecy-diggin' hussy," I swore. "First she chases after me, then ye, and now Ryan. And all because some Oracle said some nonsense about a Captain." I decided not to even bring up the fact that she'd lied to us all from the beginning; no need to rub salt in this big a wound.

"I wouldn't be surprised if Narcissus was the one who led them to us after we left the strait," James said, bitterly.

"It's possible, but I wouldn't discount magic," I replied after a moment's hesitation, unable to hide my doubts. "But then there's a lot about what's happenin' here I can't explain. Like how Ryan—the Frozen One, I mean—got so damned powerful. Or what he wants with the Vegiants."

"It's not them he's after."

"What?"

Except James didn't have time to explain; we turned the corner and came upon the battleground, met with the roar and clash of metal on metal, of ear-piercing screams and cacophonous shouts. I grabbed James by the meat of his arm and squeezed.

"Don't get yourself killed!" I yelled over the clamor.

"Wouldn't dream of it," the Neverlander replied.

Per an earlier discussion, the two of us split up as we reached the clearly drawn battle lines; James intended to report to Obelius, who presumably still led the defense of the city, while I hung back and avoided the battle. At first, James had been reticent to leave me behind, but I'd made a compelling argument, citing the possibility that more reinforcements could arrive at any moment and that having someone scout the enemy's flank was a tactical decision. The truth, of course, was more complicated: I was winded after the long uphill trek and in no condition to charge through the zombie horde, not to mention the danger I represented if the plan we'd hatched failed.

Fortunately for James, the two Laestrygonians had already carved a path through the unsuspecting sailors, leaving a wave of devastation in their wake. The Neverlander raced past, dodging the undead sailors as they rose back up from their superficial wounds, like weeds, to throw themselves back into the fray.

Up ahead, a stalwart line of giants huddled behind a makeshift shield wall made entirely of tree trunks, effectively bottlenecking the path and blocking any advance while a larger force behind them prepared to strike. I waited until I saw James pass safely through their ranks before taking stock of my own situation. Alone and exposed, it was a risk to remain out in the open. Better to stay out of sight until the Vegiants could mount an attack.

Though it took me several minutes of fruitless searching, I finally found a crevice in the rock deep enough for someone to slip inside. But it seemed fate had other plans in store for me: two sailors shambled into sight even as I tried to wedge myself into the opening. I hissed a curse, waited until they'd wandered far enough from the main force to spot me without alerting the others, and abandoned my hiding place to draw them further away. Hopefully I'd be able to take them out and return with no zombie the wiser.

Because, you know, I was lucky like that.

Yeah, right.

The first sailor I went after had been horrifically disemboweled, slowed considerably by the weight of its own guts being dragged through the mud. Aware of the odds of surviving armed only with a knife, I slashed first at the sailor's wrist, cutting away the tendons and compromising its grip on the cutlass it wielded. The zombie tried to wheel and face me but was too encumbered by its entrails, which made it that much easier to snatch up the fallen sword and hack at its exposed neck. The off balance blow caught the pathetic creature's spine, sending shock waves up my arm. But it had the intended effect: the zombie fell sideways, its head half lopped off, ensnared in the web of its own intestines.

And yes, that looked as gross as it sounded.

Seeing the fate of its downed companion, the second undead crew member rushed at me wielding its own dismembered arm like a club. Forced to leave the cutlass behind rather than pry it free from its former owner's mangled throat, I ducked and rolled beneath the sailor's swing, barely dodging the unconventional weapon. Staying low to avoid getting clocked, I lashed out with one foot—pushing more than kicking. The second sailor sprawled over its companion in a manner I would have dubbed comical were it not for the revolting odor in the air, and the fact that the banana peel in this instance was represented by a steaming pile of viscera; the zombie tried to rise using its one good arm only to slip back into the mud with a wet thwap.

I, meanwhile, took the opportunity to draw the cutlass from its neck sheath, then proceeded to chop at both zombies like I was possessed by the ghost of Lizzie Borden. Seized by bloodlust and sky high on adrenaline, it took me a couple minutes before I realized the Laestrygonian forces had descended from above; I stopped hacking and turned to watch as the giants began spearing the sailors, pinning them to the ground like they were sandwiches meant to be held together by toothpicks.

The strategy proved remarkably effective: the undead sailors fought to rise and resume their assault but failed to do much more than flail. Dimly, I thought they resembled overturned crabs trying fitfully to right themselves. It was almost enough to make me laugh. Instead, I craned my neck, scanning the Laestrygonian shock forces for any sign of James or any other familiar faces I might recognize.

And that's when they got me.

The nearly headless sailor wrapped its mutilated arms around my legs while I was distracted, pulling me to the ground. I screamed, more surprised than scared. But then the second sailor launched itself at me, the weight of its body enough to drive the breath from my lungs as it landed across my chest. The stomach-churning scent of formaldehyde was thicker now, enough to make me wretch if it weren't for the fact that I was too busy cursing and screaming. I thrust at the second sailor's chest and shoulders, trying in vain to shift him off me even as I kicked and bucked against the first. But the adrenaline which had propelled me this far was waning, as was my strength; I found I could hardly move as the second sailor wrapped its one functioning hand around my throat and began to squeeze. Looking into its soulless, emotionless face, I realized I was looking at the soft features of a creature who'd been a woman, once.

Reacting on pure instinct, I grabbed the creature's wrist with one hand and drove the palm of my other into its elbow, hoping to either break its hold or its arm—whichever gave first . But without my superhuman strength, I simply couldn't exert enough force to do that sort of damage; the zombie bore down with all its weight until my vision tunneled and it was all I could do to keep my grip on its wrist, to keep my eyes open and watch as the light dimmed.

he pressure on my throat eased the same instant I realized that the dimness was not me blacking out, but the shadow of a Laestrygonian looming over us all. It took one savage shake to yank the zombie off of me, followed by a throw so violent all I caught was the briefest flash of blue as the second sailor went soaring off the edge of the path to presumably crash upon the beach below. The first sailor was even easier to dispatch; the Vegiant merely finished what I'd started by wrenching the zombie's head clean off its shoulders and prying me from its hold.

A calloused hand that could have crushed my head to a pulp hovered in front of my face. I took it, letting the giant draw me to my feet much as he'd done days before when I nearly collapsed on Polyphemus' island. I scowled up at the Laestrygonian, doing my best to pretend like I hadn't been seconds away from dying at the hands of an undead minion on the orders of a former friend.

"Took ye long enough," I said.

"Maybe I should have waited until you passed out to rescue you," Obelius replied, grinning. "I forgot how annoying humans are when they're awake."

"Hah hah. It's good to see ye, Obelius. Though not to smell ye," I quipped, waving a hand in front of my nose. I pointed at the twitching remains of the headless sailor. "And that's sayin' somethin' with this t'ing stinkin' up the place, mind ye."

"Why shower when the stench of victory is always upon me?" The Vegiant asked with a shrug, his armor thunking as it fell back into place. The typically dour giant winked and waved me to follow, his spirits unusually high under the circumstances. But I did as he suggested, aware that my best chance of following through with the plan hinged on getting to the city's outskirts as soon as possible.

"Who authorized the armor?" I asked as we marched through the decimated remains of Ryan's crew, most of whom were being beheaded as we spoke.

"Queen Ismene thought it was a good idea."

"Did she, now?" I replied, noting the glowing way Obelius had said the royal's name.

"Nudity is all well and good during times of peace and prosperity. But war makes necessity where none existed before."

"Uh huh. And I'm sure it has nothin' at all to do with what happens to ye lads when it gets cold," I said, chuckling at my own joke. Not that it applied to Obelius; I'd seen what he hid under that armor, and it could afford to shrink.

"You know I wanted to go back for you," Obelius said, shifting the tone of our conversation so abruptly I could tell it must have been the first thing he'd planned to say to me.

"James told me. I appreciate the thought, but ye made the right choice. If you'd have come after me, you'd have been lucky to end up in the same place I did and not drowned at the bottom of the sea."

"I suppose you're right," the Vegiant replied, looking significantly relieved to hear I held no grudges. "But I still owe you for saving my life. It's a debt I hope to one day repay."

"And that didn't count?" I asked, jerking a thumb over one shoulder to indicate my recent rescue. "I'm pretty sure we're even."

"That thing would not have killed you," Obelius said, sounding surprised to hear me suggest it. "It wanted you incapacitated, not dead."

"How would ye know?"

"Because you're what those creatures are looking for."

"I'm what?"

"Your Captain didn't tell you?"

Thinking back on it, I realized that James had mentioned something of the sort before having to run off. But even then it hadn't made much sense. Why would the zombies be after me? Unless of course Ryan thought I was on the island and wanted to capture me alive. But that made no sense; Helen would have told him what happened to me, and she wasn't there when Triton told the others I'd survived. For all Ryan knew, I should be dead.

"I don't understand."

"We didn't either until we were told what happened to you. Is it true you ended up in Oceanus' prison?" Obelius was already shaking his head. "No one has even seen the River Lord since his grandson, Nereus, left the realm in search of Poseidon's trident. What's he like?"

"He was..." I flashed briefly on the image of the Titan, struck again by his massive size and improbable biology, but ultimately shrugged. "He was big."

Obelius seemed to appreciate that answer; he nodded emphatically as though I'd said something profound, even going so far as to puff himself up as though I were comparing the two beings—not that there was much to compare. The Vegiant was an impressive specimen by any standard, but I'd learned that the Titans stood quite literally head and shoulders above the rest.

"So, d'ye know what the undead want with me?"

"It's not just you. It's your crew, as well. It seems you have something the Frozen One wants. Queen Ismene believes it's an artifact of some kind, but your Captain swears he has no clue what it might be. And I believe him. He fights bravely, especially for someone so fragile." The Vegiant ushered me past the rear guard and into the city proper. "We were hoping you'd know what they seek."

Unfortunately, I only barely caught the last of what Obelius said; the city had stolen the majority of my attention. Where once I'd seen nothing but towering structures and vibrant color, I now only saw withered vines and white marble stained grey from smoke. The contrast was striking. So much so, in fact, that Obelius was forced to repeat himself as he nudged me towards the temple at the very top of the cliff.

"Sorry, what?"

"I asked if you knew what the Frozen One was looking for."

I admitted I had no idea. Frankly, until now I'd assumed Ryan had come here solely for revenge—vendettas were more or less his thing, these days. The notion that he'd chased after James and I in search of some talisman was not only odd but downright offbase. Not that it would do me any good at this point to wave the white flag and say as much to the miserable bastard, even were I in a charitable mood.

Which, to be clear, I certainly was not.

"Where are ye takin' me?"

"To Queen Ismene. She's in the temple, communing with the Great Mother. Your Captain is with her. We hoped to discuss strategy, now that you're here."

It took me a moment to decide, but eventually I nodded; for my plan to succeed, I would need to talk to the Queen, though I wasn't sure whether tactics would be part of the discussion. Frankly, strategy was the last thing I wanted to debate with the newly crowned monarch. What I required from her was obedience, not leadership. Unfortunately, the last time I'd spoken to the former princess I'd gotten the feeling that she lacked her mother's competence, not to mention Adonia's ability to make the best decision for the sake of her people, even if that meant being ruthless. And ruthlessness was precisely what I needed right now. What we all needed.

Because you can't kill anyone with kindness.

And that goes double for zombies.

27

*O*belius guided me past the guards stationed outside the temple entrance, offering clipped nods to the armored giants whose job it was to provide the last line of defense should Ryan and his forces break through. If any of them were perturbed to see a redheaded mortal tagging along, they didn't show it—clearly Obelius had earned their obedience. That, or they were the world's shittiest guards. No way to be sure, really.

Beyond the columns, we found walls of newly erected cypress, stained so dark they appeared black in the dwindling light of day, sealing off the temple's interior. While certainly more secure than the open forum had been, it pained me to see the house of worship fortified to this degree; Adonia had clearly valued the ease with which her citizens could come and pray to their hearts' content. What got my attention, however, was not the walls so much as the faint haze snaking out from the slightest gaps in them.

"Ye said Ismene's doin' what in here?" I asked, eyeing the temple's steaming exterior.

"Queen Ismene," Obelius corrected, firmly.

"Aye, Queen Ismene."

"She's communicating with the Great Mother. With Gaia, the Mother of Titans."

"Like over the phone, or on a Skype call, or…"

"What's a 'Skype call'?"

"Never ye mind," I replied, disheartened by the realization that the only being on this entire island who would have even understood that joke was the maniac I'd come to this realm to confront. How's that for irony? "Just tell me what talkin' to the Mother of Titans entails."

"See for yourself," Obelius replied as he yanked open a temple door which wouldn't have even budged for me.

A gust of scalding heat poured from the entrance. I took an inadvertent step back, caught by surprise. Sweat prickled on my brow. No, not sweat. Moisture. Obelius took one look at me, cocked an eyebrow, and strode into the ginormous sauna as though I were being ridiculous for hesitating. And maybe I was. Then again, maybe I'd simply been through enough shit to be wary of whatever fresh hell waited inside a temple that was plagued by sweating walls.

Spoiler alert: I was right to be concerned.

I followed Obelius inside only to find James and the giant lounging on the far side of the room, their faces slick and turned towards a dais that must have been erected after I'd left, eyes tracking the fluid movements of a stark naked, remarkably well-proportioned Vegiant. I, meanwhile, was left to gape in horror as Queen Ismene—de facto leader of the Laestrygonian forces—tucked her knees and rose into the most unfortunate yoga position I could have possibly imagined finding any nude person in: downward dog.

I hurriedly shielded my eyes from the unfortunate view of Ismene's exposed backside and joined James and Obelius, working my way around the platform with as much grace as I could muster while keeping my eyes lowered. From my peripherals, I noticed Ismene pop up into warrior one, both her arms extended high into the air, her fingertips spread wide, her forward leg bent and the other anchored straight behind. The monarch's body glistened with sweat, reflecting the light from braziers which blazed in each corner of the room. Suddenly, the heat made at least a little sense; Ismene was doing hot yoga.

Though what the hell that had to do with Gaia, I could only guess.

"Oy! Ye two, explain!"

"Explain what?" Obelius asked absentmindedly, his attention clearly diverted.

"What's she doin' up there?"

"Who? Queen Ismene?" James looked away first, his face betraying not the slightest indication that he felt any guilt, or even embarrassment at the sight of so much bare flesh. Indeed, the young man seemed so nonchalant that it made me wonder if he'd gone native since I first stepped foot on the *Jolly Roger*. But no, there was a big difference between hanging out with nudists and watching someone point their nether regions in your general direction, wasn't there? If so, why wasn't this skin parade bothering him as much as it did me?

Of course, it was possible I was simply being a prude.

Gee thanks, Catholicism.

"Aye, Queen Ismene! What is she doin', and why are ye two just standin' here watchin'?"

"She's channeling the Great Mother," Obelius replied, his voice full of reverence.

"Queen Ismene says this ritual brings her closer to Gaia," James added. "And she insists on having an audience."

I glanced back at the dais only to find Ismene in firefly pose, her legs mounted over her shoulders, arms planted on the floor, the line of her core visible from neck to groin. Oh, and she was staring right at me, grinning. I jerked back, then jabbed a warning finger in her direction. Her grin merely widened, though lazily.

"Listen here, ye voyeur, we're runnin' low on time!" I called. "Hurry it up."

As if on cue, Ismene uncurled, her legs arcing skyward, her head ducked until she'd executed a perfect handstand. I had to admit it was an impressive display of body control; few people can transition like that who aren't trained gymnasts. But then, I supposed that wasn't terribly surprising; the Greeks *had* invented the Olympics.

"She's nearly done," Obelius said. He nudged James, who saw what Ismene was doing and grunted. The two males stared, waiting for something to happen even as the discomfiting heat clogged the air, making me feel faint. But then I felt it: a cool breeze swirled around the room from out of nowhere, fresh with the scent of evergreen trees and gardenias. I took a deep breath, filling my lungs with the lovely aroma, and felt my exhaustion —including my throbbing throat and aching body—fade away like a half-remembered dream.

Ismene laughed, rolled out of the handstand, off the dais, and landed on her own two feet like a circus performer. She spun around like a child, moving so fluidly with the flow of the wind that I couldn't tell whether she was reacting to it or it to her. The scent lingered in the air for a moment as the heat died down, the braziers dwindling to mere embers, leaving us in a dimly lit, slightly chilly room. I shivered, rubbing the goosebumps that pebbled up and down my arms through my jacket.

"Well, look what the cat dragged in!" Ismene called, sounding in awful good spirits for someone who'd lost dozens of soldiers today alone. "Where you've been, you jive turkey?"

I glanced at James in confusion, but the Neverlander could only shrug.

"She was with Circe, my Queen," Obelius replied. "Remember?"

"Oh, right. Hey, Obie, I could use a gut waddin'. We got any of those tomatoes left?"

"Of course, my Queen," Obelius replied, his eyes darting back and forth between myself and his monarch. "I'll get you some."

"And James, could you go find some of those nuts you brought me last time? I'm going to go ape if I don't get something in my belly, soon."

"Certainly, Queen Ismene."

"Awesome. You're a cool cat, James."

The Neverlander flashed her a practiced smile and followed the Laestry-gonian out the door, leaving Ismene and me alone in the temple. Light drifted in from the open door as even more heat escaped and the braziers faded to a dull grey. I shifted from one foot to the other, awkwardly, hoping their little errand wouldn't take long; without Obelius to translate, I doubted I could make Ismene understand the gravity of our current situation, not to mention the appeal of my plan.

"You know I met your daddy, once," Ismene said, effectively shattering the silence that had crept up between us.

"Excuse me?"

"Well, more than once. He was fab. A real gas. Showed me all sorts of things, like music and movies. That's what you call them, right, movies? My favorite was *Skidoo*. I watched it every day on the tube he gave me until the thing went ape and exploded."

"Wait, he...ye..." I tried to scrape my jaw off the floor but could barely form a coherent response. "D'ye say ye met me father? When? How?"

"He was the Stranger, you dig? Came here and showed us how to grow, stopped us from eating each other. He said we should worship the Great Mother, that one day she'd shelter us. My mother didn't buy what he was selling, but I did. He was always predicting things that came true. Said you'd come, even."

"Me father mentioned me?" I demanded, my heart racing. "Specifically, me?"

"Sure he did. He told me some redheaded bird would show up and bring some heavy shit with her." Ismene folded her arms across her chest and cocked her head, looking as though a thought had just occurred to her. "Wow. Guess he got that right, too, huh?"

"Did he say anythin' else about me?"

"Oh, yeah. He said that when the time came, I should do whatever you said."

A wave of relief chased away my mounting confusion. Had Merlin really told her to follow my lead? Could I be that lucky? Flustered and horribly off balance thanks to Ismene's revelation, I seriously considered asking the sorts of questions anyone would be compelled to ask about an absent parent. For example, what was Merlin like as a person? Was he nice? Funny? A jerk? Hell, what did he even look like? But there was no time for that, not right now.

"I t'ink he meant now, Queen Ismene," I insisted.

"Oh, no," Ismene replied, waving her hand at me, dismissively. "Definitely not."

"What? Why not?"

"He said you'd say a word when it was time. He even made me memorize it by making me watch a movie with the word in the title. Before he left, he said I should watch it every day so I wouldn't forget." Ismene leaned in, grinning. "Joke's on him, though. I'd never forget, because it's my favorite movie ever."

I stared up at the Vegiant, unsure whether or not she was screwing with me.

"Was it...skidoo?"

"Damn, you guessed it!" Ismene exclaimed, looking like a little girl who'd had her nose "taken" for the first time. "Wait, how'd you do that?!"

I stood with the Laestrygonian city silent at my back, my boots sunk several inches deep in dense, wet snow. The air was significantly cooler here, the sky so grey and lifeless I could tell that there'd be no moon once night fell. The snow-covered slopes opposite, meanwhile, writhed with movement; the remainder of Ryan's undead sailors—perhaps a hundred in total—shambled towards the city in an uneven line, dragging their naked blades through the snow. I flipped the collar of my jacket and hopped up and down, repressing the urge to shiver as I waited for them to arrive.

"Are you sure this is a good idea?" James asked, his breath pluming from his mouth like a fresh exhale of cigarette smoke. The Neverlander rubbed his hands together for warmth, his button nose flushed red, eyes scanning the encroaching force as if deciphering their lumbering movements would give him some insight into what I'd insisted Ismene do if she wanted to save her people. The fact that she'd agreed before James and Obelius returned with her meal, coupled with the fact that she'd refused to reveal my request, had only made the Neverlander more curious; he'd pestered me about it ever since we left the city's warmer climate.

"If I said no, would that make t'ings better?"

James flashed me a dirty look.

"That's what I thought," I replied.

"Why won't you tell me what we're doing out here?" The Neverlander shoved his hands into the pockets of his biological father's brocaded coat—a gift from Hook's vast hoard of fashionable attire—and bounced on his heels to stave off the cold. The sword at his hip swung back and forth, slapping against his thigh.

"Because I know how much ye like surprises," I quipped.

"I hate surprises."

"Aye? Well, that's a shame. Ye should've said somethin' sooner."

"At least tell me why you left Obelius and the other Vegiant soldiers behind?" James pleaded, his teeth chattering. "The truth, if you don't mind."

"Because," I replied, sighing, "if everythin' goes accordin' to plan, they'd be a liability at best."

"And if everything doesn't go according to plan?"

"Then they'll be better off defendin' the city."

"You're not exactly inspiring confidence, here. I saw how winded you got on the cliff, and Obelius told me how he had to save you." James flung one hand in the general direction of the approaching zombies. "In case you didn't notice, that's at least twice what the Vegiants faced today."

"Oy!" I snapped, stepping close and throwing one arm across the young man's shoulders, acutely aware of how close we were in height as I met his crystal blue eyes. I flashed my best, most daring smile at him. "Tell me, Captain, d'ye trust your First Mate?"

"Define trust," James replied, nonplussed.

Guess charm was out.

"With your life," I replied, letting my smile fall away.

"Oh." James tensed beneath my arm, but he didn't try to pull away. Instead, he searched my face—though for what I had no idea. Reassurance, maybe? A guarantee that I wouldn't abuse his trust and get him killed? After a long, pregnant silence, he sighed. "Yeah, I guess I do."

"Good."

"That's all you have to say? Good?" James shrugged off my arm, glaring at me. Then, like a sun beam breaking through the clouds on a rainy day, he brightened. "As your Captain, I command you to tell me what's going to happen next. Now you have to tell, or it's mutiny, and I'll be forced to cut you down where you stand."

"Clever." I sighed, wishing I could thrust my poor hands into my pockets; the jacket I wore—like most designed for women with an eye for style—

couldn't have accommodated a tube of lipstick, let alone a human hand. Instead, I stared up at the sky, uncertain how much I should—or could—tell the Neverlander; there wasn't enough time to walk him through the logistics of what I hoped to accomplish here. To do that, I'd have to reveal the original plan I'd drawn up on Circe's island, complete with a description of everything I'd endured there.

Honestly, the fact that I'd made it this far despite a few hiccups—including an attempted massacre and the unexpected coronation of a perpetually stoned monarch—was more than I could have hoped for. How much of that my father was responsible for, of course, was a question that plagued me. Still, the only variables that remained were how long it would take the undead to arrive, how much daylight we had left, and whether Ryan would or wouldn't show to face me directly. Well, and James. "What happens next is they try to kill us."

"Obviously. So, what are we going to do about that? I know you have a plan."

"Of course I do."

"Well?"

"Me plan is simple, James. I'm goin' to stand here and wait for those undead bastards to try to kill us. And then I'm goin' to protect ye at all costs. And, if we're especially lucky, there's even a chance I'll save everyone else on this island by default. So keep your fingers crossed."

"You do realize that sounds like we've made a suicide pact, right?" James craned his neck, trying to catch my distracted gaze, his right eye twitching after having heard the sheer improbability of my plan. "Seriously? Quinn, did you hear me?"

The answer, of course, was no.

Because the sun had just gone down.

29

*N*ight descended like a lover to hold me in its dark embrace, welcoming me the way only a moonless evening could. Frigid, biting air nibbled at my exposed skin, so cold I knew with grim certainty it would kill any mortal who dared linger outside, bereft of the comfort and security of a fire. I, however, registered the sensation only dimly—no more concerning than standing in front of an open refrigerator door. But then, no chill would ever bother me.

No chill would dare.

"Quinn? Quinn, they're coming! We have to run!"

I turned to face the speaker, surprised to find a young mortal at my side. I took a moment to admire the sight of him, to peer into the pinkish flames that blazed white hot within his breast. He pined for someone, that much I knew for certain. But it seemed that his affections had turned bitter. I could taste it on the back of my tongue—his hate. Still, there was no darkness to it, no malevolence; he did not mourn his fate. If anything the mortal thrived, his turbulent emotions fueling his every thought and deed the way they so often loosened a poet's tongue or provoked a painter's brush. It was alluring, that heat. I wanted to huddle around it, to cradle it in my hands and hold it close enough to kiss.

"Run?" I echoed, amused by the sentiment. "And just what would we be runnin' from?"

The youth flung out his hand, gesticulating towards the base of the hill upon which we stood as though exposing some great and terrible evil. I followed the line of the boy's outstretched arm only to find his concern at least partially warranted; the creatures marching up the slope brandished rusty blades coated in hoarfrost, their intentions questionable at best. More concerning, of course, was their complete and total lack of fire; beyond their anthropomorphic shape, there was nothing to suggest they were alive at all. Indeed, despite my superior night vision they appeared to me like gaping wounds against the moonless backdrop, their features dark and barely distinguishable, their bodies animated by some inelegant, alien power I'd never seen before. To be honest, I found them utterly repulsive.

But not particularly frightening.

"What are they?" I asked, craning my neck for a better view, curious despite the promise of violence they represented.

"They're about to carve out our hearts and use them to start a snowball fight if we don't get moving, that's what they are!" The boy reached for me, snatching at the sleeve of my black leather jacket with genuine concern in his eyes. I let him take hold of me, let him drag me away. His blatant distress was...endearing.

"Such a way with words," I teased as he pulled us towards the light of a distant, glowing city. "Ye sure ye don't want to stop and write that down, Mr. Shakespeare?"

"Damnit, Quinn, that's Captain Shakespeare to you! I can't believe you talked me into this. Now let's go!"

"D'ye know why I enjoy mortals so much?" I asked with a chuckle. "You're always in such a hurry, as if the end of the race weren't predetermined."

"What are you talking about? What race?"

"The death race."

"We aren't dying tonight, Quinn!"

"Well, of course not." I sighed, wrenched my sleeve free, and waved the boy back as the first lurching figure crested the hilltop. The creature's boots crunched in the snow as it closed in, lurching like a piss-drunk mortal. Still, its malicious intent was clear; the instant it got within striking distance, the abomination swung its blade in a wide arc meant to take off my head. Not that I was going to let that happen.

I was rather fond of my head.

I ducked the blow, lunged forward, and took hold of the creature's wrist before it could prepare a second strike. As I suspected, there was no pulse; no fear, either. The abomination stared at me with empty eyes, its mouth clamped shut so tight that I had to wonder about the state of its teeth. How interesting. Did they feel pain, I wondered? I snapped the fragile bones in the creature's wrist, grinding them together until the blade fell into the snow, all the while staring into those unflinching eyes. Nothing.

"Who d'ye belong to?" I wondered aloud.

"Quinn! Quinn, help!"

I glanced back over my shoulder to find a handful of this one's fellows had ascended and shambled past, closing in on the hapless mortal. Why hadn't the foolish boy run off? Certainly these things couldn't catch him; they could barely put one foot in front of the other.

I felt a strange stirring at the sight of the youth trying to fend them off with his slender sword, backpedaling as if his life depended on it. But then, I supposed it did. If he were to be cut down, he'd die, and that lovely flame burning inside his breast would dim and eventually peter out. Which...would be a shame. Unfortunately for him, lovesick mortals were hardly uncommon; I could always find another. These abominations, on the other hand, represented a mystery I couldn't resist. And so I judiciously ignored the young man's pleas, determined to discover what animated these bizarre beings. Indeed, I'd only just resolved to test the creature's reaction to additional stimuli—the standard provocations to start, perhaps fire or even dismemberment—when a new voice split the night.

James. Save James!

Thinking one of the creatures had spoken, I wheeled towards the voice, only to find the mortal now on his back, kicking and screaming with three of the abominations looming over him. As I watched, they fought to grab hold of his flailing limbs, their swords lying forgotten in the snow. It seemed they'd lost the desire to cut the youth into pieces, choosing instead to pull him apart. Bit of a cringey way to go, if you asked me.

Save him.

That voice, again, only louder this time. A woman's voice. Naggy and a tad shrill, it was hard to ignore. But who did it belong to? I swept my gaze left and right only to realize dozens more had crested the hill and were marching inexorably towards that city on the cliff. Were they attracted to the light? The promise of heat? Or were they under someone else's control, as I'd originally suspected? I had so many questions that needed answering.

"Quinn! Quinn, please!"

The boy was thrashing in the grip of his captors, his mouth bloody from a cut on his lip, his skin flushed with exertion and cold. He had lovely eyes for a mortal, terrified though he obviously was. I'd been too fixated on his spirit to notice. I supposed he was handsome, too, in that unfinished way young men so often were. It really was a shame he was about to be ripped to pieces.

Protect him.

I frowned and released the creature's wrist. This time the voice had been little more than a whisper, and yet...and yet I'd heard it inside my own head. How was that possible? I shook it off, thrust the abomination back with the barest flex of power, and marched over to the cluster holding the mortal between them. He'd blacked out, though from what I could only guess. Sheer terror, maybe? Or perhaps they'd knocked him unconscious to keep him from struggling? Either way, the sight of his limp body struck a chord in me. I felt...guilty. Responsible. Protective.

We can still save him.

That damned voice again. Only this time, when it spoke, I felt something stir within; I pressed a hand to my head, bombarded by flashes of insight. The abominations were sailors. Undead sailors, bent on capturing the young man and myself, then sacking the city I'd come here to defend. They answered to someone. Someone I knew. And, if I didn't stop him, if I failed to defend the city or let this youth die, that individual would win. And I desperately did not want him to win. Indeed, in that moment what I wanted —more than anything—was to mow down these revolting creatures before they could lay another finger on anyone I cared about.

Caring...what a novel sensation.

Still, why not?

I could always take the sailors apart and see how they worked, later.

I dropped my hand, oddly disturbed by the emerald gleam of the veins flowing like rivers beneath my skin, and turned all my attention to the zombies carting away the mortal. James, I recalled. His name was James. As if sensing my regard, all three looked up as one, tracking me with their dead gazes. I waved, flashing my most brilliant smile.

Then, I pointed.

"Eeny, meeny, miny, moe, catch a zombie by its toe, if it hollers make it pay..." I sighed, realizing I'd gotten the rhyme wrong. "Screw it. Which one of ye wants to get beheaded, first?"

Fortunately, the zombie holding James' right leg volunteered by blinking before the awkward silence could stretch on for too long. I bowed my head in mock gratitude and pretended to wipe sweat from my brow.

"T'anks for understandin', it means a lot."

Resolved to kill two corpses with one tombstone, I decided in that moment to test my dismemberment hypothesis while the opportunity still presented itself; wielding a blade of pure darkness crafted from the night itself, I launched myself at the abominations with such blinding speed that the air itself was yanked along in my wake, taking the first sailor's head clean off with a single, decisive blow. Its arms went next—the essence of night sliced through the seams of its flesh, dividing the creature at the most rudimentary level. And yet, its hands did not release the boy's leg even as the torso fell away, which could only mean its limbs were independently mobile.

"Fascinatin'," I mused as I pivoted and shoved my fingers through the eye sockets of the sailor to my left, probing past the jelly of its eyeballs to gouge at its brain. When the creature failed to so much as flinch, I sent the tiniest bit of power coursing to the tips of my fingers—the barest surge.

Now *that* got a reaction.

A harsh green glare flared and sizzled as the zombie howled and fell away clutching at its face. No, *his* face, I realized; the sailor's ruined features came into sharp focus as he fell to his knees, running frostbitten fingers over a bulbous nose and sallow cheeks that had been utterly nondescript only a moment before. My power danced beneath his skin like fireflies, blinking here and there as it explored his insides. Eventually, the brief surge I'd hit him with dwindled and the light faded. And, as if on cue, the screams subsided and the sailor collapsed without so much as a twitch, his body steaming in the snow.

"Huh," I said, momentarily at a loss for words.

"What have you done to my *verschuldet*?"

The voice belonged to the third sailor, who continued to cradle the young man's head and shoulders as though I hadn't just assaulted its two companions. As I watched, an intelligence seeped into the creature's eyes—a vigor that took hold of its face and gave it the appearance of life. And yet, when the voice spoke again, I noticed the mouth barely moved and the tongue within lay flat and uncoiled. Which meant the voice likely belonged to someone else—to the zombie's master.

"Who are you?" the voice demanded.

"Well, that's different," I drawled, ignoring the question as I stepped over the first sailor's decapitated body to get a better look at this new aberration. I avoided the mortal's legs, reaching out as if to touch the zombie's oddly mobile face. What would happen if I sent my power into this one?

"Do not touch my work!" The sailor jerked back reflexively from my outstretched hand, clearly agitated.

"Are ye the one controllin' these t'ings, then?"

"They are mine, yes. Now, answer me." The sailor's eyes flicked back and forth until it spotted the crumpled remains of its steaming companion. *Mein Gott!* What have you done?"

A nagging thought occurred to me, though I didn't recognize it as one of my own. The creature's accent. German. I'd heard it before...but where? A vision of a mortal's wrinkled face, moustached and bespectacled, floated before my eyes. A face I recognized. And, with that recognition, a name… Frankenstein. Doctor Victor Frankenstein.

"Don't ye recognize me, Doctor?" I asked, taking a threatening step forward. James flopped to the ground as the creature released its grip, backpedaling. I glanced down, noticing the young man's skin had turned nearly blue from the cold; he needed warmth soon, or he'd surely die from exposure. Feeling bizarrely generous, I bent down, pressing my hand to his naked chest, feeling for the embers within. They glowed, but only just. So I fed them, pouring enough power into the young man to stabilize his flame without changing its color and binding him to me.

After all, I certainly didn't need some mortal following me around like a stray dog looking for scraps.

James gasped and sat straight up like I'd plunged a dagger into his gut, his eyes wide with terror. Poor thing. I patted the youth's head and rose, planning to resume my conversation with the mad scientist who'd engineered these monstrosities, only to discover our conversation had come to an end. That, or he wanted a larger audience; the entire horde had turned back from the city and was sprinting towards us at full speed, their blades trailing behind them, gouging furrows in the snow.

"I do not know you," Frankenstein said through his host's mouth, sounding much calmer now that he had reinforcements on the way. "But I will be glad to change that once my soldiers have torn you apart. I cannot wait to find out how you work."

"Quinn, what's going on?" James interjected, taking hold of my hand like a child looking for reassurance. "Why are they coming for us?"

"Quinn?" Frankenstein's voice held an edge of panic. "Quinn MacKenna?"

"The one and only," I replied, unable to keep the smugness out of my own voice. "Now, James…" I bent down to whisper into the boy's ear. "How d'ye feel about dyin'?"

The young man blinked up at me in confusion.

"I only ask because I'm about to go massacre all those zombies, but I'll need both hands to do it." I held up our interwoven palms, our fingers partially illuminated by the emerald blood that flowed between my knuckles. "So, unless ye want to tag along, I suggest ye let go."

James uncoiled his hand and pressed it to his chest as though I'd threatened to do him in myself. He cleared his throat and stared up at me with those crystal blue eyes, tracing the lines of my face, the way you might study an abstract painting.

"Can I help ye?"

"Are you in there, Quinn?"

"What kind of question is that?" I rolled my eyes. "Those undead must've hit ye harder than I thought. Listen, Captain Shakespeare, I need ye to do me a favor."

"What is it?"

"I need ye to stay out of the way. Wait until there's an openin', then run back to the city and tell whoever ye find that I'm busy out here and that they're to stay away." I stood and cracked my fingers, then my neck, imitating those mortals who relished a good fight. "Can ye do that for me?"

The young man nodded.

"Good lad. Now, hide."

30

here's something truly therapeutic about cutting down one's
enemies and stepping over their ravaged bodies, their blood
pooling at your feet—the harmony of their screams lulling you to sleep like
a mother's lullaby. Or at least that's what I'd always imagined it would be
like. The reality, unfortunately, was a lot messier and a hell of a lot less
satisfying; I danced among the walking dead wielding blades I pulled from
the ether, taking limbs and lopping off heads with abandon. And yet there
were no screams. No blood either, really. Worst of all, they just kept
coming.

Basically, I was getting bored.

As the next sailor came at me, I wrenched a spear out of the night sky
and flung it like a javelin, hitting the abomination square in the chest with
enough force to send it soaring into its fellows. The next I took down with
my bare hands, snapping its neck and hurling it to the ground. Unfortunately, the zombie seemed to take exception to being discarded; the sailor
wrapped its arms around my legs in a desperate hug, holding tightly
despite the fact it could have seen its own spine. Meanwhile, a handful of
ambitious zombies began closing in, perhaps sensing weakness now that
I'd lost my mobility. But I was an immortal goddess of night, not a rabid
bear. I sneered down at the offending zombie before spinning in a circle as
fast as I could. By the time I was done with my pirouette, all I had to pry off

my thighs were the arms themselves—the rest of the body had flown right off.

"This is gettin' pathetic, Frankenstein!" I called as I ripped the appendages away, scanning the undead who remained upright for signs of the Doctor's host body. When I couldn't find it, I sighed and decided on a new strategy: realizing I couldn't kill them outright, I began maiming any who dared come close, slicing off hands and legs and heads and fingers and whatever else came within easy reach. I left a trail of severed body parts in my wake as I waded among the undead, hacking and slicing and slashing to my heart's content. In a matter of minutes, I stood alone among the mutilated remains of perhaps a hundred corpses. The hilltop was littered with body parts. I watched in mild fascination as some pieces writhed and others crawled, confident none were whole enough to do more than grab at me or trip me up.

"Is that all you've got, Doctor?" I asked, letting my blades vanish back into the darkness from which they'd come. Power breathed along my skin, and I realized I was glowing with it; green light spilled across the trampled snow, casting eerie shadows that frolicked to and fro like the tongues of flames. I relished the sensation, acutely aware of my invincibility.

And it seemed I was only getting warmed up.

"Is it really you?"

I turned to find Frankenstein's host but a few feet away, its whole body caked in so much snow that clumps of it tumbled free from even the slightest movement. Frankenstein himself studied me through its eyes, his raptorial gaze a stark contrast to the zombie's complete lack of expression. A mound of snow nearby told me how he'd avoided falling to my blades: the mad scientist had buried himself like a child at a beach, waiting for the fight to end. Had he known I would win, or was he simply that cautious? Except, if the latter were true, why emerge, now?

"Why not come here and see for yourself?" I asked, holding my arms out wide in invitation. "With your real eyes, I mean. I wouldn't trust it, otherwise."

"I did not survive this long by being foolish, Fräulein MacKenna. I am not about to start now."

"Oh come now, Doctor. Call me Quinn. All me enemies do...until I kill 'em, that is."

"I am beginning to see why Herr Frost finds you so...worthwhile."

"Frost?" I frowned, struggling to identify the name. Something tickled my subconscious. Though it seemed hazier than any memory should be, I knew without a doubt that's what it was. I saw a creature with blue skin. Not a mortal or a god, but something in between. Ritual magic. The smell of machinery. A wound sat square in the middle of the creature's forehead while a pool of blood the same shade as his sightless eyes congealed along his cheek. A wound I'd caused. And yet, for some reason, the vision came with an unexpected sense of relief. "Sorry, Doctor. I'm pretty sure I killed him, already."

"Oh, yes. His predecessor. I had nearly forgotten." The zombie tapped his temple as if mimicking Frankenstein's gestures in real time. "It happens to the best of us if we are not diligent. But then, you are young, still. I expect you will not have to find this out for yourself."

"Is that so?" I scoffed at the deranged doctor, though I had to admit I was amused by his warped perception of both me and the situation at hand. "Doctor, ye may very well have defied the limits of your fellow men by staying alive as long as ye have, but I am immortal. A goddess. Daughter of the Morrigan and Last of the Tuatha de Dannan. I will not age, nor will I succumb to the dementia which so obviously plagues ye. Which means I do not forget, and I will not forgive. Coincidentally it also means that, provided no one beats me to it, I will kill ye for what you've done tonight."

"A goddess, you say?" Frankenstein asked, bypassing my threat altogether. The doctor fell silent for a moment, and I got the sense he was speaking to someone else on his end of things. Someone I couldn't hear. "Prove it."

I showcased his butchered army with a sneer.

"Was this not enough proof?" I asked.

"Oh, no." Frankenstein chuckled, wiping at dry eyes. His zombie mimed cleaning off a pair of glasses and replacing them on his host's face, then pointed over my shoulder towards a pair of distant hills divided by a low valley. As I watched, a dozen figures came pouring through the gap—each far too large to be human. And, behind these, a silhouette so massive its shoulders brushed the hilltops. "Please do me the kindness of showing me what a goddess can do against more than mere cannon fodder. I would very much like to see what you think of my latest works."

31

The ground trembled as Frankenstein's latest creations came thundering towards us, trailed by a sluggish behemoth—little more than an ominous shadow in the distance, at this point. Though arguably the greater threat of the two, it was clear I couldn't worry about that lurching figure until I'd first dealt with the advance party; heavily muscled, the stark naked giants loped with an easy grace that had eluded their predecessors. The fact that they were also quite obviously the living dead—and therefore immune to things like reason or pain—didn't bode well.

"Looks like I've got me work cut out for me," I remarked, appreciatively.

"The Laestrygonians were formidable in life," Frankenstein replied proudly, as if I'd complimented his handiwork. "In undeath, I think they will be unstoppable."

The Laestrygonians. Bizarrely, the name struck a chord. But it wasn't the race of the undead creatures I was meant to destroy so much as the latter sentiment which stuck in my craw. Unstoppable, were they? I craned my neck to study the sprinting giants, marveling at their long, smooth strides. They'd been crudely refashioned, their flesh sewn up and seared with naked flame, but I knew Frankenstein was telling the truth: I'd never be able to dispatch these creatures the way I had the sailors. The Laestrygonians were too big, their reach too long, their reflexes too swift. That—coupled with my strong suspicion that the giants were the diluted descendants of a divine bloodline, and therefore far more durable—made me hesitant to go on the offensive.

Of course, not all battles could be fought in the trenches. In fact, when facing a foe who could not be stopped, the most effective tactic was often the least intuitive. With that in mind, I scanned the grotesque hilltop upon which we stood, then the valley on the other side. That would do nicely, I decided.

"Tell me, Doctor, can they see whatever ye see?" I tapped my temple. "Is that how they know where we are?"

"I am always in control," Frankenstein replied dismissively, as if that answered my question.

Which, in a way, I supposed it did.

"Well, that's unfortunate," I said, with a long, drawn out sigh.

"And why would that—"

I didn't let him finish. Instead, with a mere flick of my wrist, I shaped a razor sharp shard of night and drew it across the eyes of Frankenstein's host. The zombie reeled from the blow, clutching at its face as though the doctor himself had actually been blinded—likely nothing more than a knee-jerk reaction.

Not that I'd have regretted the alternative.

"What the hell was that?" Frankenstein shouted, clearly enraged.

Unfortunately for him, I was over our little tête-à-tête; rather than answer and give away my location, I slipped off, working my way down the slope opposite the one the zombies had ascended. Had I not blinded the mad doctor, he'd have watched me creep across the snow towards the deepest, darkest section of the valley. Once there, I bent over, scooped up a handful of fresh powder, and fashioned a snowball. After adjusting slightly, I set my feet, took aim, and fired.

The snowball took Frankenstein's blind host right in the nose; snow exploded in its ruined face and sent it stumbling backwards, clawing wildly at the air. I threw another, this time hitting it in the shoulder. At last, I saw the zombie point in my general direction. The mad doctor screamed something in German, clearly frustrated with his current impairment, and the ground began to quake once more with even greater force than before.

The Laestrygonians were close, and they were coming for me.

I fell to my knees as if I were a mortal beseeching divine intervention and buried my arms in the snow to the elbow, my eyes raised to the heavens even as the giants rushed over the hilltop and came barreling down the slope at a full sprint, their skin pale and faintly blue, their faces slack and pitiless. I lowered my gaze and met the dead eyes of the forerunner—a giantess who, unlike her companions, wore finely crafted pieces caked with dried blood—and let her see how sorry I was to see what had become of her and her people. Mortals were one thing, but the descendants of gods were not toys to be taken apart and put back together on a whim—a lesson Frankenstein would learn before the night was through.

I'd make sure of it.

Once the last of the giants came sprinting down the slope, I withdrew my arms from beneath the snow. Viridescent light, so bright it would have momentarily blinded any mortal caught staring, shone from every pore in my arms and hands. The power I'd stored covertly strobed as the first wave of giants hit the valley. I heard the doctor's panicked yell urging his creations to halt, but it was far too late for that; as he'd said, they were unstoppable.

Which meant they couldn't slow down now if they wanted to.

The giantess leading the charge lunged for me only to end up impaled on a jagged spike made of pure darkness that took her through the belly and raised her completely off the ground. Spitted, it was all the giantess could do to stare down at me as her fellow Laestrygonians met similar fates. One after the other, the giants careened into the wall of spikes I'd forged. Skewered by their own recklessness, some merely hung in place, while others were ripped entirely in half or held aloft to twitch and fight gravity's pull.

The whole affair made for a pitiful sight.

Feeling sickened, I pressed my blazing hands into the dark shadows I'd created, shoving my power into the wall itself. The whole thing went up as though I'd poured fuel on a bonfire; green flames ignited along each of the shards, then climbed the wounded remains of the Laestrygonian force sent to tear me limb from limb. I watched them burn through teary eyes, my throat tight, gripped by a grief I couldn't rightly explain. The giantess was the last to go, her flesh initially shielded from the all-consuming flames by her accessories. For a moment, I could have sworn I saw something like gratitude ripple across her otherwise blank face. But then it was gone, lost among the smoke.

I released the power and watched the wall disperse like a mirage, leaving nothing but charred remains in its wake. I let my hands drop to my sides and bowed my head, drained from channeling so much power all at once. Was this truly the limit of what I could do? Or was I simply out of practice? I honestly couldn't remember.

"You tricked me, Fräulein MacKenna."

"Is that ye out there, Doctor?" I called cheerfully, straightening. I didn't dare let the madman know how close I was to collapsing; the mad scientist didn't strike me as the type to honor a timeout.

"I will admit you have proven more formidable than I would have thought possible, goddess or no. But it seems our game is at an end." Frankenstein's host emerged from the smoke, staring sideways at me through an oddly discolored—but seemingly functional—eye.

"D'ye steal that from one of the other corpses?" I asked in mock horror. Truthfully, I was a little impressed; retrofitting an organ under the circumstances was a pretty bold move.

"Needs must, Fräulein." The host dipped its chin in acknowledgment. "I feel I should tell you that Herr Frost has caught wind of our little altercation and is coming here. Sadly, I cannot let him take such risks at this stage in his coalescence. Forgive my rudeness, my dear Fräulein, but it is time for you to die."

As if on cue, the hulking, shadowy figure I'd spotted earlier appeared, only partially obscured by the thick wall of smoke. A face—horribly ugly and dominated by a great gaping hole where a single eye had once sat flush in the middle of its forehead—rose above the plumes.

A Cyclops.

Worse, an *undead* Cyclops.

Falling somewhere south of god but considerably north of mortal, I knew without a doubt that the newcomer would prove a greater challenge even than the host of undead Laestrygonians I'd defeated only minutes before. Indeed, as exhausted as I was, I wasn't certain I had enough juice left to even escape, let alone fight.

Hide and seek.

The thought came unbidden, but I had to admit it wasn't the worst idea; if taking the Cyclops down by force wasn't an option, perhaps finesse would suffice. A quick glance revealed Frankenstein had turned away to admire his handiwork, giving me the opportunity I needed to call the darkness without his noticing. Only this time I crafted neither a wall nor a blade, but a cloak—a thick blanket of night that hid anything it touched from sight.

Moving swiftly, I wrapped the cloak around me, slipping the excess over my head like a hood. Shrouded and invisible from the naked eye, I slipped away, dancing lithely past Frankenstein's half-blind host as the smoke cleared and the behemoth was revealed in all his gory glory.

Standing in nothing but a loin-cloth, the Cyclops was a beefy wall of flabby muscle and frostbitten flesh, his hair matted with frozen blood, his eye teeth capped with golden fangs. In his right hand, the enormous beast held an uprooted tree with its uppermost branches torn off like a club, dragging it behind him as he shuffled forward, plowing up whole swathes of snow in the process.

"Where…" Frankenstein turned a quick circle, swearing in German. "No matter, Polyphemus will find you."

As if trying to honor the mad doctor's prediction, the Cyclops scented the air, leaning forward like a dog sniffing out a trail. My trail. Inwardly, I cursed; my cloak hid me from sight, not smell. I'd hoped to avoid the creature while I recuperated, but it seemed I wouldn't have that kind of time. So, what were my options? I returned my attention to the Cyclops, himself, looking for weaknesses.

I quickly realized there was something different about this zombie—a liveliness his predecessors had lacked. It was there in the curl of contempt on his lips, his occasional grunt, even the way he shifted impatiently from side to side.

Still, I had to believe the same rules applied: without limbs, he'd be as debilitated as the rest. The question, however, was whether I had enough power left to cut up a creature of his size. I eyed the Cyclops' bulging arms and thighs, the knobby gristle of his wrists and ankles, his impossibly thick neck, searching for any vulnerability. Unfortunately, as far as I could tell, my best hope was simply to slow the creature down.

Sweep the leg.

Shaking my head to clear it of any distraction, I took a deep breath and centered myself. In my mind's eye, I bent over the last of my considerable reserves, assessing what it would take to do what I had in mind. It wasn't pretty; at this rate, I'd have to empty every reservoir of power I had left. If I failed, I'd be a sitting, legless duck.

Good thing I liked to gamble.

I opened my eyes to find the Cyclops had lumbered considerably closer —so close I could smell him at least as easily as he could me. The rank stench of sweat and body odor permeated the air, mingling with the faintest whiff of rot.

Damn, it was now or never.

Moving as surreptitiously as I could, I slipped one hand from the confines of my cloak and envisioned what I wanted: a bolt of pure, roiling power. My hand began to glow, then shine, as the image in my head manifested. The power surged, the bolt expanding from the size of a pencil to a lance to a cannon barrel.

"There she is!" Frankenstein yelled, threatening to break my concentration. "Get her!"

I gritted my teeth but stood my ground; I'd never get another chance at this. The Cyclops whirled with shocking speed, only to hesitate at the sight of my shimmering creation. Uncertainty flitted across the monster's face.

"Do as I command! Now!"

The Cyclops shuddered and raised his improvised club, preparing to strike. But his momentary hesitation had given me the time I needed. I screamed as the last of my power was drawn from me, the result a flaming green spear of energy as thick as a tree trunk and as long as a canoe.

Straining to contain so much power, I let loose the bolt, putting every last scrap of energy I had into its flight. It soared like an arrow, striking the Cyclops' belly with enough force to emerge out the other side, shredding through fat and muscle and bone in the process.

The one-eyed monster howled in rage and pain, toppling to its knees, clutching at its bowels. I, too, fell to my knees as the impact of his collapse shook the earth. Bleary-eyed from exhaustion, it was all I could to huddle beneath my cloak, hidden once more—not that I expected that to save me. Frankenstein knew where I was, and his horrific creation was far from dead; still, I'd slowed the damned thing down, at least. Without a functioning spine, the Cyclops presented a significantly diminished threat to me and anyone else he came across. Or that's what I told myself, at any rate.

"Oh, that was quite the display, Fräulein MacKenna!" Frankenstein called, followed by the sound of clapping hands. "Completely pointless, of course, but still."

I raised my eyes to see the mad doctor's host staring at the smoking hole in his undead monster's gut from only a few feet away. The host stroked at an invisible moustache, tapped its lips, and stepped away as though there was nothing of note to see. Except, suddenly, there was; the gaping wound I'd created began to fill with golden ichor that glowed like molten metal, seeping into the cavity like maple syrup.

I watched in disbelief as the hole closed, the flesh reknitting before my very eyes. I slumped in the snow, disheartened. All the energy I'd put into that shot, all that power...wasted.

And for what?

"I confess it took some doing, finding a god willing to give up his blood for my experiments. But I am glad to see that my theory was correct." Frankenstein's host rocked back and forth on its heels, thrusting its hands into pockets that did not exist. "The sailors were not terribly difficult to fetch from the sea floor, though I was relieved to find them so well preserved. To my regret, neither they nor the Laestrygonians were able to survive the transfusion process. I believe it has something to do with the integrity of the vessel. Further tests should shed more light on that." The host showcased the Cyclops as it clambered back to its feet, its body hale and whole once more. "As I am sure you are aware, Polyphemus, here, was a son of Poseidon. I rightly assumed he was made of superior material, but I must admit I am grateful for your participation in my little experiment. It is not often I can rely on someone to fail so spectacular—"

But the Doctor didn't get a chance to finish; having crept to within a few feet of his host body during his tiresome monologue, I discarded my cloak, reached out, and planted my bare hands on either side of the zombie's ravaged face. Then, before Frankenstein could utter another word, I squeezed. Hard.

Flesh burst between my fingers as bones shattered and brain matter pulped. The result was terribly unappealing, and yet I felt a surge of supreme satisfaction. With the last of my energy, I stepped back, planted my foot, and lashed out with a kick that sent the headless corpse careening into the base of the hill with enough velocity to cause a small avalanche. Snow buried the body.

"Ye talk too damn much," I muttered.

I felt more than saw the Cyclops turn towards me, its nostrils flaring. I sighed and faced the behemoth, prepared for whatever assault was coming. Thank the gods, being immortal had its advantages; even if Polyphemus struck me with that tree of his, I'd likely survive. Maybe long enough to escape, now that Frankenstein was out of the picture. Of course, I could always try to make a break for it...but no. There was no point. The Cyclops wouldn't even break a sweat chasing me down.

Then why is he sweating, now?

I shook my head, trying to clear my suddenly foggy thoughts. But the phrase continued to repeat itself over and over again inside my head like the toll of some gods forsaken bell. I gritted my teeth and glanced up at the monster's brow, only to realize the voice was right; he *was* sweating. And was that steam I saw rising from his body? How was that possible?

Blood.

That voice again, like a whisper. Then again, and again, each time louder than the time before until it was a crescendo pounding in my head. But no matter how blaring it got, I still didn't understand. Whose blood? Mine? Frankenstein's? The monster's?

The blood of a god.

I frowned, eyes drawn inexorably to the pink flesh of the Cyclops' belly, to where I'd seen the golden ichor drip and pool. A transfusion...hadn't that been what Frankenstein said? Had he truly pumped the blood of a god into this creature's body? I'd only barely listened during his one-man soliloquy, but something about that made no sense. The blood of a god couldn't be given away, or even transfused—not that I knew of. It could be taken, of course, but only by force.

Such was our way.

On a hunch, I reached out with my senses, probing the night air, and that's when I felt it: heat. Spanning the length of the Cyclops' body, flowing through its veins, flared the brilliant inferno that roared inside every one of us. And yet, there was something very wrong, something utterly grotesque, about those flames. Unlike those that lived within me, these burned wild, consuming everything they touched.

Frankenstein had been wrong: the Cyclops could not contain this power. Already, Polyphemus' skin was regaining its bronze, sunkissed coloring. Soon, his lungs would fill with air, and his heart would pound. Only that wasn't where it would end. The blood of a god did not bestow life, it bestowed power. Power so formidable it kept its host from tasting death, so potent it could bend reality to its will, so overwhelming it could devour the unworthy whole. And Polyphemus—for all his strength—was not worthy.

But I was.

I took a step forward, reaching out with both hands, calling to that immortal heat. Except it seemed that wasn't all I'd called to; somehow, the instant I opened myself to beckon the power, it was as if Polyphemus' suffering had suddenly become my own. Raw and faintly intimate, I listened to the son of Poseidon as he raged inside his own head, castigating the cruel being who'd killed him. Beyond his muttered threats, however, lay a loneliness so pervasive I had to shy away from it or else end up drowned in its murky depths.

I began to see visions of life through his eye, the lens oddly warped. I saw Polyphemus sitting alone on his island, mourning the loss of his sheep. Their bones lay in a neat pile beside the fire; he'd picked them clean, driven by hunger to eat his only friends. The other Cyclopes had disappeared long ago, but he didn't care about that. They'd never been his friends to begin with. Until he'd gotten his new eye from his father, they'd even gone so far as to mock him—teasing him about the time Odysseus had tricked him and escaped. He was glad that they were gone.

Still, he felt it would be nice to have someone or something to boss around, to lead across the hillsides during first light, to track down when the sun at last began to fall. I saw the idea form in his head, watched in snippets as he walked the bottom of the ocean floor, as he snuck onto the island of the cannibals, as he stole into the home of a young giantess. He took her, stealing her away from everything she'd ever known to come and be with him. Though smaller than he was, and of a different race, he was sure she would come to depend on him. Maybe even to love him, one day.

But she did not love him. She hated him. And so he was forced to eat her, as he had his beloved sheep, and to try again. And again. Soon, the pile of bones he kept as a tribute grew so large that he had to make his cave bigger. That is until, one day, the cannibals began to fight back. Enraged at first, he eventually came to crave their battles, to enjoy the terror he could cause. He'd grown larger, fiercer, from consuming their kin.

Life was good.

Until the chill winds came, and with them the dead men. They'd invaded his island, ignored his threats. He'd only just decided to sink their ship when the beast found him in his cave. From then on, all he could recall was pain. So much pain.

"I can take that pain away," I whispered, drawing away long enough to reassert myself. Still, I didn't sever the connection; I wanted Polyphemus to know I meant what I said, that my offer was genuine. "I can ease your burden."

"Yes," Polyphemus replied, his voice like a crack of thunder. "Please."

"Come, then."

This time when the Cyclops fell to his knees, I was ready for it. I'd already begun walking when Polyphemus slid down to all fours, the cavernous wound in the middle of his forehead bleeding freely now that his heart had begun to beat. Soon, if nothing was done, he'd grow feverish and sick. He'd thrash and seize as the blood of a god cooked him from the inside. He knew it, had seen it happen before.

"I won't let it happen. Not to ye, I swear it."

I pressed my palm flat against his cheek as blood—no longer red, but thick and golden—oozed down his face. When it hit my forearm, it felt as if I'd been struck by a bolt of lightning; I collapsed to one knee, twitching, though my hand remained firmly in place. So much power. Where had Frankenstein gotten this much blood? More importantly, who had he gotten it from? What god would volunteer to help do something like this?

I felt Polyphemus begin to pull away, distressed by my questions, so I leaned into him, planting a kiss along the corner of his mouth. I let him feel the comfort of my touch, let him know that I would be at his side until the very end. And I waited until he no longer shivered with fear, until his mind quieted, before I did the one thing that would end his pain, forever.

I leaned in to lick the ichor.

32

*M*y tongue burned with stolen power.

Energy, raw and intoxicating, flooded into me through that single point of contact. My skin began to ache as Polyphemus' foreign power continued to pour into me, filling me up like a balloon about to burst. And yet, I did not pull away; I straddled that line between pleasure and pain, between ecstasy and torture, aware that it would be like this—that it had to be like this. I pinched my eyes shut, focusing on leeching the last of the ichor's potency from Polyphemus' very veins. After what felt like an eternity, I drew away and licked my lips. They tasted of honey and bay laurel leaves.

When I finally opened my eyes, it was to find an emaciated face beneath my hand—little more than a thin veneer of pale flesh over a mass of chipped bone and deteriorating cartilage. Polyphemus, the faintest smile tugging at his dessicated lips, slumped to one side as the fire within dimmed from mere embers to cold ash. The Cyclops was dead. Well and truly, this time; there would be no more resurrections. Soon, his bones would freeze and crack under their own weight, leaving nothing behind but a charnel house worth of remains. One day, I expected this place would become known as the Valley of Bones—a shrine not unlike the one Polyphemus had created to honor his victims.

I sensed he'd have been glad to know that.

Rising to my feet, I finally caught sight of my own body, now practically radiating power; green light glimmered and danced along my arms and down my hands. But there was a tinge to it, a sickly yellow cast, which spoke of borrowed energy. Of course, that was to be expected; the blood of a god could be taken, perhaps even stored, but never kept.

A chill wind gusted through the valley, bringing with it a strange new scent.

Someone was out there.

"I know you're here!" I called, amplifying my voice with so much power that it rang out like the cry of a battle horn. "Come and see what I've done to your masterpiece, Frankenstein!"

Except it wasn't Frankenstein.

A figure appeared at the top of the hill. About my height, he stared down at me with electric blue eyes that sat in stark contrast to his cerulean skin and navy blue hair. Light played beneath that skin, drifting across his face in lines that reminded me of waves. It was an attractive face, full of strong lines and aesthetic curves. And yet, despite his handsome, otherworldly features, I found myself even more repulsed by this creature than I had been the sailors. I couldn't be certain, but I sensed there was something *wrong* with him.

Something broken.

"You aren't her," he said.

I sensed his power flare the second before he lashed out at me, catching me by surprise. I gasped at the sudden assault, feeling as though I'd been shoved headfirst into an ice bath. But the sensation didn't last long; I chased away his power with the merest flex of my own, pissed that he'd caught me off guard. Who the hell did he think he was?

Ryan.

The name came to me just as I'd brought my own power to bear—thick tendrils of night twirling around my left hand like the spiral of a whirling galaxy. Pain unlike anything I'd experienced thus far quickly followed; forced to release my burgeoning power, I cradled my pounding skull as a swarm of memories began playing like a reel before my very eyes. I saw a beautiful elf laughing, the sun bright on his face as he toasted me, amber liquid sloshing down the side of his glass. I saw the same elf behind the bar of a crowded establishment waving a dirty towel in my general direction. The elf crossing the street to greet me. The elf watching mortal women pass by, his eyes gleaming with mischief. The elf passed out on a couch with a child-sized blanket draped over his legs.

Then the memories changed.

I saw the elf screaming at me from the deck of a ship as fire and mayhem broke out around us. I saw him clinging to the edge of a ship falling from the sky, the wind pulling at his hair. I saw him with his blade at my throat, his once lovely face a rictus of pure hate. I saw him glance back at me from the other side of a cell, his gaze utterly devoid of hope.

Suddenly, the elf was gone, supplanted by a creature with his face. Blue-skinned and cold, I saw the Winter Queen's servant at the end of a long hallway, his arms held wide as shards of ice frolicked around his fingertips. Then again, this time on a beach, poised over the body of a downed Laestrygonian, his eyes tracking our ship as we fled.

Ryan O'Rye.

Jack Frost.

The Frozen One.

Between one breath and the next, I knew his many names, knew his face and his moods, knew that we'd once been friends. And yet, there was so little of him that I recognized; he might as well have been a stranger to me. Still, the sense of nostalgia lingered.

"D'ye come all the way to see me, Ryan O'Rye?" I asked, embracing our easy familiarity.

Ryan's eyes narrowed.

"I came to find Quinn. Where is she?"

"Is that supposed to be some sort of joke?" I asked, scoffing. "Ye know, I shouldn't be surprised. Ye never were very good at tellin' jokes."

"Tell me where she is before I get angry."

I opened my mouth to call the blue bastard's bluff when another figure materialized at Ryan's side. Older and significantly shorter, I recognized him immediately as Frankenstein, in the flesh. The mad scientist flicked his gaze from me to the carcass of his prized Cyclops, snarled in contempt, and thrust an accusing finger in my direction.

"What have you done?"

Ryan held out an arm, cutting the little man off.

"Let her answer my question, first, Doctor. Where is Quinn MacKenna?"

Frankenstein, who'd begun to throw his hands up in frustration, stilled.

"I'm right here," I replied, evenly.

"Don't be ridiculous."

"Herr Frost," Frankenstein interjected, glancing back and forth between his companion and me, "I believe it is time we leave this place and resume our journey. As I have said before, the woman you seek is quite clearly not on this island, or she would have sought you out by now. It is as the Greek said: Quinn MacKenna was lost at sea."

"Ye can't be—"

"We must find her, Doctor," Ryan replied, ignoring me altogether. "As you know, I need her by my side when we reach the gates, otherwise this will all have been for nothing."

"Yes, I know. Do not worry, Herr Frost, we will find a way," Frankstein replied. To my surprise, the mad scientist reached out and patted Ryan's shoulder, his expression like that of a doting father. What's more, Ryan leaned into his hand, seemingly comforted by the mortal's touch. "Come, now. It will do you a great deal of good to move on from this. You have stretched yourself quite thin, I think. Against my advice, I might add."

"Yes. I am sorry, Doctor."

"Think nothing of it. We will get you back to the ship and I will look you over." The mad scientist pulled at Ryan's sleeve, drawing him away from the valley. "I must say, it seems you are adjusting to the changes exceptionally well. Is your half of the eye giving you any trouble?"

"Wait!" I called, rushing after them. Panic I hardly understood clutched at my chest, urging me to capture Ryan at all costs. There was something I wanted from him. No, something I *needed*. "Don't go! It's me, Quinn! I'm right here!"

But it was too late.

A whirlwind of snow and ice began to form around the retreating figures, growing in size and scope until it reached the heavens. Thinking to charge into those winds and drag Ryan out by force if need be, I raced forward, propelled by stolen power. But, before I could so much as step foot within, the funnel disappeared, leaving nothing behind but the faint impressions of their footprints in the snow.

The Laestrygonians found me the following day, clutching a handful of finger bones I refused to let go of for reasons I couldn't rightly explain. James, who'd come running as soon as he heard I was alive, had met us on the outskirts of the city and helped put them in a pouch he happened to be carrying. Even now, I wore the thing around my neck like a trophy, aware only that I wasn't allowed to let anyone else touch the phalanges under any circumstances. James hadn't thought to question my reasoning, though he had demanded I tell him what happened after he fled.

I told him the truth.

"I have no idea," I admitted.

"What do you mean 'you have no idea'?" James hissed, drawing me to the side. The band of Laestrygonians escorting us towards the city halted, displaying an unexpected degree of deference in the process.

"I mean it's...fuzzy." I tapped the side of my head, keeping my voice low so as not to be overheard. "I wasn't exactly in me right mind. Honestly, I'm not even sure what happened after the sun went down."

"But...but you had a plan. You said so yourself!"

"Well, sure. But bein' out of me mind was a big part of it."

Of course, that had been Circe's idea, not mine; originally spawned before our heated exchange in the atrium, the witch had come up with the idea that I could sway the goddess within me much in the same way my Wild Side had influenced me in the past—a heady mix of psychic whispers and foreign compulsions. What she'd needed, however, was to figure out how to trigger them. And it seemed I had my former personas to thank for solving that mystery; by defending their agendas, I'd inadvertently revealed what motivated me more than anything: my desire to protect. And so, after conferring with Barca on the subject, the two of them had put their heads together and drawn up a battle plan designed to accomplish one goal, and one goal only: to give the goddess within me no choice but to defend Telepylus from Ryan's forces.

"You'll have to put her back against a wall," Circe had insisted. "Find someone you care about, keep them close until nightfall. Then, make sure you're both under imminent threat of death. If you do that, you should be able to sway her decisions."

"Should?" I'd countered.

"Probably."

James brought me back to the moment at hand by holding me at arms length, staring into my face like I'd gone mad. Then, unexpectedly, he laughed. No, he more than laughed. He *guffawed*, tears pricking at the corners of his eyes. Suddenly I felt like I was the one looking at a batshit crazy person. I shied from the Neverlander, eyebrows raised.

"Ye do know we're in public, right?" I asked. "Get ahold of yourself."

"Sorry," James wheezed, barely managing to suppress his chuckles. "It's just I can't believe you did it. I mean, look around!" James showcased the grass beneath our feet, then the clear blue sky, and finally the city. Bright, warm sunlight bathed the whole of Telepylus, baking the newly laid red clay tiles, reflecting off the freshly scrubbed marble; the Vegiants must have been busy since the sun rose to reveal a world untouched by winter's chill. "Look, I don't care how you did it," James continued. "The fact is you saved them, saved the whole island. Saved us! Now we can finally go home."

I faked a smile, clapped the young man's shoulder, rejoined our escorts, and resumed our trek. Now wasn't the time to confess I'd brokered a deal with a witch that I'd yet to honor, not to mention the fact that I'd come here to do something which remained undone. While it was true I remembered very little from the night before, I knew in my gut that Ryan was still out there, that I hadn't stopped him so much as chased him away—if that. Not that I planned to disregard the needs of my two beleaguered crew members. I simply wanted more time to come up with a solid plan. Time I'd have once we'd wrapped things up with Ismene and her people.

Maybe they'd throw us a parade.

Then again, maybe not.

Whispers, not praise, greeted us as we entered the city. The few citizens we encountered along the path leading to the temple eyed us with blatant suspicion, even contempt. And I wasn't the only one who noticed; James scanned the faces of the Laestrygonians, clearly perplexed.

"What's their deal?" I asked under my breath.

"I have no idea. I reported to Queen Ismene like you asked me to and stuck by her side until a runner told me they'd found you. You'd think they'd be happier."

"Aye, you'd t'ink."

I heard a pot smash and someone hurl a curse in our general direction, followed by the sound of a door being slammed. Our escort fanned out immediately, putting themselves between us and whomever was out there. But the street remained empty.

What the hell was going on?

Thankfully, Obelius was waiting for us at the temple entrance; if anyone could clarify what was happening, I assumed the Queen's de facto general could. Except—rather than greet us with an explanation—the giant ignored us completely, choosing instead to bark orders at our escorts.

"The Queen is inside, communing with the Great Mother. Guard the temple."

The Laestrygonians exchanged concerned glances but did as they were told. I'd only just opened my mouth to ask what was bothering the guards when I caught Obelius' warning glare. The Vegiant shook his head—a quick, almost imperceptible jerk. Something was clearly wrong, and it appeared he didn't want me making it worse by talking. I clamped my mouth shut, prepared to be patient.

For now.

Once our escort had dispersed, Obelius waved us forward, his expression stern. I hesitated, uncertain. James, catching the tension, waited for me to make the first move. I waffled back and forth, my hard earned instincts insisting I find out what was going on *before* putting myself within the giant's reach. I pictured the giant standing over me with his hand held out, his toothy smile practically bisecting his face as I gulped air. The guy had saved my life once. Shouldn't that alone give him the benefit of the doubt?

I did as the Vegiant asked.

"Look humble," Obelius urged under his breath the moment we were within speaking distance. Then, in a much louder, booming voice. "Our Queen demands your presence, mortals."

"As the Queen demands," I replied, bowing my head in mock deference while conveniently hiding my irritated expression behind a curtain of hair; I didn't do humble well. "Lead the way, big guy."

Obelius scowled at me before turning on his heel to pass through the columns and throw open the temple door. Steam poured from the interior, which suggested what Obelius had told the guards was true, but I didn't bother trying to verify one way or the other; whatever was going on, it was clear Obelius wasn't keen to talk about it publicly. In fact, it seemed entirely possible that we were being watched—though for what purpose and by whom, I had no idea.

"The Queen awaits," Obelius said, beckoning us through.

"Well we wouldn't want to keep her Majesty waitin'," I muttered as I slipped past. "Come on, James."

Seconds later, the door slammed shut behind us with a clang, leaving us in the dimly lit antechamber. I turned to find Obelius pressed against the door, gazing at us with the same expression I'd seen on the faces of the Laestrygonians.

James, who'd done well to stay silent throughout, gave up and threw his arms up in confusion. "What was all that about?" the Neverlander asked. "What's going on, Obelius?"

"Precautions had to be taken," the Vegiant replied. "The Laestrygonians want your heads."

"They what? But why? Quinn saved them!"

"That's not how they see it," I guessed. A look flashed across Obelius' face, and I knew I was right. "So, they t'ink what, exactly? That I'm takin' credit for somethin' I didn't do?"

"That's one theory," Obelius admitted. "There are others. Some say you made a deal to save yourselves, and that the Frozen One will return to finish the job as soon as you leave. There are others who believe you brought him here in the first place. That you're a spy, working for him."

"But that's ridiculous," James insisted. "You know that isn't true, Obelius."

"Do I?" Obelius shook his head. "Besides, this is not about what I believe, James. The citizens discovered Quinn had an audience with Queen Ismene, and that the Queen agreed to do whatever she wished." Obelius flicked his gaze to me, gauging my reaction, then quickly looked away. "Public opinion says you used magic to sway her. That you've turned our monarch into a puppet."

"And Queen Ismene? D'ye bother askin' *her* why she agreed?"

"She refused to tell me," Obelius replied, scowling.

"Ah," I replied, realization dawning. "So, was it ye who leaked that bit of information? Hopin' to keep your Queen from bein' blamed if t'ings went wrong, or were ye just upset she didn't include ye in the plannin' process?"

Obelius flushed but didn't respond.

"And the rumors? D'ye have anythin' to do with those?" I accused, feeling more betrayed than I'd have thought I would; you'd think I'd have been used to it by now.

"How could you stop him when we could not?" Obelius asked, his voice laced with suspicion. "The Frozen One was looking for you and your crew. We knew this. But we did not know why." The Vegiant shook his head, violently. "I did not start the rumors, but I must admit they don't sound all that far-fetched. James says you fought off the undead, and yet you bear no wounds. Do you honestly expect me to believe such a ridiculous story?"

"Aye, because that's what happened," I snapped.

"You knew the Frozen One by name," he accused. "You called him by it on the boat, after spending a great deal of time alone with him in the cave. You even warned us not to explore Polyphemus' island. Was that because you didn't want us to confront your master?"

"Are ye even listenin' to yourself?" I countered, prodding my temple. "Ye must have lost your damned mind. If you'll remember, I called Ryan by his name when he was chasin' *us*, tryin' to kill *us*. Oh, and that was *before* I saved your sorry, ungrateful ass. And you're damn right I told ye to leave that island alone. If you'd have listened to me back then, Ryan would never have known to come here!"

"So you admit it!"

"Admit what, ye big, daft oaf? That I t'ink you're too stupid to function?"

"No! That you and he planned this from the start!"

"Enough!"

Ismene's voice cut through the din of our argument like a knife through flesh. Power brushed against my skin, as that peculiar aroma—the smell of pine and honeysuckle—permeated the air. As one, the three of us turned towards the sound of that voice. The Queen stalked towards us, and yet it didn't look like Ismene; where I'd come to expect nudity, I found a gown of freshly bloomed flowers held in place by swirling vines that curled around her waist and along the naked skin of her arms. A garland of autumn leaves sat atop the Queen's head, and her eyes blazed with power.

Though the makeover should have earned a comment or two, I had more pressing concerns to worry about—like not being accused of mind raping the Queen, for example. What I needed was for Ismene to settle this dispute; all she had to do was tell Obelius the truth, and he'd see what a colossal jackass he'd been. In fact, I'd already opened my mouth to demand she nip this nonsense in the bud when my throat suddenly closed up.

"No, you are not to speak unless I wish it," Ismene said. Except that voice didn't belong to Ismene. It was as though another voice had slipped beneath the Queen's, creating a strange, autotuned effect that reverberated throughout the antechamber. "My priestess has called, and I have answered."

"The Great Mother," Obelius whispered before collapsing to his knees, his forehead brushing the floor. To my surprise, James followed suit; the Neverlander trembled beneath Ismene's stare. Distantly, I felt the pull of this alien creature's power sweep the room, tugging at me like a child hoping to drag me along in its wake. Was I supposed to believe this was really a manifestation of Gaia, Mother of Titans? The Great Mother? It was hard to fathom, and yet the pull continued to nag at me.

"Stop that," I insisted.

"You refuse to kneel?"

I gave the possessed Queen the look that comment deserved.

"It's bad for me knees," I drawled.

"I see." She gave me a once over, her gaze lingering on my face. "So, it's true, then. You are the one who chased away the Frozen One's influence."

I heard Obelius' sharp intake of breath but chose to ignore it; I was plenty petty enough to consider saying I'd told him so, but the potential presence of a Titan in the room took precedence. I considered her question, wavering, though I eventually nodded. Obviously I wasn't sure what I had or hadn't done, but I knew better than to contradict her with the stakes as high as they were. If the Laestrygonians' go-to deity wanted to call me the island's savior, I certainly wasn't going to contradict her. Unfortunately, she must have caught my hesitation.

"Is that not what happened?"

"I...if that's what ye say happened, then yes."

"Ah," she said, skepticism giving way to mild amusement. "You do not remember."

"How d'ye know that?" I asked, alarmed.

"I can see it," she replied, using the verb as though it meant something different to her than it did to me. "You are shielding yourself from your own memories."

"I am? I mean, no I'm not," I replied, defensively. "What makes ye say that?"

"That."

The creature, who I was beginning to suspect truly was Gaia shacked up within Ismene's nubile form, pointed at my forehead. Pain, sharp and immediate, surged just behind my right eye. I cursed, raising my hands as though to protect myself, but it was no use; my brow continued to throb.

"What the hell is that?" I hissed.

"That *was* the wall you built to keep yourself sane. And I've just torn it down."

"Ye did *what*?"

"You do not need it."

"But I don't even—"

Sadly, that was as far as I got before being assaulted by my own memories. Or, I should say, my inner goddess' memories. They came in a rush, but haphazardly, like flashing back to a drunken night out the following morning—complete with a relentless, pounding headache. Indeed, the more I recalled, the more hungover I felt; I slumped to the floor from the pain, shocked by the sheer impossibility of all I'd done. Wielding sheer night as though it were a weapon, butchering the undead, setting fire to the corpses of Queen Adonia and her Laestrygonians, drinking the blood of a foreign god, and finally confronting Ryan only to have him slip from my grasp. Hell, I even knew what the finger bones were, though not what they were for. But it was Ryan who haunted me, whose apathetic face I couldn't get out of my head.

"He didn't recognize me," I said, my voice strained and my nerves fried. "After everythin', he was right there, and I couldn't save him."

"Do you mean the Frozen One?"

"Huh?" I glanced up, realizing I'd ended up on my knees, after all. Damn it. "Aye. His name is Ryan. Or it was, once."

"And you wished to *save* him?"

"He is…was a friend."

"I see. I am afraid that will not be possible."

"What?"

The Titan inhabiting Ismene's flesh snapped her fingers, and the smell I'd associated with her power intensified. I felt the pain behind my eye recede, my nausea ease. Before I could ask what she'd done, however, a noise brought me round. Snoring. Obelius was snoring. Indeed, further inspection revealed both he and James had passed out, their bodies curled awkwardly next to each other like they were having a sleepover and had crashed in the middle of the floor.

"What d'ye do to 'em?" I demanded.

"What I have to say now is for your ears, alone. But first, you must come with me." She waved for me to follow and stepped into the temple proper without waiting to see what I'd decide to do.

"Ye arrogant mother…" I started, gritting my teeth. "What d'ye mean when ye said it wouldn't be possible?"

She didn't answer.

I groaned in frustration, rose to my feet, and followed after her. Not that I had much of a choice; what I needed right now were answers, and who better to pump for information than a being who'd reputedly given birth to time itself—or at least the god we associated with it? Assuming that this wasn't her luring me to my death, or that she'd let me ask those questions, or that she'd bother answering.

I really wasn't living my best life, lately.

"Oy! So, what can ye…" I drifted off, realizing I'd left the antechamber and stepped—not into the center of the temple like I'd been expecting—but into a freaking tropical rainforest.

Unbelievably lush and vibrant and vaguely claustrophobic, I found myself hemmed in on all sides by broad, sweeping fronds and thick, moss-covered trees, the air dense and heavy with moisture, the buzz of insects and the peculiar warbles of all manner of birds merging together to form a chaotic orchestra of sound. I spun, searching for the way back, but the antechamber was gone. The temple was gone. It seemed I'd stepped into another world. Again.

Except this time, I was alone.

You are not alone.

The voice fell from the heavens like rain, soft and sibilant. I raised my face to the sky, expecting some sort of angelic light, or some other wild phenomenon, but all I could make out was the dense canopy overhead. Where the hell was Gaia? Had this all really been some sort of elaborate trap? I gulped, recalling the various ways someone could die in the rainforest; people like to think its the wildlife that'll get you—the jungle cats or the alligators—but there were dozens of ways to go that were much less flashy: snakes, poisonous toads, leeches, disease-laden mosquitos, bacteria-filled water, or even just plain getting lost and dying of exposure.

Do not be absurd. I did not lure you here to see you die of dysentery.

"Gaia? Wait, is that ye?" I asked, wheeling in search of the Titan. "Where are ye?"

I am here. This is me.

"As in...ye mean..." I suddenly felt a little sick. "Are ye sayin' I'm inside ye, right now?"

Of course not. Do not be disgusting. I am simply too large for your mind to fathom. So, when you look at me, this is what you see. I believe you have come into contact with some of my offspring. Were they not also hard to look upon?

I thought about it, then nodded. I'd only met two Titans who really qualified as direct descendants, but both had been larger than life figures. Typhon's existence, as I recalled, had been especially difficult to wrap my head around; the Father of Monsters' body had both defied the laws of physics and given me one hell of a migraine.

Yes. Typhon does not hide his true form. It is not in his nature to pretend to be something he is not. Besides, he was never worshipped. Feared, yes, but never adored. Oceanus is different. He always enjoyed the company of sycophants. It is why he keeps his nymphs so close by.

"It's not polite to read someone's mind, ye know," I called out, feeling slightly violated—not to mention nervous. Could you imagine someone hearing your every innermost thought as you went about your day-to-day?

Talk about a complex.

I am allowing you to hear my thoughts. It only seemed fair.

"Uh huh," I replied, nonplussed. "Why don't ye tell me what ye brought me here for?"

I had two reasons. The first was to be certain we were not interrupted. My priestess, the one you call Ismene, is very devoted, but I cannot fill her vessel for long without endangering her life. I did not wish to bring her any harm.

"And the second?" I asked, my tone significantly less caustic now that I knew compassion had played a role in my abduction.

I needed to be sure you believed me. After all, it is likely your life and the lives of everyone in this realm will depend on what I tell you. I believed that if we spoke like this, you would have no choice but to accept the truth.

"The truth?"

Yes. The truth about the Frozen One.

"Ah, right. Ye said I wouldn't be able to save him."

No, I said that saving him is not possible. The distinction is paramount.

"Go on, I'm listenin'." I waggled my hand about, indicating the rainforest as a whole. "It's not like I can go anywhere."

No, you cannot. Very well, I will begin at the beginning.

"Do we really have that much time?" I quipped.

Not my beginning. Quit being silly and listen. To the best of my knowledge, the Frozen One, the creature you call Ryan, first sailed into this realm a little less than five years ago. He—

"Hold on, d'ye say *five years*? That's not possible. We were right behind—"

Time does not flow here as it does in the mortal realm. Or even the Fae realm. I am not saying you are wrong, only that I am certain the Frozen One has been terrorizing the Eighth Sea for half a decade. At first, we Titans thought him harmless. We were certain he sailed here by accident, as have more than a few before him, and so we let him be. Most are mortal and perish so quickly we forget they were ever here. You see, we did not understand what he was, what he had come for. Worst of all, we did not know who—or perhaps I should say what—he had brought with him.

"Frankenstein," I guessed.

Yes. I believe it was his magic, his spells which brought all this about.

"His magic?" I shook my head, lips pursed. "No, Frankenstein is a scientist. A doctor. Only like the crazy-murder-spree, pull-wings-off-a-butterfly kind. Not the do-no-harm kind."

That may be what he calls himself, even what he believes himself to be, but we know from experience that is not true. Frankenstein is a warlock. A necromancer. A thaumaturge. Without him, we believe the Frozen One would never have risen to such power that he could prove a threat to us.

"How so? D'ye mean the army he created?"

You realize this would go much faster if you stopped interrupting?

"Right. Sorry."

It all began on Ogygia. The Frozen One and his small crew sailed there initially, though I do not know if it was by design or mere chance. Ogygia was Calypso's island. If you will recall, it was in her arms that Odysseus spent seven years of his exile. And it seems her charms were not diminished, seeing as how the Frozen One spent his first three years in her company.

"Aye, that sounds like the Ryan I knew."

I do not know what transpired between them during that time, only what happened immediately after. It was Typhon who discovered Calypso's body drifting on the open sea. Her heart had been pulled from her chest, and yet she mustered up the last of her strength to speak to him. The nymph told Typhon all about the Frozen One, including the fact that she had fallen in love with him. In the end, however, it was his strange companion—the mortal who had ripped out her heart while she slept, rowed her out to sea, and dumped her body—whom she cursed with her last breath. Typhon was furious at them both, as you can imagine.

I shuddered at the thought, recalling Typhon's thunderous voice as he denounced Ryan and swore his vengeance.

Since then, the Frozen One has invaded at least three other islands, leaving behind nothing but death and devastation in his wake. But it was not until he returned to claim Polyphemus that I began to understand why. I believe the Frozen One desires power. Stolen power.

"Afraid I don't follow that bit," I admitted. "What's Polyphemus got to do with that?"

His eye was taken. Do you know why?

"No...but I t'ink Frankenstein said somethin' about an eye to Ryan before they disappeared."

It is likely. You see, the eye was a gift from Poseidon to a treasured son. Coupled with the loving heart of a powerful nymph and several other artifacts cultivated by the one you call Frankenstein, they make incredibly potent ingredients for a spell. And I think Frankenstein has woven that spell into the Frozen One's very flesh.

"Wait a second. Are ye really sayin' Frankenstein's been experimentin' on Ryan?"

That is what I have come to believe. And it seems that, with every new addition to his body, our power in this realm wanes. Once, I could have buried him beneath the earth with a simple thought. We could have drowned him beneath the waves. Now, I find it difficult even to know where he is and what he plans. Indeed, when he arrived on the island of the Laestrygonians, I found I could hardly shut him out.

"That can't be right. Oceanus said—"

He lied. He is too proud to say so, but Oceanus is as powerless as I am to stop him. That is why he sent you to the witch, why Typhon let you live. You are a foreign entity, bound to different rules. The Frozen One holds no sway over your power. Which is why you are the one who must stop him before he wipes us out and it is too late.

"Stop him, how?" I asked, flabbergasted. "If what you're sayin' is true, I'm not even sure what he wants, anymore. You're tellin' me he's been amassin' power here in your realm for years, when I thought his whole plan was to find Atlantis."

Atlantis?

"Aye. I was told he was after somethin' that had been left there. A weapon powerful enough to decimate one's enemies and end a war."

That is impossible.

"Which part? The weapon, or what it can do?"

Neither. I meant Atlantis. The city cannot be found.

"Why? Just because it's a lost civilization, or whatever?"

I am afraid you have been misled. But then, I should not be surprised. Mortals have been getting such things wrong since Prometheus came down from Olympus to thrust fire into their grubby hands. A failure in translation, perhaps. Or simple misdirection. Either way, it's not the Lost City of Atlantis. Its true title is Atlantis, City of the Lost.

*a*tlantis, City of the Lost.

I sat with my back against a mossy tree trunk as thick as a grain silo, marveling at the distinction the simple rearrangement made, trying hard not to think about the fact that I was leaning against Gaia's essence— or whatever you'd call it. Fortunately, I had plenty to distract me; the Mother of Titans had gone on to explain the difference between the two titles in greater detail only moments before. The first, of course, was the popular notion embraced by the public at large—that the remains of some ancient civilization with all sorts of advanced technology lay hidden somewhere, just waiting to be discovered by an enterprising soul. The second, however, had proven far less appealing...and somehow more cryptic.

Atlantis is the place where lost things go. It cannot be found, because to find it you must be looking. And if you are looking, then you are not lost.

"I feel like you're askin' me a riddle," I'd admitted when Gaia finished. "Is the answer the moon? Time? I feel like it's always time."

Further elaboration on the Titan's part had, fortunately, proven more fruitful; Gaia had gone on to say that the only way to reach Atlantis was to accidentally stumble upon it, though apparently even then you had to be either a raving lunatic or utterly dissociated. Two sides of the same shell-shocked coin, if you asked me. Of course, that meant no one with a sense of direction, with a sense of purpose, would ever be able to reach it. Ironic, really, considering how many explorers were out there even now trying to uncover the mythical city.

I quickly realized that was why Oceanus had been so dismissive when I'd mentioned Atlantis in his throne room beneath the sea: gods were, by their very nature, driven creatures. They had aspects. Worshippers. Purpose. Or, should I say, *we*. But if that was the case, why had my mother's ghost insisted I go there? And how much of this did Ryan know?

"Oy! Gaia!" I called as I jerked forward, struck by a sudden, disturbing thought.

I am always here. Which means there is no need to shout.

"Sorry. Listen, ye said the only people who can enter Atlantis are either deranged or detached, right?"

That is a bit simplistic, but essentially correct.

"So, on a scale of one to ten, from say Mr. Rogers to Dr. Mengele, how insane d'ye t'ink Ryan has become with all these parts Frankenstein keeps addin' to him?"

Silence.

"Still there?" I asked, mockingly.

If that is their goal, it would be an extremely roundabout way of doing things. It would be simpler to...but no. I do not think that is their intention. Besides, the nature of Atlantis is known to very few.

"Is it a secret?"

No. It's simply not something that is often talked about. The Olympians, by and large, did not concern themselves with it. Especially not once they began taking an interest in mortals.

"Would Calypso have known?"

It is possible.

"And is it also possible Calypso might have told her lover, especially if he asked about it?"

Silence, again.

"For the sake of argument, let's say it is," I continued, musing aloud. "Say Ryan found out what it would take to reach Atlantis from his lover. Ye said he spent three years on her island, so it's possible she refused to tell him, or he never thought to ask. Or maybe he found out and gave up. Hell, maybe Ryan fell in love with her, too, and so he kept the knowledge to himself for a while. Regardless, what if Frankenstein found out and killed her to get Ryan movin'? Or maybe the doctor did it to make him grieve?"

I shook my head, seeing the flaws in my own argument, recalling Ryan's face. His hard eyes, his flat tone, his forgotten smile. "No," I said, hesitant. "Not grieve. Ryan isn't goin' insane. He's becomin' detached. Cold and distant. That's what's happenin'."

These are speculations, not facts. They still do not explain what Frankenstein hopes to achieve. If the Frozen One truly disconnects from reality, he may reach Atlantis, but he will not remember why he wanted to be there in the first place. He will wander, lost, as all who reach it are doomed to do.

"Unless he's bound to someone," I replied, struck by the fragmented conversation I'd caught between Ryan and Frankenstein. "The doctor said 'your half' of the eye. What if that's part of it, somehow? Like a lifeline, somethin' to make sure he can follow?"

I confess I do not know. Atlantis is a realm of Chaos, and therefore outside my influence. I only know that it exists and that it may be reached in the manner I have told you. Whatever the Frozen One and his master have planned between themselves has proven beyond our understanding. Beyond our influence. This is why we entrusted it to you. I only brought you here to be sure you understood that the Frozen One is beyond saving. That what he has become is no longer salvageable.

"You're probably right."

And yet, you will try to save him, anyway.

"Blame human nature?" I suggested.

I believe you will have to grow out of that.

"We'll see." I shrugged. "So, what's left? Any advice on how to stop 'em?"

Seek out the witch. Oceanus claims she has a plan of some sort.

"Ye don't seem to care much for Circe," I noted. "Why is that? Family squabble? D'ye play her in *Monopoly*?"

She used her power to shut me out, to ban me from her island, long before your time. I find her...impertinent. But if she has found a way to help save us all, then perhaps I can overlook that. Though I doubt it. I blame Titan nature.

"Fair enough," I replied with a snort. "So, how exactly do I get out of here? Down the hall, second door on the left?" I clambered to my feet, gesturing vaguely towards the dense forestation as I stretched to loosen up the tension in my shoulders and back before closing my eyes. "And what about the Vegiants? Are ye gonna tell 'em the truth about what happened?"

The twittering sounds of the rainforest died out so abruptly it was as if they'd been nothing more than a sleep aid, only to be replaced by a cacophony of shouts. I opened my eyes to find myself in the dim temple interior where I'd first seen Ismene "communing" with Gaia.

"Welcome back. Trippy place, am I right?"

I turned to find Ismene lounging on the dais, completely nude once more, looking a tad dazed and faintly euphoric. She waved at me, curling her fingers one by one, grinning like the cat who ate the canary.

"Ye can say that again." I frowned, distracted by the shouts. After a moment, I realized they were coming from outside the temple. Except they weren't shouts, at all. They were more like chants—the sort of thing you'd hear at a rally or a ball game. Cries of "come out or else" and "we want our Queen" and "die humans die" were being repeated one after the other. Apparently, while I'd been off visiting their goddess, the citizens had grown tired of waiting—and of us breathing, for that matter.

"What's their damage?" Ismene asked.

Obelius and James came barreling into the room before I could answer, each with equally protective looks splashed across their faces, albeit directed at two very different people. Obelius spotted the two of us, first. He jabbed a finger my way.

"If you laid a finger on her, I swear I'll—"

"Oh, calm down." I waved at him, dismissively. "She's fine, just look at her. Now, go tell your fanatics outside that everythin' is alright, and that we'd appreciate it if they'd pipe down."

The crash of something colliding with the wall and shattering drew us all around. The chants became more chaotic, and I could have sworn I heard someone scream. Obelius glanced at Ismene, taking peculiar note of her lethargic position. He cleared his throat.

"My Queen, what do you wish me to do?"

"Sounds like they're having a gas out there," Ismene replied as she sat up. "Obi, go on and take these two through the tunnels to the beach. They'll need their ship to get where they're supposed to go. The Great Mother told me to wish you luck, by the way."

"She didn't say anythin' about any of that to me," I countered, annoyed that Gaia had left out details after I'd asked her point blank what my next move should be. "What about the rest of our crew? Tiger Lily and Tinkerbell?"

"I, uh, moved them to the *Jolly Roger* last night," James interjected, looking sheepish. "After you sent me back. I thought it would be safer for them aboard the ship."

"In case I lost and everyone in Telepylus ended up dead," I supplied, giving the Neverlander the look that thought deserved.

"To be fair, you weren't exactly being upfront with me up to that point. Plus, you almost let them take me away. I saw your face when they came after me. For a minute there it was like you didn't even know who I was, and you certainly didn't seem to care whether I lived or died. I didn't want to risk their lives, too."

I winced at that, painfully aware what James was referring to. But now wasn't the time to defend my actions—or the actions of my inner goddess. What we needed now were concrete escape plans; I wasn't interested in being attacked by a mob of outraged giants.

"You're right," I told James. "That wasn't fair of me, I apologize. Now, what was it I heard about tunnels?"

"Your Majesty..." Obelius said, shuffling from side to side, his armor clanking with the movement. "I don't know if it's in our best interest to show them the tunnels."

"Oh, I almost forgot. The Great Mother had a message for you, too, Obi. She said 'remember Thebes.' What happened in Thebes?"

Obelius clammed up immediately, his eyes so wide I thought they might pop out of his skull, his face as red as the embers that lit the room. The Vegiant gulped, scratched at his scraggly beard, and coughed something which sounded an awful lot like an apology—though to whom, I wasn't sure.

"Follow me," he said, crooking his finger at James and me.

The Neverlander did as he was told, filing past me with a raised eyebrow. He waved at Ismene, then—rather brazenly, I thought—blew her a rather salacious kiss while Obelius' back was turned. I managed not to snicker, though I did stop to bid farewell to the reigning monarch.

"T'anks for believin' in me, Ismene. If it wasn't for ye, I don't know that we'd have been able to stop Ryan."

"All part of the plan, man," she replied, with a wink.

As I turned to follow the others, I felt a nagging suspicion that somehow Ismene had helped to engineer this whole thing. That it was entirely possible she had a much firmer grasp of what was going on than I'd given her credit for. I glanced back over my shoulder, wondering if I'd catch her staring after us with that tell-tale glint of intelligence twinkling in her eyes.

Instead, I found her bent over backwards in bridge pose.

So much for that theory.

35

The tunnels, it turned out, were actually staircases built into the foundation of the temple, accessed through a nondescript alcove and hidden beneath a stone slab that even Obelius struggled to lift on his own. The stairs we took descended into the very belly of the cliff, winding all the way down to a slight spar on the far side of the beach. Calling them tunnels had been Queen Adonia's idea, according to Obelius, who'd become a great deal more personable since we left the temple.

"She wanted a way for her loved ones to escape if something happened," the Vegiant had explained. "Now, only Queen Ismene and I know it exists."

Frankly, after finding out that bit of trivia, I couldn't blame Obelius for being so reticent to share; if someone were planning to attack Telepylus, this stairway of theirs was as much a liability as it was an advantage. That being said, I had no intention of revealing its location to anyone—or ever coming back, for that matter—and I made sure Obelius knew that as we waited for James. The Neverlander had left to retrieve the ship, which he'd docked on the other side of the cove following the attack.

"Ye have to know I didn't intend to involve your people in me and Ryan's business," I added for good measure, eyeing the burnt out husks that had washed up on shore—the remains of Laestrygonian ships.

"I know. And you were right to be angry with me for accusing you otherwise," the Vegiant admitted. "As I was right to suspect you. Even though," he went on, one massive hand raised to silence my objection, "I should have trusted you."

"I accept your apology," I replied, snarkily.

"That's not what...nevermind. So, where will you go next?"

"Well, I came here to save a friend. And now it seems I may have to kill him. But first I need to see to the state of me crew. Then I have to steal a flower for a witch. And then I'll worry about Ryan."

"I hope your friend dies a painful and ignoble death, whining like a malnourished dog," Obelius said after spitting into the sea.

"Tell me how ye really feel," I teased.

"Did you know we still have not recovered the bodies of the former Queen and her bodyguards? I fear they are lost forever, and that we will never be able to lay them to rest."

"Out of curiosity," I began, choosing my words carefully so as not to tip the big guy off, "how d'ye lot feel about cremation?"

"Cremation?"

"Ye know, burnin' your dead."

"Ah. Yes, we used to do that, before the Stranger came. He showed us the value of rotting flesh. How our remains could help make things grow."

"I guess what I'm askin' is whether it would offend ye to be burned, instead?"

"No. But I have been around a long time. The old ways still appeal to me, as they did to Queen Adonia. She set fire to the King, despite the Stranger's arguments. Why do you ask?"

I considered telling Obelius the truth, but frankly I couldn't be sure how he'd take it. The fact that I'd burned his former monarch to a crisp along with her loyal bodyguards might not sit well no matter how open-minded he was to the idea of being cremated. Fortunately, I didn't have to explain myself, because a second later the *Jolly Roger* came into view with James at the helm. James, and someone else.

Someone fishy.

"Triton," I muttered. "What's he doin' here?"

Obelius shot me a long, considering look.

"For a fragile mortal, you are awfully popular," he noted. "First you're freed from Oceanus' prison, then you're granted an audience with the Great Mother, and now it seems you have yet another god hoping to speak to you. What is it they see that I don't? What am I missing?"

"Oh, Obi," I said with a sigh as I reached up to swat the Vegiant's beefy arm, slapping it hard enough to see the flesh go red. "Tact. You're missin' tact."

"I don't understand. What is tact?"

"Ask Ismene," I called as I walked away. "Then ye can tell her all about Thebes."

"That's Queen Ismene," I heard him mutter in reply.

I waved over my shoulder as I strolled along, walking parallel to the pounding surf. I noticed Triton lowering the dinghy we kept aboard the *Jolly Roger* to get from sea to shore whenever we laid anchor and angled myself to meet him. Thankfully, I wouldn't have long to wait; the tiny row boat was moving at an impossible clip with Triton aboard. I supposed being a fish god had its privileges. Once he was close, I waded out and clambered in, too impatient to bother removing my boots this time around; I had more important shit to worry about right now.

Like what in the Eight Seas Triton was even doing here.

"You said to return this morning," he replied after I'd settled in, sounding uncharacteristically hurt by my accusation.

"I said you'd know whether I succeeded or not by mornin'. Somethin', I might add, ye should have been able to see from a lot farther away than the deck of me ship."

"I thought it was that young mortal's ship?"

"Semantics. Now quit avoidin' the subject. What gives? Why were ye waitin' for me?"

"It's Circe," Triton admitted, hanging his massive, misshapen head. "She sent me here with a message, and a task."

"I didn't realize ye answered to Circe."

"I do not. Or I did not. She...well, she promised—"

"To change ye back," I finished for him, seeing the obvious connection an instant before he could say it aloud. "She's made ye her errand guppy, and in exchange she swears to return ye to your original form, is that it?"

"Yes, though I resent being called a guppy. But do you think she can really do it?" Triton asked, his voice overflowing with so much hope I found I couldn't even tease him, let alone lie.

"Aye, if anyone can, it's her." I held up a hand. "But, before ye start plannin' your makeover, maybe ye should give me her message."

"Oh, right. Yes. Circe says she needs the flower you promised to deliver before you do anything else. That it has become, to use her words, time sensitive."

"I see," I replied, mulling that over. "And how am I supposed to get there? D'ye have a map?"

"No, I am to lead you to the island. That is the task Circe has asked me to perform."

"Aye? So, you're comin' with us, then?"

"Yes. Part of the way."

I frowned at the fish god, noting his overall shiftiness.

"What aren't ye tellin' me? What is this island, anyway?" I asked, realizing I'd never actually gotten that tidbit of information out of Circe.

"Circe made me swear not to name it. She said to tell you that you stand a better chance of succeeding in your task if you do not know."

I began muttering curses under my breath.

"Lady?"

"Fine, let's do this. I don't have all night."

"But it is daytime—"

"I know what I said," I snapped. "Just get me to the ship, quickly. I have to speak to me crew before we set sail."

Here's hoping my Captain allowed the detour.

Mutiny is such an ugly word, after all.

I cracked open the cabin door and peered out onto the deck of the *Jolly Roger*, alerted by a series of strange sounds echoing throughout the fog that had followed us ever since Triton pointed us north and bid our ship farewell. The mist curled and writhed, so thick I could barely see my hand in front of my face as I stepped out onto the deck, tracking what sounded like fog horns. I made my way to the railing. The bleating horns grew louder, more insistent. But the fog was too dense; the sounds bounced around, making it impossible to tell where they were coming from.

"James? Ye out here?" I called.

The Neverlander didn't answer, but then I hadn't expected him to; James had been giving me the silent treatment for the past few hours. The Neverlander hadn't been pleased to learn we had priorities that didn't include leaving the Eighth Sea, even after I'd walked him through the conditions of the deal I'd made with Circe—including the exceptionally complicated revelation that I was, in fact, a goddess. Part time. Of course, I didn't blame him; one look at Tiger Lily and Tinkerbell was all it took to expose the flaws in my argument. The two were down in the cabins below decks, likely twitching and feverish, their skin clammy and flushed. Neither had been responsive when I'd spoken to them, though it seemed Tiger Lily had it the worst. Probably from trying to fight it for so long, if I had to guess.

Honestly, I felt so wretched about it that I'd been racking my brain trying to come up with a solution.

And I had—albeit a convenient one.

"Once we get the flower," I yelled over the blaring horns, hoping James could hear me, "we'll take 'em to Circe. I'm sure she'll have a potion or somethin' that will help!"

Still no answer.

"We'll make another deal, whatever it takes, I swear!"

Several more horn blasts passed.

"Where the hell is that comin' from?" I muttered, scanning the fog once more. And where was the island Triton had assured us we'd reach before nightfall so long as we stayed the course? It'd been hours since then. I frowned, then spun round, realizing there was no way James could be down below taking care of his fellow Neverlanders because that would mean no one was at the helm steering the ship. So, either he had heard and ignored me, or there was something very, very wrong.

I bolted for the stairs that led to the aft end where the wheel stood, calling for James. The horns grew louder as I ran, their blasts lasting longer and longer until I felt like I was inside a train tunnel with a locomotive barreling down on me. I clamped my hands over my ears as I hit the poop deck, cursing, then froze. No one stood at the helm; the wheel rocked slowly to and fro as if piloted by a ghost.

"Son of a bitch!" I snapped, snatching at the helm.

"I'll have you know my mother was a nice lady."

I whirled, startled, my heart racing, to find a masculine figure looming not ten feet away, his features obscured by the fog. Hell, between the fog and the horns, even his voice seemed muddled—like the filter they use to protect anonymous sources on *60 Minutes*. Still, I kept the helm as steady as I could, for whatever good that would do me; there was no way we were on course, not now. For all I knew, we were mere seconds away from crashing into the damned island. The thought made me reconsider the presence of the horns. Maybe someone was trying to warn us that we'd gotten too close, that we were in danger?

"Who's there?" I demanded. "Stay back, I'm warnin' ye!"

The fog began to slip away like layered sheets being torn away one at a time until I could make out the man's height and general build. He was taller than me by a smidge, his shoulders broad, waist trim. Ordinarily, I'd have noted these details with interest. As things stood, however, I had no choice but to perceive him as a threat. Unfortunately, the racket crescendoed as the fog dispersed, drowning out whatever response I might have received. I turned towards the source—audible now that the fog had passed —and felt my jaw drop of its own accord.

"Where the fuck…" I mumbled.

"Hey, since when do people sail pirate ships down rivers?"

I flinched, caught off guard by how close the man had gotten while I'd been distracted, and raised a threatening fist as if to pop him in the face. Thankfully, his was a face I recognized. Unfortunately for him, his was a face that I'd wanted to sock for a long time, now. Deciding that it would be a bit premature under the circumstances, I pushed him away, instead; the wizard rocked back on his heels, anger flashing in his eyes.

"What the hell are ye doin' here, Nate?"

"I asked you first," the wizard growled, wiping self-consciously at his immaculately tailored suit. Then, he frowned. "Wait, I felt that. How did you do that?"

"Push ye?" I asked, cocking an eyebrow. "Please don't tell me that was the first time a woman's rejected your creepy advances?"

"What? No, I meant…" Nate drifted off, his attention diverted by the skyline that had so confounded me. He pointed to a bridge which spanned the river we were indeed sailing on, its base supported by what appeared to be rusted red metal beams and mildew-coated stone. "Hey, that's the Eads. What the hell are you doing in St. Louis?"

I'd just opened my mouth to tell the nosy bastard that I'd never even been to Missouri—AKA Middle Earth—and had absolutely no idea how I'd gotten here, when I spotted the traffic jam which spanned the length of the four lane bridge, leaving the vast majority of cars bottlenecked on either side, forcing a total gridlock. Except for one vehicle, it seemed, which had come swerving onto the bridge like a spastic dog out of a kennel. A vehicle —I might add—that was being chased by a silver freaking dragon the size of a townhouse.

A real, live dragon.

"That's not possible," Nate said, his voice riddled with disbelief. Police sirens joined the fray as the wizard stepped up to the railing, staring up at the mayhem like an enraptured child. As we watched, a humongous ball of flame came soaring—not from the dragon's mouth as I would have expected, but from the passenger side of the hulking SUV—at the chrome-plated lizard, catching it full in the snout. Nate made an involuntary noise that sounded a lot like a snicker.

"What was that?" I asked. "What's so funny?"

"A reptile dysfunction," Nate said, gesturing to the fight with a sort of manic glee dancing in his eyes. I tracked his gaze, watching in awe as some crazy cop actually tried to ram the dragon with a police cruiser, though the result was somehow even less ideal than I'd have thought: the cruiser shot up into the air at an angle, spinning end over end, spitting out shards of glass. I grimaced, dreading the inevitable collision with the ground. And yet the crash never came; the dragon snatched the cruiser up in mid-air as it leapt off the bridge, beating its wings. The dragon banked, coming back for another strike, while the SUV wove between several stalled out cars.

"And now it's bullet time," Nate mumbled, his voice barely audible beneath the sounds of sirens and screams coming from the bridge.

I almost turned to ask the wizard what he was babbling about when I heard the shots; the cop inside the cruiser was firing at the dragon from point blank range. From where we were, I could even see the face of the officer doing the honors: she was a woman. A woman I thought I recognized, in fact, although I wrote that off almost instantly; I sincerely doubted I knew any female cops in St. Louis. Not unless she was one of Jimmy's friends, maybe a transfer from his unit? In the end, it seemed her existence was a mystery I was destined never to solve; the dragon launched the cruiser into the river with a gleeful roar—practically guaranteeing the heroic officer a watery grave.

Nate scowled, his eyes darkening. He began scanning the river, then the *Jolly Roger*, the wheels in his head churning at an almost visible clip. Then, without so much as a word of explanation, he thrust me aside, yanking the wheel hard to starboard. I yelped, stumbling backwards. I grabbed at the railing to keep from falling and pulled myself back up, seething.

"What the fuck was that?"

"We have to move!" Nate replied, eyes locked on the fight taking place almost directly above our heads. "Now, get out of the way, or you'll die!"

"Is that a threat? Are ye really threatenin' me right now?"

"There's no time," Nate muttered, though it was clear he wasn't responding to me. The wizard grunted, grabbed me by the lapel of my jacket, and yanked me along in his wake, supposedly headed for the ship's portside. Acting on reflex, I slapped his hand away and put him in a quick wrist lock, bending his hand in ways a hand was never meant to bend. I forced his arm behind his back, putting added pressure on his shoulder. I felt him struggle, then curse.

"What have you done to my magic?" he demanded, voice strained.

"I didn't do anythin' to it! Now, tell me what this is all about! Why am I here?"

"You honestly expect me to believe you don't know? You brought me here!" Nate glanced over his shoulder, not at me, but at the battle being waged above. "Oh, shit."

I spun, following the wizard's gaze just in time to see the silver dragon lock up in mid-flight, the gaps between its scales coated in a thick sheen of ice that made it impossible to move. It was a brilliant tactic; I had to admit whoever was up there had put on one hell of an impressive magical display. Unfortunately, a dragon that couldn't move also couldn't fly.

And guess who sat directly beneath it, ill prepared to break its fall?

"Run!" I yelled, releasing Nate's arm and thrusting him towards the ship's railing. The wizard barked something about that having been his plan all along, but I was too busy booking it to pay attention. Together, we leapt overboard just as the metal-coated reptile came crashing down, spearing the ship with its head and snapping it in half like the *Titanic*.

"James!" I screamed as I surfaced, spitting out grimy river water, seized by sudden panic as I realized who'd been left onboard when we jumped. "Tiger Lily! Tinkerbell!" I began paddling towards the seething water, fighting the current, but there was no use; I wasn't strong enough. Besides which—assuming they'd been below, after all—I sincerely doubted there would be much left of the Neverlanders to find.

I flailed, too shocked to be properly upset, until I heard Nate calling out to me from downriver. I treaded water as best I could, looking for the wizard, but we'd ended up under the bridge where the shadows were thickest. On the other side of the river, however, I could have sworn I spotted the female cop from earlier being fished out of the water by a couple of well-dressed passengers on an old-timey riverboat.

"Nate!" I screamed.

"Here, I'm here!"

I swam towards the sound of his voice, playing the world's least fun game of Marco Polo ever, until at last I flung out my hand and caught his.

He pulled me close, and I could tell by his breathing that he was struggling to stay afloat as hard as I was; my clothes weighed like a thousand pounds and my boots felt like concrete blocks attached to my feet.

Then, suddenly, there was light.

I blinked and shielded my eyes, kicking my legs until I could look up at the bridge. We'd come out the other side, and already onlookers had gathered along the railing to stare down into the Mississippi river's murky brown depths. As I watched, at least a dozen pulled their phones out to either snap pictures or call the police. I waved with my free hand, wildly, trying to get their attention.

"We're down here!"

But then a new, absurdly familiar face appeared over the edge, his blue-green eyes scanning the water for signs of life, looking harried and more than a little pissed off. He was also younger than I'd ever seen him, not to mention blonder. I dropped Nate's hand immediately, kicking myself free to stare sidelong at the wizard, wondering which of the two faces belonged to an imposter.

"Who are ye?" I hissed.

But Nate was too busy staring at his doppelgänger to reply.

I slapped the water, splashing the wizard across the face, trying to elicit a reaction. He sputtered, paddling to face me, only to disappear beneath the river's surging surface with a yelp of his own. And that's when I felt it: something coiling around my ankle. I struggled, but whatever it was pulled me under with so much force that my scream was lost to the Mississippi's depths.

God, I hated Missouri.

*N*ate and I collapsed on top of one another in the middle of a grungy, rundown street, our tangled bodies partially illuminated by the light of a street lamp. We were also, somehow, completely dry. I rolled away first, groaning, clutching at both my aching side and throbbing ankle. Nate, meanwhile, seemed to have suffered injuries of his own; he sat up cradling his head, dabbing at a small cut above his right eye and staring at his fingers as though he'd never seen blood before.

"Where are we?" I moaned, sitting up.

"How should I know?" Nate replied, hackles rising. "I went looking for help, and I found you. Again. Just so we're clear, *this* does not count as help." The wizard waved his bloody fingers in front of my face, clearly agitated. "This shouldn't even be possible. I've never gotten hurt doing this, before. And that memory of mine, how did you do that?"

"I have literally no idea what you're talkin' about," I hissed as I rolled to my knees, then my feet, looming over the irate wizard. "Last I knew, me crew and I were on an errand in the Titan realm. Then suddenly you're on me ship, and I'm in St. Louis, and there's a damned dragon fallin' from the sky. Oh, and then I see a younger version of *ye*, which means this is probably your...what the hell are ye doin', now?"

Nate glanced up at me with unfocused eyes, as though he hadn't been paying attention to anything I'd said. Instead, he seemed remarkably fixated on his hands; he began flicking them about once more, muttering something under his breath that sounded like the murderous ramblings of a madman.

"I've lost my magic," he said, at last.

"Aye?" I planted my fists on my hips, rage swelling up to fill the hole I thought I might fall into the instant I began to dwell on what might have happened to my crew back there—wherever and whenever *there* was. "And I lost a whole Goddamned ship!"

"Wait, I know this place," Nate said as though I hadn't spoken. The wizard climbed to his feet to study the distant skyline, eyes narrowed. "Why do I know this place?"

For a moment, I seriously considered choking the wizard out while his back was turned. It wouldn't be terribly difficult; I could slide up behind him, sling my forearm across his throat, trap it with my other arm, and hold tight until he went purple.

The image alone gave me immense satisfaction.

But then I noticed what had gotten his attention.

The bright lights of Boston harbor.

"That's home," I said, disbelieving. Recognition surged, chased away almost immediately by relief and concern. God, how long had I been gone? Were my friends alright? I began to worry about whether Christoff's kids had been able to recover from the loss of their mother, about whether Scathach had gained full control of the Chancery, about Robin's relationship with Camilla now that her brother was in a coma. In fact, I was so overwhelmed that Nate had to repeat himself a few times before I realized he was asking me a question.

"Home? What do you mean, 'home'?"

"Boston. We're in Boston."

Nate flinched.

"What's wrong?" I drawled. "Not a fan?"

"It's not that," Nate snapped. "I had some fond memories of this town, once. That's all."

"Had?"

"Things change. People move on."

"Ye can say that again," I muttered, sensing I'd broached a topic that still stung the wizard. "I still don't understand, though. How'd we get here from St. Louis?"

The tell-tale whirr of sirens brought the two of us round before he or I could take a stab at the question; six or seven cruisers and at least one unmarked tore through the residential neighborhood at a breakneck pace. One of which, at least, I could have sworn belonged to someone I knew.

"Come on," I insisted, taking hold of his suit jacket. "We have to follow those cars."

"Are you crazy? No way! What I need is to find a phone. I'll call Alucard, or Gunnar. One of them can come get me until I figure out what's going on with my magic." Nate flashed me his trademark smile, the cocky one that must have worked on most people. "Maybe I'll turn it into a friendship game. First one to save Nate wins a prize."

I scowled at the mention of the hunky Daywalker I'd more or less shacked up with before sailing into Fae, before my whole life was turned upside down. Part of me wanted to ask how the vampire was doing—the same part which hoped he'd become a miserable, unlovable ass in my absence. Mercifully, I had more important things to worry about than Alucard's relationship status.

"I know one of the cops headed to that scene," I argued. "She'll have a phone ye can use."

Or at least I hoped she would. Since discovering she was at least partially gifted in witchcraft, Detective Maria Machado had been far more cordial to me than I'd come to expect. She'd even sent me a funny cop meme via text message once, though I suspected that was by accident. Either way, I was almost a hundred percent sure that the unmarked vehicle had been hers, and I was also desperately hoping she'd be willing and able to give me a ride home—especially considering I had no license, no wallet, and no cellphone.

"That seems a little convenient, don't you think?" Nate asked, sounding doubtful.

"Hmm..." I thought about it. "Maybe. Is convenience that t'ing when you're sailin' downriver and someone grabs the wheel to put your ship directly under a dragon fallin' out of the sky? Oh, wait, I got that mixed up. That's *inconvenient*. Silly me."

"Okay, first of all, that happened years ago. I couldn't be sure where she was going to land. Besides, how was I supposed to know you're supposed to turn the wheel the opposite way you want to go? I blame whoever designed that shit backwards."

"Wait, you were bein' serious?" I replied, choosing to ignore the rest. "That actually happened?!"

"Obviously. You saw it for yourself."

"Aye, but I assumed it was some sort of illusion, not a memory. I mean, fightin' a *dragon* in the middle of the day on a bridge filled with people? Who does that?"

"It wasn't like I had a goddamned choice," Nate replied. "She came after me on her Lord's orders. Don't give me that look, there was a lot going on at the time. One of my best friends was betraying me. There was a book everyone wanted that they thought I had. I was trying to figure out who killed my parents, and why..." Nate drifted off, grunted, and stared into the middle distance with a pensive frown plastered across his face.

"What is it?" I asked, alerted by his sudden shift in expression.

"Nothing. Just realized chaos is a common theme in my life. Stuff like that happens a lot."

I nudged the wizard, sensing the deep pain lurking behind his eyes.

"So, are we goin', or not?" I asked, not unkindly.

"Sure, fine," Nate said, gathering himself. "It's your town, you lead the way."

I jerked a nod and began working my way towards the sound of sirens and the steady strobe of flashing lights in the distance. Something nagged at me, however, as we drew closer—a suspicion that I'd been here before. Not simply this part of Boston, but this exact neighborhood, with its busted out streetlights and derelict houses. But when? And why?

We came upon the fleet of police cruisers camped outside a residence, blocking off all traffic on either side of the street. Uniforms milled about, clearly on edge about something though it looked like whatever crime they'd responded to had run its course; no one shouted orders and there were no barricades to obstruct us from walking right up to the scene. Struck by a sense of nostalgia, however, I slowed as we approached.

"What is it?" Nate asked.

"That house...I feel like I know it." I sped back up, beelining towards the nearest officer—a rookie with a clipboard in hand, either taking notes or doodling. "Oy!" I called. "What's goin' on here? Whose place is that?"

The cop didn't even so much as look up.

"I'm talking to ye, damnit. Where's Detective Machado?"

Still no response. I turned around in frustration, looking for Nate, only to find him rabbit punching a cop in the face. Or at least that's what it looked like; his fists vanished the instant they reached the officer's flesh. Seemingly satisfied with that turn of events, Nate let his arms drop, took a step back, and fired a cringeworthy kick into the officer's groin. The toe of his boot appeared on the other side of the cop's slacks, sticking out like a tail.

"What are ye doin'?" I hissed.

"Testing a theory." Nate pointed to the rookie in front of me. "It's your turn. Kick him in the nuts."

"I am not goin' to kick a cop in the nuts just because ye say so! Besides, how's that supposed to help get ye access to a phone?"

"Just do it!"

I mumbled curses under my breath, reached out, and waved my hand directly in front of the rookie's face. When he didn't react, I moved to flip his hat off his head. But when my fingers passed right through as if I were touching nothing but air, I jerked my hand back like I'd been shocked.

"I thought so," Nate said, sounding smug. "Now come here and let me touch you."

"Absolutely not."

"I need to see if my hand passes through you," Nate said, his voice laced with frustration and the first quivers of anger. "Why are you being so difficult?"

"Besides the fact that ye got me ship sunk?"

"You're really going to have to let that go."

"How about ye acknowledge the fact that ye just told a woman ye hardly know to come round so ye could 'touch her'?"

"That line has never failed me," he said dryly.

"Listen, I've had about enough—"

I clamped my mouth shut as a stirring among the uniformed officers stole my attention. Two figures appeared in the doorway of the besieged house. The first I recognized immediately as Detective Machado. The second took me a little longer to wrap my head around; standing comically tall next to the Detective, her arms cuffed behind her back, her clothes tattered and blood-soaked, with fiery red hair and skin so pale it practically glowed, the girl looked more like a domestic violence victim being carted off to the station than my double.

"Jesus, what happened to you?"

I flinched to find Nate at my elbow, peering over my shoulder. The wizard had a lock of my hair between his fingers and was rubbing the strands together, idly—which I supposed meant we could at least interact with each other.

Was it too late to exchange that gift?

"Stop that!" I hissed, slapping his hand away.

"She could be your twin. Well, your *much* younger, prettier twin," the wizard quipped with a mischievous grin that explained the wrinkles tugging at the corners of his eyes and left me wondering whether Nate knew how hard I could punch. "So, what's this? You're getting arrested again? What'd you steal this time?"

I rolled my eyes but had to admit Nate had a point. Not about the theft, but about the girl, who was indeed the spitting image of me not but a few years ago. And, from where we stood, it seemed painfully obvious that she'd gotten herself into some trouble. The truth, however, was far more complicated. I flicked my gaze from the house to Maria to an unoccupied section of unlit street not thirty feet away.

"I didn't steal anythin'," I countered. "This was after me fight with Gladstone. He'll be right over there, lyin' in wait."

"Who's Gladstone?"

"Seriously? He's the wizard who wanted to kill ye so badly he blackmailed me into stealin' one of those portable portals your company makes so he could break into Hell and broker a deal with a demon."

"They're called Nate's Tiny Balls. And I've never heard of him."

Seconds later, as if we'd conjured him out of thin air, Gladstone himself appeared. He looked as I'd last seen him, though from this angle I could see that the blood which had soaked the front of his body after slitting a man's throat had missed the back. Even knowing what to expect, I relished his shocked expression as Maria marched my doppelgänger forward, getting a great deal of pleasure watching the thuggish wizard fling his hands about in much the same way as Nate had only minutes before.

"Is that him?"

"Aye."

"Yeah, I've never seen him before. Why'd he want to kill me, again?" Nate asked, as though there could be any number of plausible answers to that question.

"Somethin' about overhaulin' the Academy?" I shook my head, struggling to remember. "Whatever it was, he took it personally. Very personally."

"I hope you beat him like the Celtics beat the Yankees every year," he growled, appearing ironically murderous at the mere mention of violence. "In the Super Bowl."

I blinked at the wizard, unsure how any one person could get so many facts wrong in a single statement. But, since I honestly had no idea where to begin, I dismissed it. "No, that was mostly from me fight with his henchman."

"And where's he?"

"Dead."

Nate shot me a sharp look.

"I didn't kill him," I snapped, defensively. "Gladstone did. He needed a sacrifice, apparently."

"Your wizard is casting something," Nate said, apparently more interested in Gladstone now that he knew what the bastard had been willing to do to exact revenge. "Elemental magic, looks like."

I followed Nate's gaze and saw Gladstone raising his arms. The air was suddenly charged, reeking of burning ozone. Gale force winds began to beat at us, whipping my hair across my face and threatening to bowl me over. I saw Maria dragging my younger self to safety behind a cruiser even as Nate drew me away, cursing; his suit jacket flapped madly in the wind, his hair tousled. The St. Louis native shouted something at me, but I couldn't hear it over the crack of thunder overhead. Nate froze and pointed to the sky, his face slack. I looked up just in time to see a fork of lightning arc towards us in a burst of brilliant light that sent us both soaring backwards into space.

38

I collided with a wall, bashing my head against the cement with an audible thunk that sent shockwaves rippling down my spine, only to collapse against a tile floor covered in scuff marks. I shook my head, dazed, and caught a grunt of pain to my right. Nate leaned over his knees, palming his forehead, his eyebrows singed. The wizard's suit—which should have been a wrinkled mess and smoldering from the lightning blast—bore no signs of wear besides the creases down his slacks. I rose on all fours and took stock of myself, distantly aware that my own outfit had survived without a mark. The aches and pains from leaping overboard, being pulled under, landing on a sidewalk, and being thrown into a wall, however, were seriously beginning to take their toll.

"Where are we, now?" I asked, blinking up at the harsh fluorescent lighting. Further inspection of the room revealed pale cement walls, an unoccupied desk, and two doors—one painted green, the other brown. I frowned, realizing I could hear snippets of what sounded like a heated exchange behind the green door. Something about a key.

"This is the St. Louis County police station," Nate replied, sounding somehow both awed and annoyed. "I've been here, once or twice."

The conversation on the other side of the door got more animated, though it was still hard to decipher. Moments later, the stench of sulfur drifted on the air. Nate jerked, swiveling towards the source of what could only be described as an argument, at this point. The wizard rolled to his feet, his fists balled so tightly his knuckles were white.

"There's no way this is happening," Nate said. "No one saw this but me."

"What?"

Nate didn't answer me. Instead, he marched right up to the door, eyed it, and slid his foot forward like a man testing the water out with his toe. His shoe disappeared, seemingly swallowed. Apparently satisfied, Nate hurried through to the other side, leaving me kneeling on the floor wondering whether it was safe for me to stand, yet; I'd hit my head often enough by now to know better than to hop right up and keep going like nothing happened.

You couldn't rush a concussion.

The sounds of a struggle reached me as I climbed gingerly to my feet. I felt a tad wobbly but mercifully better than I would have if I'd done some real damage. The sudden screech of metal tearing, followed by maniacal laughter, spurred me to action; I rushed to the other side of the door, heedlessly, worried Nate had gotten himself in more trouble.

And it turned out I'd been right.

Sort of.

"The Key is not up for grabs. Tell your boss I said so," the prisoner said as he pried the claws of a literally Goddamned demon from his chest. Well, half a Goddamned demon, anyway; the other half was lying several feet away in a pool of steaming blood. I let out a sigh of relief, realizing the fight I'd thought to stop had already come to an end. The prisoner, meanwhile, discarded the unholy remains, moved to the corner of his cell, sat, and hugged his knees like a lost little boy. Sitting like that, it was painfully clear that I was looking at a younger, blonder version of Nate.

"Well, would ye look at that?" I crowed, turning to Nate. The wizard stood outside the cell, avoiding eye contact with his younger self. I put on my best, fake valley-girl accent. "Oh my God, is that Nate Temple behind bars?"

"*Mardi Gras* in Saint Louis is no joke," the wizard replied, though I could tell I'd gotten under his skin. "Second biggest party town behind New Orleans."

"Let me guess, ye get thrown in jail for showin' someone your tiny balls?"

"No. I think it was for starting a fight at Achilles' bar. Or pissing off a dickhead cop. Or murder. Or...horsenapping?" Nate shrugged, clearly too distracted by something on his arm to notice how awful that list sounded when said out loud. "I honestly don't remember which accusation they went with, in the end."

"And the demon?"

"She wanted the Key to the Armory. And payback. Pretty sure I killed her brother." Nate shook his head. "That was a bad week. Went broke, lost my magic, almost died. Twice."

Frankly, I believed him; Nate seemed like the kind of guy to get himself into that sort of trouble. Of course, none of that explained the blonde streaks in his freaking hair—which, for some reason, I couldn't let go.

"Oh, I'm guessin' ye dyed it more than twice."

"What are you talking about?"

"Your hair, Justin Timberlake. Go ahead, ye can tell me the truth...d'ye have more fun?"

"Huh?" Nate flicked his gaze to his doppelgänger, then to me, and finally back to his arm. "That's just how my hair gets in the summer. Besides, I'm not sure you have room to talk, Princess Merida."

"Oh, like I've never heard that one before." I eyed the younger wizard's dirty blonde locks, trying to think of an equally witty comparison and failing; I'd expended all my ammo by leading with the pop star reference. "So it's been like, what, six years since you've seen the sun?"

Nate grunted, still picking at his arm.

"Jesus, what the hell are ye fidgetin' with? Let me see."

Nate showed me. A long, jagged cut ran the length of his forearm from wrist to elbow, splitting the sleeve of his suit jacket neatly in two. Blood welled along the wound, but didn't spill, which meant it wasn't very deep. The question was, how'd he get it?

"The Demon caught me by accident when I tried to get closer," Nate replied when I asked him. The wizard shook his head and flung his good arm out at the bars, not the least bit surprised as they passed through each metal rod without fail. "This doesn't make any sense. I can't touch them, but the demon could touch me? How unfair is that? And why aren't we falling through space, if we can pass through objects? None of this makes any sense!"

I didn't have an answer for any of that. Honestly, I had no idea what was happening, or why. First we'd sailed into the middle of an old battle between Nate and a dragon, then we'd stumbled upon the tail end of my altercation with Gladstone, and now we stood looking at the aftermath of a violent disagreement between Nate and a pesky demon. What *was* the point of all this?

And why was the demon cut in half?

"How'd she get like that?" I asked, eyeing the corpse even as it turned to ash and collapsed, leaving behind nothing but a pool of sizzling blood.

"What?" Nate, having clearly been lost in his own thoughts, looked up in a daze. "Oh, I basically stopped mid Shadow Walk, which meant her top half teleported with me, but her bottom didn't."

"Wait, ye can *do* that?"

"I mean, I guess so. I never really did it again, after this."

"Why not?" I asked, floored by the notion that Nate could essentially tear beings in two whenever he was in a bind. Or, hell, whenever the urge struck. "Seems like it'd give ye a huge advantage in a fight."

Nate opened his mouth to respond but was interrupted by the lights going out. I listened intently for the faint whirr of all things electronic but heard nothing, which I assumed meant the power had gone out. Fortunately, the station had a generator; emergency lights flickered on a moment later, and I was able to spot Nate's younger self lurking near the bars, looking tense.

"Ah, right. Here comes Othello," Nate said, pointing to the door we'd phased through.

"Othello?"

"She rescued me. Will rescue me. Whatever."

The door opened, except behind it was not Othello. It was two men, both of whom I recognized. The first, taller and well-built, wore a mercenary's uniform. The other, slight and severely balding, wore a tailored suit. They chattered back and forth in Russian as they walked towards—and then through—us. I whirled as they passed and rounded the corridor, only to realize we'd gone from the police station in St. Louis to an even less pleasant location.

A prison in Russia.

"This memory's mine," I said, before Nate could ask the inevitable question. I sighed, wishing I understood why we were flitting about through time and space like Ebeneezer Scrooge sans spirit guides. "We should follow them."

"Hold on, let's stop and think about this." Nate peered down the dark corridor, rubbing at his arms. His sleeve, I noticed, was intact once more—albeit stained with fresh blood from a wound that was apparently still there. "First off, where are we now?"

"Somewhere outside Moscow."

"Of course we are," Nate replied, groaning. "What the hell are we doing in Russia? Or, should I say, what the hell were *you* doing in Russia?"

"Savin' friends from Rasputin with Othello and her cousin."

"Wait..." Nate held out an arm like a mother stopping her child from crossing the road. "Did you say Othello has a cousin? I didn't know she had a cousin."

"That's because she likes me more."

"Oh yeah? Well, did she ever break *you* out of jail?"

The lights went out before I could reply. But then, in a way, I supposed that meant Nate was about to get his answer; Othello was about to do just that. Orange strobe lights and alarms came on seconds later, dispersing the gloom and shattering the silence, followed by a flash of light from the direction the two Russian men had gone.

"That'll be Othello!" I yelled over the piercing screech of sirens. Uniformed guards came filing into the hallway where we stood, slinging assault rifles down off their shoulders before running off towards the commotion. Before I could say anything else, however, Nate began jogging after them, calling out his friend's name.

Surprised by Nate's sudden willingness to forge ahead, I had to sprint to catch up, my poor hip and aching skull flaring in pain with every jerky step. By the time I reached him, however, he'd already run out into the main hallway and was standing behind the firing squad as they aimed at Othello and a decidedly less ragged version of me.

Nate, yelling at the top of his lungs, tried to stop them, snatching at the nearest guard's throat with his bare hands as though he planned to throttle the young man to death. Of course, when the wizard's hands inevitably passed harmlessly through, Nate only got angrier.

"This is bullshit!" he complained.

The prison guards unloaded their magazines. The stench of hot metal and smoke filled our end of the hallway as bullet casings spewed all over the floor. Nate, meanwhile, kept trying to assault the gunman; he jabbed his fingers into the young man's eyes over and over again like Patrick Swayze trying to move a picture frame in *Ghost*.

Funnily enough, even had he succeeded, I knew it would make no difference; Othello was on the other side of that barrage using a Gateway glove to soak up all the bullets, saving both her and my younger self in the process. Bullets, I recalled, which she would be sending right back this way, shortly.

"Nate!" I shouted as the firing stopped. "We need to move!"

Unfortunately, the wizard had lost his cool completely by this point; Nate was busy kicking and punching everything in sight like a kid after his first karate lesson. I rushed to his side, trying to grab his arm and lead him away, but the moron was simply too animated.

"I...won't...let...you...hurt...my...friends!" Nate snarled as he waged his ineffectual assault.

"Nate, look!" I pointed down the hall. "She's fine. I'm fine."

Nate turned and saw the truth to my claim; Othello had her hand raised, a Gateway forming around her hand like a vortex. Gripped by a sudden panic, I wrapped my arms around Nate's torso and yanked him backwards as the first wave of reflected bullets came ripping into the guards, tearing into them with blood-curdling shrieks and Russian curses. One projectile even grazed my shoulder, sending searing pain down my back. I screamed, unable to stop myself. Nate tried to rise, maybe even to help, but I continued to hold him down until, at last, I heard nothing but silence.

Followed, inexplicably, by the howling of wolves.

*S*unlight spilled over Nate and me as I flipped off of him. I whimpered, feeling like someone had run a hot poker up my spine before jabbing it into the meat of my shoulder. The bullet may only have grazed me, but that didn't make it hurt any less. Nate, meanwhile, hadn't moved at all; I found him on all fours, staring out at a forest of golden trees with a strange, almost primal look splashed across his face.

The howling of wolves, distant but unmistakable, was quickly joined by other, equally primal sounds: the spitting and hissing of cats, the grunts of boars, the clomp of horse hooves, and even the shouts of men. Except it couldn't be men, because men lived in the mortal realm.

And that's not where we were.

I sat up, gingerly, as the ruckus grew louder and louder. Whatever was out there, they were somewhere beyond the nearby ridge and closing in fast. I nudged Nate, jerking my chin towards the forest. Maybe there we could find cover and hide from whatever was coming.

"Thinkin' about makin' a break for it?"

"We wouldn't get very far," Nate replied, a deep, somber timbre in his voice that I'd never heard before. "The Wild Hunt will be here soon."

"The what, now?" The bestial din cranked up in volume as I struggled to stand, my thoughts sluggish. The Wild Hunt...where had I heard that before? "So, this is your memory, then?"

Nate leapt to his feet without answering, still staring at the forest.

"They come," he growled, smiling wickedly, a manic gleam dancing in his eyes.

I scowled, baffled by his excitement, but followed his gaze to the edge of the forest. At first, I saw nothing out of the ordinary. Well, nothing unexpected, at any rate; the Fae realm had a great many jaw-dropping sights to its credit, and the breathtaking clearing we occupied was no exception. Sadly, when you're about to be trampled to death, you tend to prioritize things like help over aesthetics.

"Who's comin'?"

Nate simply pointed. I squinted and finally saw who he meant: blood-soaked pixies emerged from the forest in what seemed like endless ranks, brandishing tiny blades. Leading the charge, her features barely distinguishable, flew a silver pixie I thought I recognized.

"Barbie?" I wondered, aloud.

"You know her?" Nate asked, suddenly interested.

"Of course I do. Wait, ye know her, too? How?"

"It's a long story. She helped me fight a war, once. And now she's about to put herself between me and King Oberon. Soon, I will kiss her," he added in a tone that sounded more ravenous than smug.

"Oberon's here, too?!" I asked, pointedly ignoring the part about him making out with a pixie the size of his thumb; whatever kinky stuff he did with someone that size was his business, after all. Nate faced me directly before answering, giving me more eye contact than I was prepared for. In fact, there was a savageness to his expression, a ferociousness, that I found decidedly disturbing. Gone were the antics and the jokes, the sarcasm and the asides.

Indeed, it felt almost as if I wasn't speaking to Nate, at all.

"How do *you* know King Oberon?"

"Talk about a long story," I muttered, dismissing the wizard's suspicious tone. "Listen, I'll tell ye, but first let's move away from here. Whatever's about to happen, I don't want to end up caught in the middle."

Apparently seeing the sense in that, Nate nodded. Together, we ran perpendicular to the ridge and away from the horde of pixies beelining towards it.

No, not a horde.

A bunch? A flight?

"A stick," I said out loud, triumphantly, once we'd gotten far enough from the front lines to feel safe from the impending clash. "A stick of pixies!"

"What was that?"

"Nothin', nevermind."

Nate grunted.

"What's your problem?" I asked, catching the faintest air of irritation in his otherwise noncommittal response. "Look, This is obviously your memory. What happens next?"

"I was not conscious when this happened," he replied, folding his arms across his chest. "I ended up there, in the forest. I tried to Shadow Walk, but it didn't go as planned."

"So ye don't know what happens next?" I asked, my eyes drawn to the ridge where even now figures—mostly goblins, but also a contingent of elves dressed in hunting garb holding the leashes of grotesque monsters that reminded me of the rotting dogs from *Pet Cemetery*—gathered to launch an assault.

"The pixies took our blood. They stayed behind and fought..." Nate fell silent as the forces collided. The pixies, who had the clear advantage of being able to fly, zipped and zagged, scoring blow after blow with their razor sharp blades, nicking and cutting with abandon. But their strikes were too weak, too ineffectual; the goblins swung haphazardly, taking out any pixies foolish enough to get too close.

Meanwhile, the elves—probably the Hunt's trackers, if I had to guess—lingered on the crest of the ridge, holding back the horrifying hounds. Were they reserve forces, I wondered, or were they non-combatants? Whichever, it seemed I wasn't the only one to notice them; Barbie and a stick of pixies burst away from the battle towards the elves, intent on bringing them down. The trackers scattered, bolting away in whatever direction their dogs were willing to run.

One came sprinting directly towards us, panic written plain across his face as he looked back over his shoulder again and again, confirming his worst fears: the pixies had given up on the others and were after him. Barbie and two of her companions got him just as he reached us, slashing at his legs over and over again until he collapsed. Then they were on him, stabbing and slicing until his pleas for mercy had long died in his throat. Still attached to his wrist, somehow, his ragged hound dragged the elf's corpse a bit further before the beast finally broke its leash and sprinted off.

Barbie and her pixies, covered in even more blood, turned to find their forces routed, the majority of their companions dead or fleeing. Without a word exchanged between them, the three headed straight for the trees, leaving the elf's corpse to rot.

Drawn by an awful suspicion, I approached the body, already dreading what I would find waiting for me when I got a chance to study the elf's face. It was exactly as I suspected; though lifeless, his eyes staring up at nothing, I could see Ryan's reflection in it clear as day. They had the same jaw, the same nose, even the same ears—pointed and small-lobed. I remembered, suddenly, where I first heard mention of the Wild Hunt: Cassandra had mentioned it to Ryan the day he left, citing this very battle as the one which had claimed his father's life.

"Good riddance," Nate said, joining me over the body. "Those who are too weak to fight should stay home. Though I guess I should thank him. It's possible Barbie only survived because she left the battle to chase him down."

"Shut the hell up."

"Excuse me?"

"I said shut up!" I shoved the wizard, hard. He stumbled backwards but kept his feet, raising his arms in self-defense. But I wasn't going after him. There was no point; he clearly had no idea how callously he'd come across. "Can't ye see that this was all your fault? All this?" I showcased the gory results of the battle, tears pricking at the corner of my eyes.

"My fault? The Hunt was after me. After my friends. Everything that happened here was because the Queens feared me and strong armed Oberon into joining their crusade. What was I supposed to do? Die?"

"Of course not," I snapped. "But d'ye even try to solve this by some other means? To do anythin' but pick a fight? Why d'ye have to win so badly? Can't ye see it gets everyone ye know and love killed?!"

I clamped my mouth shut, distantly aware that my speech could just as easily have been directed at me as it could to him. Overwhelmed by the surge of emotions flooding through me, I slid to my knees beside the corpse of Ryan's father, wishing desperately that I could bring him back. How many things in my life might have changed if Ryan had never returned to Fae? Would Dobby have gotten close enough to kill Dez? Would Ryan and I have been enough to save Christoff and his family before Rasputin's men got ahold of him? Would Ryan have kept me from visiting Fae with his dire warnings, or at least postponed my trip?

Would I be who I was?

Or would I be someone else? Someone better, maybe?

"This was the father of a friend of mine," I said, my voice so hushed I wasn't even sure whether or not Nate could hear me. "By all accounts, he was a good father. T'anks to what happened here, his son wants to kill the Manlin' he t'inks was responsible. To that end, me friend has become a servant of the Winter Queen, has tortured and betrayed his own kind, has even invaded and terrorized an entire realm in search of the power he t'inks he'll need to bring that person down. And now here ye are, standin' over his father's body, and ye can't even say you're sorry for your part in it?"

"I..." Nate drifted off.

"I would say me friend's name, but I doubt you've ever heard of him, so why bother? Ye know, one day your gravestone will read 'Here Lies Nate Temple, He Had More Enemies Than Anyone Has Friends.'" I chuckled at my own joke, but the laughter died almost immediately in my throat. I closed my eyes, fighting back the urge to sob. "But at least ye have friends. That's got to count for somethin', right?"

"Quinn?"

"No, please. Just leave me here for a minute."

"I can't do that."

"Why not?"

"Because," Nate replied, yanking me to my feet beneath a cloudy grey sky, pointing first to one and then a second army squaring off on either side of a completely new battlefield, "it looks like they're about to kill each other, and we're in the way."

*T*he second battle in as many hours kicked off before Nate or I could discuss where we'd landed, giving us only enough time to come up with one viable plan: move. Horns blew as warriors on horseback came marching forward on our left from perhaps a half mile out, their bodies covered in what appeared to be thin layers of wool and calfskin, bearing broadswords and targes. At least two hundred yards out to our right, meanwhile, plodded an army of spear-wielders dressed as though they planned to invade Russia—nothing but fur piled on top of fur.

The Curaitl.

The name hit me like a bolt of lightning—something I could actually say now that I'd been struck by one. Other names followed, registering one after the other as Nate and I sprinted for the battle's sidelines, where we figured we'd be the least likely to end up trampled or impaled; neither of us were sure what could hurt us, at this point, and had no desire to find out. As we went, I found myself scanning the spear-wielding army for familiar faces. Blair. Tristan. Lady Aife. Even Rhys.

But the Curaitl's forces were too far away, their numbers too great. Hell, even if I abandoned Nate now and booked it for their front lines, I doubted I'd make it in time; the battle was about to kick off at any given moment. In fact, I realized I dimly recalled this clash; I'd seen the first stirrings of it from the relative shelter of a cluster of rocks...

"There!" I shouted.

"The rocks?" Nate called over his shoulder, his suit jacket clutched in one hand, his shirt stained with a light sheen of sweat around the collar and along the small of his back. "Why them?"

"We can hide there! It should be safe."

"Are you seriously telling me this is *your* memory? When did you travel back in time to the goddamned Middle Ages?"

"Just go!" I shouted, my own breathing labored. My hip, back, and head throbbed with each and every step, as if threatening me to slow down. "I'll explain later!"

Nate switched gears, angling towards the odd configuration of rocks at the edge of the battlefield. We'd almost made it, in fact, when a slightly younger version of myself bolted out from the gap between two stones, screaming "Scathach" at the top of her lungs, waving her hands in the air like she just didn't care. She blasted past us, moving with that inhuman speed I'd possessed until a few short days ago.

"Go, Princess Merida, go!" Nate shouted as we reached the stones before promptly planting his hands against the rock and sucking in air.

"Don't be mad," I wheezed, "because in this scenario...I'm a princess...and you're the comic relief...slash sidekick."

"Who's mad?" Nate replied with a snort, seemingly having returned to normal ever since we'd left the Fae realm behind. "I always wanted to be a...*what the fuck is that?!*"

A great big, black beast appeared as if by magic on Nate's right, its muscled chest coated in a shaggy mane of hair riddled with druidic markings the color of ash, its amber eyes locked on my doppelgänger. The wizard, meanwhile, yelped like someone had stepped on his toe, backpedaling until he practically ran into me.

"Keep her safe, what a joke," Cathal growled as he crept towards the battlefield, stalking forward like a lion in the savannah, utterly oblivious to the two of us. Which was great because I was laughing so hard I wouldn't have been able to explain the situation if he *had* noticed us.

"Okay, seriously, what the hell was that thing?"

"There, there," I said, patting Nate's shoulder, still chuckling. "Don't mind Cathy. He's a good boy. I've only seen him chomp on, like, five men your size. Ten, tops."

"Hah hah." Nate continued to stare, clearly transfixed. "You know, he sort of reminds me of Grimm."

"Your rainbow-hatin' alicorn, ye mean? I can see it. They do both have that whole 'murder ye for fun' vibe goin' for 'em. Though, as I recall, Cathal doesn't cuss as much."

"Hold on, you know Grimm?"

"'Know' is a strong word." I tugged at Nate's arm, pulling him into the recesses between the rocks. It was a tight fit, but at least we weren't likely to catch any stray projectiles. "I saw him break Neverland's rainbow, once. Apparently he found it recreational, if not downright therapeutic."

"You were in Neverland?" Nate shuddered, looking exceptionally perturbed. "When was that?"

"Before it died. Or nearly died, I guess." I shook my head, still finding it difficult to think about Cathal and Eve and whether or not I'd ever see them again—in the flesh, that is. "I went to Fae lookin' for me family. And I found it. Turned out me parents weren't who I thought they were, and that me whole life was pretty much a lie."

"Yeah," Nate said. "I know what that's like."

For some reason, I believed him.

"Listen," I began, "about what I said before—"

"I'm sorry about your friend," Nate interrupted. "I mean it. I never intended for anyone to get hurt, but then I never do. The truth is, you're right. I have a shitty tendency to pick fights and lash out, especially when I could be building bridges instead of burning them."

"More like settin' fire to whole cities and pissin' on the ashes, from what I hear," I teased, making it clear from my tone that I hoped to lighten the mood. Frankly, I was still a bit ashamed of how I'd gone after him in Fae. Sure, he'd had it coming...but so had I.

"What can I say? When I do things, I tend to do them well or not at all," Nate replied, smarmily. "Anyway, weren't you going to tell me how we ended up here? When this memory took place, that is. Unless you have any more of an idea why this is happening than I do, in which case, I'm all ears."

"Not a clue," I admitted. "As for the when, I'm not entirely sure. I'm not even sure time is a t'ing, here. This isn't the Middle Ages, it's the Otherworld."

"The what now?"

I spent the next twenty minutes giving Nate the skinny on everything I knew about the Otherworld, including how I'd reached it and why I'd been sent there. To his credit, Nate stayed silent for most of the spiel, interrupting only twice. The first occurred when I mentioned the Highland Games and the Huntress in the same breath, while the second took place in the middle of the bit featuring the round table discussion between Manannan Mac Lir and my mother's ghost.

"I'm sorry, could you back up and say that again?" Nate had asked, holding up one hand to stop me.

"Morrigan. The woman who gave birth to me. One third of the Celtic triple-headed goddess." I cocked my head. "Didn't Othello fill ye in on any of that? Feels like the sort of t'ing she'd mention."

"Of course not. I think I'd remember..." Nate screwed up his face. "Unless she told me while I was under attack. Or getting shot at. Or trying to outwit a god. Or gods, plural."

"I suggest checkin' your Inbox," I replied, dryly. "Search for 'goddess Quinn' and see what ye find. Knowin' her, she'll have sent ye a whole dossier, complete with blood work and birth certificate. Not that you'd glean much from that."

"Why not?"

"Because the one I have is obviously a forgery. Not that I would have expected anythin' else, given the circumstances. It's not like they could just sign it 'Morrigan and Merlin' and expect everyone to play along."

"Back up," he said, pinching the bridge of his nose with two fingers. "Merlin?"

And that's how we got so sidetracked that we skipped over all things Otherworld and moved right on to things like my lineage and my newfound divinity. To say the wizard was skeptical would have been a colossal understatement, but—by the time we'd run out of immediately pertinent questions—he seemed to have at least a partial grasp of my situation.

"Merlin..." Nate said, shaking his head back and forth. "He gave my parents a table once, you know. I even used his blood to fix my Horseman's mask."

"Your what?"

"Oh, you mean Othello didn't tell you about that?" Nate asked, his lips curling.

"Pretty sure I'd remember, if she had. Unless I was too distracted because I *am* a goddess."

Nate slipped a hand into his pocket, then frowned. He began pawing at himself frantically, patting down his various pockets. Which, in our tight confines, was less than ideal.

"Hey! Watch it!" I snapped, swatting at his hands.

Nate froze as a shout came from the other side of our hiding place. Had we been overheard? But how, no one could see or hear us, right? Just to be safe, I signaled Nate with a finger to my lips and pressed myself as far from the gaps in the stones as possible. Which is all that saved me as a spear came jabbing into the aperture, mere inches from goring my side.

"Shit, run!" I yelled, thrusting Nate out the side exit Cathal had used earlier, only to end up frozen like startled rabbits as a band of wild, riderless horses broke from the battle and headed straight for us. Froth dripped from their lips, their muscled flanks slick with sweat, eyes bugged out with panic as though they were being chased by some beast. For a moment, I could have sworn I saw Cathal cutting across the field in the opposite direction.

Damned mutt.

"Now might be a great time to run," Nate said, sounding nervous.

"Agreed."

"Great. So...which way?"

Instinctively, I turned on my heel and faced the slope that led to the beach, recalling the path Cathal and I had taken to reach the rocks. Would my boat be down there, still? Was it possible Nate and I could get in it and flee, maybe even find a way to escape these hellish landscapes for good? There was only one way to find out.

"Follow me!" I urged.

"So bossy," Nate replied, offering me a little half-bow to go with his shit-eating grin. "But you know what they say: Ladies first."

41

I sprinted towards the sound of the surf, running downhill with Nate puffing along at my side, the herd of wild horses hot on our heels. The slope was steeper than I remembered from my uphill trek with Cathal, but at least my sense of direction wasn't totally impaired; the black sand beach lay at the base of the hill just as I'd remembered it, spreading out to meet the sea like an oil spill. Unfortunately, I didn't see my boat, but at this point it didn't matter; all we had time to do was run headlong into the tide and pray the horses—freaked out as they were—changed course rather than throw themselves into the sea.

If not, then it looked like we'd be testing that trample theory, after all.

"Almost there!" I shouted, pointing. Nate acknowledged me with a grunt. The pounding of the horses' hooves grew louder with every passing moment until it felt like they were right behind us, seconds away from running us down. A glance over my shoulder told me I was right.

We weren't going to make it.

Nate, apparently sensing the same thing, broke away from our intended path, barreling into me like a linebacker just as we hit the beach. Together, we crashed into the sand, skidding across its surface as the herd blew by— wheeling just enough to avoid us as they turned to gallop across the beach. Still, we kept our heads low, shielding our faces from the buckets full of sand they kicked up, waiting for their neighs to fade. At last, we were left with nothing but the tide's lulling whisper.

Until, that is, Nate tapped my shoulder.

"Looks like another one of yours."

I raised my head and took a look around, realizing he was right; the sand on this beach was as white as sand could get—the ivory to the Otherworld's ebony. What's more, my younger self was on it, staring out at the waves like she was about to pull a Virginia Wolfe, looking somehow even more wretched than she had wearing Maria's handcuffs. I groaned but managed to get my feet under me quickly, thanks to a helping hand from Nate.

"Nice tackle," I acknowledged.

"Oh, thanks. I played lacrosse, once. That's the one with the helmets, right?"

"Ye literally just described a half dozen sports."

"Hockey? Baseball?"

"Was there ice involved? Or...bases?"

"Yes?" Nate gave me an indifferent shrug, grinning. "Hey, who are you talking to over there?"

I followed Nate's gaze and saw my younger self having an in-depth discussion with an old man in a corduroy jacket and threadbare slacks. I waved Nate forward, eager to catch what was being said. For some reason, this memory barely registered as a memory, at all; I couldn't recall how my younger self had gotten here, or even what the old man and I had talked about. What I recalled most from this brief conversation was being too grief-stricken to ask logical questions, too focused on saving Jimmy to properly listen.

"...I think about this a lot," the old man was saying, his gravelly voice barely audible over the whistle of biting wind and the crash of waves upon the shore. "Whether all mortals perish with some tiny regret in their hearts. Not those frivolous bucket lists with their skydiving and travel, but real regrets—people they wish they didn't have to leave behind, stories they never got to tell, versions of themselves they never got to be."

"That's deep," Nate whispered as he leaned in to me, one hand propped on the other side of his mouth as though they could actually hear us. "Who is this guy?"

I realized I wasn't certain I knew the answer to that question a moment before the old man's jade green eyes slid—eerily—towards the two of us.

This time, when he spoke, it felt less like a replayed memory and more like a message; the hairs on my neck stood straight up, and I felt Nate stiffen beside me under the old man's hefty regard.

"We cannot interfere directly," he intoned. "It must be your decision. They were your friends. You will have to take responsibility for bringing them back. You will pay the price."

The old man snapped his fingers and the sounds of violence rang out at our backs. Nate and I jumped and spun as one, prepared for a fight. Except it became clear right away that we weren't the ones under attack; we stood in an open coliseum between two marble pillars among a crowd of shadowy, featureless figures who seemed fixated on the outcome of some sort of all-out brawl taking place. Disturbed by the abrupt shift, I began to turn back when I noticed the impossibly beautiful sky above our heads, not to mention the very scary, bearded deity hovering amidst the clouds. I grabbed Nate's arm for something solid to hold onto as I met the god's eye.

"Nate, who the fuck is that?"

"My butler in disguise," Nate replied, patting my hand. "Don't worry about him."

"I'm serious," I snapped. "Where are we?"

"Right. Welcome to Mount Olympus." Nate caught my awed expression and nodded sagely. "And now you can't say I never take you anywhere nice."

Sick and tired of his nonchalant behavior, I punched the wizard's arm—admittedly a little harder than I needed to. Nate winced, rubbing his injured limb, but he didn't complain. Which led me to suspect he was putting up a good-humored front for my sake; I doubted he'd have baited me quite so much, otherwise.

"What's wrong?" I asked, keeping my voice low.

"Nothing," Nate lied. "So, was it just me, or did that last guy act like he was talking to us?"

That's because he was.

The voice slid over me like honey—somehow both sweet and cloying. I felt Nate tense, but that was as much as he could do. As much as either of us could do, I realized. We were frozen, locked in place by that sibilant, vaguely disturbing voice. I thought I caught the slightest movement at our backs, but that could have been anything. Or anyone.

Relax and look.

As if by magic, the shadowy figures obscuring our view of the fight drifted away, parting like a curtain. I gasped, surprised to find Nate—albeit a brooding, unkempt version of the wizard, his skin covered in flaking warpaint—standing over the fallen body of a goddess; golden ichor pooled around her face, her neck bent at an odd angle.

"Athena," Nate whispered beside me, sounding far less triumphant than you'd expect from the man who'd killed her.

You mourn her? The one who took so much from you?

Nate scoffed at that.

"I wouldn't go that far," he replied. "I guess I understand her, that's all. More than I ever thought I would."

How so?

"How about you tell me who you are and what *you* want? Or why you brought us here? I promise I'm a great listener."

When it suits you.

"Alright, so you know me," Nate reasoned. "Or at least you think you do. Which narrows this down a little."

Would you like to know what I think?

"I'm on pins and needles."

I think you fear becoming like her. Bloodthirsty, craving war for war's sake. You know you're capable of it, so you push them all away. You give them the excuse they need to leave, then get angry when they don't, and angrier still when they do. You, dear Catalyst, are the very definition of a self-fulfilling prophecy.

Nate was silent—though whether that was because he actually bought into what was being said, or because there was no point arguing with a being you couldn't fight or even see, I had no idea. What I did know was that Nate's silence didn't bode well for either of us. Seconds later, I felt the being's focus shift to me like a physical blow; my knees weakened beneath its attention.

Do you see her?

"Who? Athena?"

Look close and tell me what you see.

"I see a dead goddess. I'm guessin' Nate broke her neck, somehow." I studied Nate's doppelgänger as he loomed over the body, his muscles straining, the very air around him brimming with wild magic. "What's your point?"

That is how she died, yes, but not how she was defeated. Would you like to know how he bested her?

I licked my lips, sensing a trap. Did I really want to know how Nate had killed a goddess? I had to admit a large part of me was curious; now that I technically was one, I felt a certain kinship—a connection—to these archaic, all-powerful creatures. Had Nate weakened her the way Circe would have? Had he out-maneuvered her, out-strategized?

"I want to know."

Tell her.

"Sex," Nate said, matter-of-factly. "I channeled Aphrodite's magic and used it against Athena. Then, when she begged me for a warrior's death, I gave it to her."

He exposed a weakness, you see. Found the crack in her facade.

"I did what I had to. And I didn't go as far as I could have," Nate growled, defensively.

How does that make you feel?

I could sense the question was directed at me, but frankly I wasn't sure how to feel about any of it. Was I supposed to be outraged on Athena's behalf? Was that the point of all this, to drive a wedge between Nate and me? Nate had used Athena's weakness against her—so what? It'd been a tactical decision, and it had worked. I couldn't—wouldn't—fault him for that.

So, why did I feel a little queasy?

Would you like to know what I think?

"Are ye goin' to tell me, anyway?"

I think you're wondering what your flaw is, deep down. Only you believe you've got too many flaws to count, meaning you could never pin down your greatest weakness, even if you tried. But you've missed the point.

"Oh?" I coughed, my throat suddenly dry. "And what's the point?"

Ask me again when this is over.

I opened my mouth to respond, but the voice interrupted.

Time's up.

"Wait, I have more questions for—" Nate began.

But a crack of thunder cut him off. A bolt of lightning—golden, not blue —descended from the heavens, cracking the stone at our feet. Nate and I stumbled backwards, half-blind. Panicked, I grabbed for Nate and found him reaching for me. But we were unable to lock our hands together in time; we landed a dozen feet apart in a field of fresh, purple grass.

I sat up first, which turned out to be a mistake; a shockwave of energy flattened everything in our immediate vicinity, swatting me so hard I felt like I finally understood what it was to be a pulverized fly. I moaned, rolling to my side in time to see Nate—not my Nate, but yet another replica—beating the ever-loving shit out of a gangly goat-man twice his height. Laughing maniacally, the wizard looked to be trying to snap off one the creature's horns with a block of wood. And the fight only got uglier from there.

"What the hell is that you're fightin'?" I asked, cringing as the goat-man picked up a freaking boulder and chucked it at the wizard, who had the good sense to turn it to dust, but not enough sense to stop before breathing it all in. The wizard bent over double, hacking his lungs out.

And that, ladies and gentlemen, is why you should never inhale.

"Not what. Who," Nate replied, his voice breaking, unexpected grief written raw across his face. "That's my best friend. *Was* my best friend."

The goat-man—more accurately known as Pan, the Greek god of the wild—had just flung Nate's doppelgänger into the side of a cave as the wizard filled me in, very briefly, on what was happening between the two friends. According to him, Pan had started the bout to teach Nate a lesson—one that required one hell of a tough love approach.

"It was my fault," Nate said, rushing towards the epic tussle with me in tow. "He was trying to help me, but I didn't see it. Not until it was too late."

The raw emotion in Nate's voice, the pain, didn't just surprise me—it shocked me. Not so much because I thought him above those sorts of feelings, but because he'd been so jovial only moments before. Realizing that this grim memory had been lurking beneath his stoic facade all this time, well...it was eye opening.

"What happened?" I asked.

But Nate didn't get a chance to respond before his double—who'd apparently had enough—raised a boulder twice as big as he was overhead and hurled it at Pan, clearly imitating what the god had done earlier. Except when this massive block struck, it did so with enough force to send Pan careening backwards, tumbling end over end until he toppled over the edge of a ridiculously high cliff. As we closed in, I realized the god was hanging on for dear life; Nate's double raced to the god's side, fear and guilt splashed across his face.

"Not again," Nate snarled venomously as we ran. "I won't let it happen again."

"Nate!" I called as he began to outpace me, churning his legs so fast I was fairly certain he would pull something before he reached the two struggling figures. "Wait! Ye know ye won't be able to touch him!"

But the wizard was beyond reason; he was shouting Pan's name over and over again until it became one sound: a bestial roar unlike any I'd ever heard a human make. The doppelgänger looked around frantically, screaming for help.

Help that I knew—based on Nate's reaction—wouldn't come.

By the time I caught up to him, my Nate was inconsolable, his eyes red-rimmed, his jaw clenched so hard I thought he might crack his own teeth if he weren't careful. The wizard stared down at his hands like they were broken, useless things. Disgust rode his face like a mask, and for a moment it was as if all hope had fled from his eyes.

"I tried to help," he whispered, his voice so raw it sounded like dead leaves rustling through an abandoned cemetery. "But you were right."

I glanced over to see Nate's double holding Pan's horn in a white-knuckled grip, urging him to hold on even as the two exchanged words, going back and forth as they discussed all manner of seemingly crucial matters, as they prepared themselves to say goodbye. And yet, I knew from Nate's face that he'd never forgive himself for what was about to happen. That—like the old man on the beach had said—Nate would live with this little regret until the end of his days.

"Help! Gunnar! Talon! Somebody! He's slipping!" Nate's double croaked, his throat clearly raw from screaming.

"They won't come." Beside me, the wizard clenched his fists open and closed. Open and closed. He refused to blink, not even through the tears streaking down his cheeks. "No one comes."

I don't know what came over me in that moment. Maybe it was the simple urge to try—especially if trying meant I could actually do *something*. Maybe it was that old man's voice in the back of my head, reminding me what it was like to live a life full of regret. Or maybe it was less complicated than that.

Perhaps it was like hearing a child's cry emerge from a filthy, abandoned alley on a rainy night. Or catching the forlorn whimper of a single woman surrounded by a trio of jackal-like drunks in an empty parking lot after last call. Or...listening to a man whose remorse was so great he'd have traded anything for a second chance.

Whatever the reason, I moved before I could think about what I was doing.

I launched myself towards the tragic pair, diving to snatch at the god's wrist a moment before the god's grip gave out. I felt flesh beneath my hand and looked down to see Pan staring up at me in wonder. Nate's double, on the other hand, seemed to have not the slightest clue I was there; from his perspective, I had to imagine Pan simply stopped weighing so damned much.

We stayed like that for a moment, my mind reeling at this development, before I realized how freaking heavy Pan was; I snatched his wrist with both hands and began to pull. Together, Nate's double and I were able to lift him, inch by inch, until his forearms rested on the rock shelf.

My Nate was already at my side by that point, staring at me like I'd invented Christmas. I waved him back, still straining to keep the god from slipping. After several long, stressful minutes, however, we had Pan lying on his back on the rocky shelf, safe and relatively sound—if you didn't count his mangled horn, or the fact that he was laughing like a maniac. Nate's double, meanwhile, lounged beside him, crying from either joy or pure stress relief.

I was bent over, trying to catch my breath while Nate flicked his gaze back and forth between his double and his friend. I could tell from his expression that he wanted to know how this had happened as badly as I did —if not more so. Had I really saved Nate's best friend? Or was this all some sort of cruel illusion—a spell cast on us to keep us busy or teach us some "valuable" lesson? I honestly couldn't say. Neither, I thought, could Nate; the wizard looked somehow both happy and miserable, like he'd been given a badass gift but feared it would be immediately taken away.

"I'm so sorry, Pan," Nate's double said, at last. "And I'm so glad you're alright."

"Me too," Nate said, echoing the sentiment with significantly less relief.

"For every time there is a season," Pan replied ominously, turning his head to stare—not at Nate's double—but at us. "For every act there is a reason. Selfish, selfless, all the same. But damn it's fun to play the game."

"What's he babblin' about?" I asked Nate, sidelong.

"No idea."

Pan flashed us a manic grin, his gums bleeding so profusely it was as if his teeth were crimson-rimmed, and slapped the ground next to him. Stone cracked, splitting down its seams, as the ridge beneath our feet gave way. Nate and I pinwheeled, screaming bloody murder as we tumbled off the cliff to our deaths.

Or so I thought.

We hit rock bottom and bounced right back up, buffeted by the plush surface of a Queen-sized mattress, our bodies immediately tangled up in sheets and covers. Pissed off and tired of this bullshit, I swore like a sailor as I fought to get free, only to slip off the bed and collapse to the floor. Caught off balance yet again from the brutal transition from one place to the next, it took me almost a full minute to realize I was standing in my childhood bedroom. The walls were exactly how I remembered them: purple and plastered with posters of various rock bands. My old stereo sat awkwardly on the dresser, poking out on either end; it had always been too big to sit up high, but I'd hated having to bend down whenever I wanted to pop in a tape or change the station. That, and a large part of me had enjoyed baiting Dez; she'd always insisted my clumsy self would run into the appliance and end up breaking it one day.

Funnily enough, I never had.

As if conjured from my very thoughts, my aunt Dez—my sole caretaker after my mother died—walked into the room, a bundle of folded blankets under her arms. Dark-haired and small-boned, Dez was one of those women who'd always aged better than her girlfriends; she looked fifteen years younger than she had any right to. In fact, I'd even had a few of my guy friends make inappropriate comments to that effect while I was growing up. Back then I'd felt a little like Oprah handing out cars: you get a bloody lip, you get a bloody lip, you get a bloody lip!

But, at this precise moment, seeing her stroll into the room, humming under her breath, I wasn't the tough, bratty kid pouncing on the first person to talk smack about my family. Instead, I felt like a lost little girl, struggling not to fall to her knees and cry. Nate slid off the bed with far more grace than I had and came up beside me, craning his head this way and that as if trying to take in everything at once. Until, that is, he caught sight of my face. He placed a gentle hand on my shoulder.

"Quinn, what's wrong?"

I tried to answer but couldn't get past the lump in my throat.

Dez looked exactly as I'd last seen her: her hair in a loose bun, makeup-less, wearing a green cardigan and her favorite pair of jeans—the ones I always told her hugged her body a little too tight for my liking. What's more, as she tidied about the room, I realized she was working on rear-ranging things so my room looked exactly as it had before I'd moved out. As if it were yesterday, her dying words began to play back in my head, stab-bing at parts of me that no one else could see; they reminded me that she'd wanted me to visit more, because of course I'd been too busy to make time for her, and so she'd recreated my childhood home. She'd wanted to give me a haven, a sanctuary, a place to feel safe. Except, in the end, this was where she died, her green cardigan stained with blood from a stab wound, her pale face going paler until her eyes stared out at nothing.

Which meant today was the day she died.

The day Dobby betrayed me.

The last day I would ever see Dez alive.

I turned to Nate, stricken, but the wizard's eyes were tracking something else across the room. With a sudden lurch, he lashed out at what appeared to be a knife floating in mid-air. His swat connected, sending the blade skidding across the ground and under my bed. From there, all hell broke loose: Dez screamed, backing away from the two of us as though we'd appeared right in front of her, while an invisible creature I knew very well spat out a curse and bolted down the hall and down the stairs, judging from the sound of his footsteps.

"Quinn, ye scared me half to death!" Dez exclaimed, one hand pinned to her breast, her cheeks flushed. She used her other hand to point at Nate, who at least had the wherewithal to pretend like he hadn't confronted an invisible assailant. "Who's this that you've invited into me home without askin', then?"

I had no words.

Somehow, some way, Nate had spotted the spriggan imposter as he snuck into my bedroom to assassinate my aunt. Or maybe he'd simply spotted the knife floating ominously at her back and had taken action on his own. Either way, Dez was alive.

Alive...and pissed.

"Quinn MacKenna, I asked ye a question!"

"I...uh...he's a...well..."

"A friend," the wizard interjected smoothly, holding out one hand to shake, his head bowed just so. "Nate Temple. It's a pleasure to meet you. You know, Quinn never told me she had a sister."

"Is that so? D'ye really t'ink ye can sweet talk me into forgettin' that ye two snuck up on me just now?" Dez's eyes narrowed but a grin tugged at the corner of her lips. "Although I must say, it is nice to see Quinn bringin' home such a strappin' man, for once."

"Dez!" I said, my cheeks flushed. "It's not like that."

"Oh, I know how ye lot get on these days." Dez rolled her eyes, throwing up air quotes. "We're not 'official' because we want to 'see how it goes' and 'keep t'ings casual.' Whatever any of that means."

Nate coughed a laugh into his fist.

"Say, boyo, would ye mind goin' downstairs to get me a glass of water?" Dez asked. "I'd like to talk to me niece alone, for a moment."

"Uh, sure thing." Nate shot me a questioning look.

I responded with a shrug and a nod, as uncertain about what was going on as he was. First, I'd saved Pan, and now Nate had saved Dez—albeit with a lot less fanfare. Had we really altered history, or was this all some big, horrific cosmic joke played at our expense? Were we supposed to be learning some sort of lesson, or were we being punished? I honestly had no idea. What I did know, however, was that Dez—who I thought I'd never get to speak to again—wanted to have a heart-to-heart.

And that, frankly, there was nothing more I wanted in all the world.

"Is everythin' alright?" Dez asked as soon as Nate left the room, her brow furrowed in concern, her eyes scanning my face. She'd always been able to tell when I was hurting, even when I'd been loathe to admit it to myself. When I was a little girl, she'd been quick to soothe, to put salve on the wound—both figuratively and, when necessary, literally. She reacted that way, now, moving closer to take my hand and rub the skin between my thumb and forefinger. "Quinn MacKenna, talk to me."

"I've missed ye," I said, voice breaking. "I've missed ye so much."

"Oh, dear. What's this all about? Is it somethin' that Temple fellow did? D'ye need me to gut him?" Dez patted my hand, eyes twinkling. "It'd be a shame to see all that man go to waste, but I'd do it for ye."

I laughed through a sob, shaking my head despite myself. I was being silly; I finally had the chance to talk to Dez again, and it was all I could do to fight back tears. I sniffled and got ahold of myself, bowing slightly to meet her gaze. It was funny, I'd forgotten how much smaller than me she was. But

I supposed that wasn't all that surprising: in death, our loved ones tend to become larger than life.

I put on a brave smile for her sake.

"I like what you've done to the place," I said, glancing around the room as if seeing it for the first time. "Feels like home."

Dez cracked a genuine smile at that.

"I know I haven't been around much," I went on, dabbing at the corner of my eyes with a crooked finger. "But I want ye to know that's goin' to change. I don't want to take anythin' for granted anymore, especially ye."

"I'm glad to hear ye say that. But ye should know I'm not lettin' ye move back in. You're a big girl now, and I need me privacy for all me gentlemen callers." Dez flashed me a wicked grin and a wink. "Besides, it looks like you'll have your hands full yourself, with that one."

"Oh, hush. He really is just a friend, Dez. A really good friend," I added, realizing how much I meant it the moment I said it aloud; at some point along the way, Nate Temple and I had bonded. Maybe it was the constant teasing, or having faced death together numerous times, or having saved each other's closest friends...but it turned out I genuinely liked Nate. We had our differences, sure, but we were uncannily similar in ways I hadn't expected, ways that could define us. At our core, I believed we both wanted to keep the people we loved safe, and would risk anything to do it.

"Well, why don't ye go down and help your 'friend' with that glass of water. I don't want Master Temple pokin' around me house without supervision. The man may be a hunk, but he's got trouble written all over him."

"Ye have no idea," I replied, grinning despite myself. "Ye sure you'll be alright up here?"

"Aye, I'll be fine," Dez replied, shooing me away. "Just need to finish gettin' the bed made. And maybe see about movin' that stereo. That thing is a hazard just waitin' to happen, ye mark me words."

I turned to leave but hesitated just outside the doorway, staring back at the woman who'd been there for me from the beginning, who'd raised me at the expense of meeting someone, of starting a real family, of finding her own brand of happiness. I loved her. No matter what my mother's ghost had said about Dez's affections being manipulated, *I* loved her. Thinking to hurry back, I turned and strutted down the hallway, resolving to tell her as much as soon as I returned.

Feeling whole for the first time in years, I went down the stairs grinning

from ear to ear. Suddenly, it felt as if the world *wasn't* one giant disappointment after another, as if I could believe in things I'd given up on—things
like good Samaritans and responsible dog owners and reputable news
outlets. And yet, something nagged at me the further I descended, making
each step harder and harder to take.

Master Temple...why had Dez called him that?

Thinking back, Nate hadn't given her his title. Sure, it was possible she'd
caught his name scrolling across the bottom of her television screen on one
of those breaking news bulletins; the wizard had certainly earned his fair
share of bad press in the past. But I knew Dez. She'd have said something,
made some quip about him needing to mend his relationship with Jesus. So
why had she called him that? And what *was* taking Nate so long to get a glass
of water? Had he gone after Dobby, instead? By the time I reached the base
of the stairs, I was so immersed in my own thoughts that it took me a
moment to realize I'd wandered into a completely different room than what
I'd intended.

A room that didn't exist in Dez's house.

I whirled, but the staircase was already gone. I was in an empty corridor,
utterly alone. Panicked, I raced up and down the hallway, running my hands
along the wallpaper, feeling for secret doors or hidden latches or something
—anything—that would lead back to Dez.

"Dez!" I screamed, bashing my fists into the walls until they felt mangled
and pulped, until my bones ached and my knuckles bled. "Dez, where are
ye?!"

A sound, like a woman's voice, echoed down the corridor.

I chased after it, turning first left, then right. I took turn after turn,
desperate to find someone who could tell me where I was, someone who
could tell me how to get home. But deep down, I knew it was no use; I was
the only one in this labyrinth, and I wasn't ever going home again. Panting,
my hopes crushed, I pressed my back against the nearest wall and slid to the
ground, clutching my knees to my chest as I sobbed, feeling the loss of Dez
all over again.

And that's when I saw the door.

Ten feet tall and made of living stone, the door seethed with depictions
of nocturnal wildlife—each critter moving as they would in real life across a
woodland scene complete with foliage that swayed as if caressed by the
slightest breeze. Ripples spread in concentric circles in the center of a pond

as a fish leapt beneath the light of a full moon, tracked by the eyes of a wolf on the bank. Magic. It had to be magic.

Up in the corner of the mural, a bird cawed, and I realized what I'd mistaken for a woman's voice was actually a solitary crow soaring across the night sky. Compelled by the oddest notion that the crow was trying to communicate with me, I approached the door, reaching out as if to touch her. To my surprise, the crow seemed to settle on my finger, perched as though it were a tree limb.

"Well, aren't ye the loveliest—"

The crow pecked me, hard, drawing blood.

And then the motherfeather fucking evaporated.

"Son of a bitch!" I cursed, forced to jump back as the door ground open like one of those ancient death traps in the Indiana Jones films. I flinched, waiting for some boulder to come bowling down the corridor.

But there was nothing like that.

Instead, golden light spilled out into the hallway, reminding me vaguely of the briefcase in *Pulp Fiction*. And I'd always wanted to see what was in that briefcase. Between my natural curiosity and a lack of any viable alternative, I ducked inside. Predictably, the moment I passed the threshold, the door slammed shut behind me. But I didn't care; what I found inside was so marvelous, so unexpected, that I didn't care how I'd gotten there, or who I'd left behind, or what I'd come for. Or any inbound death traps.

For years, I'd dedicated myself to finding, buying, and even stealing the world's most precious, most valuable artifacts. I'd traveled the world and the realms hunting down whatever my clients could afford. Magical herbs, rings of power, spellbooks, occult paraphernalia, you name it. But never in my wildest dreams had I imagined a treasure trove like this one existed; I bounced around the room like an unaccompanied child inside Willy Wonka's chocolate factory, swinging mythical swords and touting impossible shields, running my fingers over fur and jewelry and anything else with even the slightest sensory appeal.

Look, to say it was paradise would have been a bit of a stretch.

But it *was* a damn close second.

"Well, hello there," a pale, dark-haired woman said from the far end of the room, her eyes dancing with amusement. "I've been expecting you, Quinn MacKenna. My name's Hope. Welcome to the Armory."

I opened my groggy, heavy-lidded eyes feeling faintly weightless and even slightly euphoric—like I'd taken something the night before to knock me out that had done its job maybe a little too well. And those dreams...so vivid I felt I should turn over and write them down, recording them before they slipped through my fingers, forgotten forever.

The last, especially, lingered in my mind. Dez had been in it, and Nate, and then a woman named Hope. She'd told me something. Something important. And she'd taken something from me. No, I corrected, I'd given her something. A weapon...or a tool...I couldn't remember. There'd been so many dreams. I remembered them in snippets: Nate laughing at something I'd said, me clutching the wrist of a goat-man, our ship being smashed to bits by a falling dragon, being chased by a stampede of wild horses, Dez holding my hand, a room full of treasure behind a magic door, and so many more.

I yawned, stretching, my muscles tight and oddly stiff. I felt something prickly slide across my shoulder, brushing against it like the hairy leg of a giant spider; I rolled and jumped to my feet, heart hammering in my chest, prepared to fight off some *Land of the Lost* monstrosity before it could wrap me in a silk cocoon and gnaw on me like a burrito.

But there was no spider.

What I'd felt was grass—thick blades of blue grass like you might find in

Kentucky, their faint blue hue accentuated by both the faint mist that coiled along the ground and the dim light of dawn. I scowled at the offending vegetation, wishing it *had* been some sort of hideous monster. At least then I wouldn't have felt so silly.

Except...why had I been sleeping on the ground to begin with? And where was I? I turned a slow circle, seeing nothing at first but rolling hills and a rising sun, the sky painted majestic shades of purple, red, and gold. But then, tucked between two of those hills and expanding into the horizon, I saw the sea. And a ship sitting on the water like a mirage, its hull enveloped in fog.

The *Jolly Roger*.

I began to remember. I could see my hands untying the ropes that bound the dinghy to the ship, saw myself climbing in and taking hold of the oars. In my mind's eyes, I saw James waving as I rowed towards the island Triton had guided us to. I recalled the Neverlander hadn't been pleased to be left behind, though he'd seen the sense in it; someone had to watch over Tiger Lily and Tinkerbell until I returned with the flower.

The flower...

That's why I was here! I remembered searching for it as the sun fell, desperate to find this mythical blossom Triton had described before heading back to report to Circe. But with every step I'd grown more and more tired, my thoughts sluggish, drifting. One second I was scouring the island, the next I was on my knees trying to find the energy to stand. I'd been *so* damned exhausted. Honestly, it'd felt like something was dragging me under, like being hit with a hefty dose of anesthesia.

The question was, had I been drugged, or had I simply been that tired? Distantly, I realized the latter was possible; I'd spent two consecutive nights running around doing goddess-knows-what without catching more than an hour of sleep after pushing myself to my physical limits on the previous and following days. It was plausible that, eventually, something had to give. And yet there was something about those dreams, something I couldn't quite put my finger on, that made me doubt that explanation.

They'd felt so *real*. In fact, I realized I could still remember them if I tried, even though some were a bit hazy, the details fuzzier than I'd have liked. But the emotions, including the overall sense of camaraderie, hadn't gone anywhere.

A creaking sound snapped me out of my reverie, drawing my attention to the other side of a nearby hill. For a second, I thought I heard someone singing a lullaby—a man, his voice drifting on the wind, sweet and cloying as honey. I felt my eyes grow heavy again, as if I hadn't slept nearly as long as I could have. Then again, I probably hadn't; I'd need to pass out for a couple days at this rate if I ever hoped to catch up.

With some effort, however, I shook that off and marched towards the sound of the voice I'd heard, climbing the hill until I stood at the very top. From there, I was able to see a good portion of the island, including a nearby valley where there were dozens of what looked like lotus flowers dipped in metallic paints—their seeds brilliant gold, their petals solid silver, and their stems burnished copper—growing. Among them, reclining in a hammock strung between two trees, lay a god reading a book.

I couldn't tell you precisely why I was so certain that's what he was, but somehow I knew it the second I laid eyes on him. It was like I could feel him in my mind, could sense a heat coming from him that normal people just didn't exude. It sounded like shoddy reasoning, even to me, but I decided to trust my gut as I approached, warily, searching for any signs of a trap. Fortunately, the god didn't seem to care I'd found him. Or even notice, really; he licked his finger and flipped a page the way people do when they want to be creepy. As I drew closer, I found I was able to read the title of the book he was so preoccupied with: *The Interpretation of Dreams* by Sigmund Freud.

Gross.

"Ye do know he's been largely debunked, right?" I called from a good twenty feet away, still prepared to make a run for it if things went south.

The god snapped his book shut and turned to me, revealing a finely molded face, tousled blonde hair, and owl's wings where his ears should have been. Startled, I took a step back. The god rolled out of his hammock with a smooth, practiced motion that looked easy but wasn't— as anyone who's tried to do it would vouch for. He wore surprisingly comfortable clothes for a deity. In fact, if I hadn't known any better I'd have said he was in his pajamas. An open velvet robe a la Hugh Hefner rode his slender shoulders, while his shirt read "Don't Give Up On Your Dreams...Go Back to Bed" in bold black letters. A pair of plaid sweatpants and fuzzy slippers completed the ensemble.

And yet, despite how absurd he looked, I sensed there was more power lurking in his little finger than all the minor gods I'd met put together. But of course that was the thing about deities: looks could be incredibly misleading. The question was, who was he? And why was he here?

"Took you long enough," he said. I immediately recognized his voice as the one who'd been singing a moment ago, but there was something else about it that stuck with me—something familiar besides that.

"Do I know ye?"

"Consciously? No. But unconsciously, it's possible."

"Don't ye mean subconsciously?"

"No, I meant *not* conscious." The god tossed his book onto the swinging hammock and stretched, yawning so hard it made me yawn on reflex. When he saw that, he laughed. "So, did you sleep well?"

"Excuse me?"

"The witch warned me you do that," he said, smirking. "Answer a question with a question. But, if it's all the same to you, I'd like a straight answer. How. Did. You. Sleep?"

I started to ask him whether he was talking about Circe or not when I caught the faintest gleam of malevolence behind his eyes; the wings on either side of his face flicked once, brushing against his shoulders in agitation. So, rather than pick a fight, I thought about it. How *had* I slept? Despite feeling rather abused within the dreams themselves, I realized I'd woken up feeling better than I had in a long, long time.

"Good."

"Good?"

"Well," I corrected. "I slept well."

"Good!" The god turned and wandered back to his hammock, retrieving his book and hopping back in it like a spry teenager. When he noticed I hadn't gone anywhere, he waved his book at me. "Well don't just stand there. Take your lotus flower and go."

"I don't understand," I admitted, ignoring his half-hearted command. "Who are ye?"

"You know, a great deal of this," the god said, showcasing Freud's work, "is just flat out wrong. So, so wrong. But would you like to know what I find so interesting about it?"

"Sure..."

"His ideas. The science, blah, who cares? But ask any mortal with a modicum of education about their id, their ego, their superego, and they'll have all sorts of insight." The god tapped the book's cover with his finger.

"People like to believe their unconscious minds hold significant truths. They *love* their symbolism, their pageantry, their abstracts. And what's more abstract than a dream?"

"I do know ye," I said, stepping forward as the truth came to me, my hackles rising. "It was ye on Olympus with Nate and me. Your voice. Ye trapped us, talked to us. Told us t'ings about ourselves."

"Oooh, well done. So, have you figured it out yet?" The god waggled his eyebrows like we were playing some sort of game. "The point?"

For some reason, that struck a nerve.

But I couldn't put my finger on why.

"Were ye the one who did that to us?" I demanded, my fists balled in anger. "D'ye know what it was like in there? We could have died! I got shot. We got hit by lightning for fuck's sake! And where's Nate?!"

"Relax."

That one word hit me like a shot of whiskey, burning on the way down, making me feel warm and oddly pliant. It was his power. I could feel it, dimly, but I didn't want to fight it; there was something natural about this sensation, something comforting.

"*If* you almost died," he began, "it was because you were both too caught up in the moment to realize it was dream. In dreams, our imaginations make the rules. You can imagine passing through objects, for example, but falling through space for eternity? Not so much. Besides, the only things that can hurt you when you're dreaming are the things you're afraid can hurt you when you're awake. Bullets, being run over, demons, being stabbed...all very logical fears. The lightning..." The god bounced his head from side to side, his pointer finger dancing. "Let's just say a passed out Catalyst isn't what Zeus had in mind. Not fond of sharing, either, our Zeus."

"Our Zeus?"

The god shrugged.

"Why?" I asked. "Why d'ye do it?"

"Well, it could be that I owed Circe a favor. Or it could be that I have a vested interest in seeing you and Master Temple make love, not war. Or—and I see this thought in the back of your mind as we speak—I'm lying about everything and can't be trusted." The god patted his book, his smile lazy. "But then that's what I'd expect from someone with *your* nightmares. Awful stuff...and trust me, the bar is high."

"Who are ye, really?" I whispered, feeling oddly exposed.

"I have many names. Here, they call me Morpheus." The god shook his head, grimacing. "No, not like *The Matrix*." He cocked an eyebrow. "Of course I can hear your thoughts."

"Well stop it," I demanded. "I'm tired of ye lot doin' that shit. It's rude."

"Fine, fine," Morpheus laughed. "But you should know I wasn't lying."

"Was any of it real?" I asked, anxiety clawing its way up to combat that numbing sensation he'd hit me with. "Did we save Dez? Pan? Are they alive?"

"Reality is such a funny thing," Morpheus replied, rocking side to side so the hammock would swing back and forth on its own. "Do you know how many brilliant ideas come to people in their sleep? How many mortals are able to get up and plod through their sad, dreary days simply because they got enough rest? How utterly *insane* they get without it? And yet, it's just sleep. They're *just* dreams."

"That literally answered not one of me questions."

"That's because I don't have your answers. They weren't *my* dreams. What you have to ask yourself is whether they felt real or not."

"*That's* the point, isn't it?" I said, struck by the way he'd phrased that, by the words he'd emphasized. "When ye were talkin' about weaknesses on Olympus, I mean. Ye told me I'd missed the point."

"Oh, solved it on your own, huh?"

"Ye meant belief. Ye talked about it when ye mentioned Freud, too, but I didn't catch it. What makes us weak, any of us," I went on, captivated by the idea, "is what we believe to be true that isn't, and what's false that is true. Our unconscious beliefs."

"Well, my work is done here," Morpheus said, stretching his arms wide, the wings on his head spreading and flapping like mad. "Be sure to schedule another appointment with my secretary on your way out. And seriously, don't forget to take a flower."

"Wait, I—"

But between one blink and the next, Morpheus was gone.

Almost like he'd never been there at all.

44

*C*irce waited for us on the beach, alone, dressed in a button-up and a pair of khaki shorts that exposed her long, tan legs; her wild mane of hair was billowing in the wind. The Goddess on Safari, I thought, uncharitably; the witch had some serious explaining to do before I crossed her off my shitlist. Together, James and I hopped out of the dinghy and towed the boat towards the shore. Tiger Lily and Tinkerbell lay inside, swaddled in plush, red velvet blankets I'd swiped from Hook's cabin.

That man really had been a fabric snob.

"That her?" James asked, tipping his head in Circe's general direction.

"Aye."

"Do you really think she'll help us?"

"The truth? I'm not sure. She's got her own agenda, that much is obvious. But, if what Gaia told me is true and she planned to send me after Ryan whether we made a deal or not, then she owes me."

James made a noncommittal noise as the bow hit land, grinding into the sand. As one, we turned, yanking until the boat sat far enough inland that the tide wouldn't take it away. Once finished, the Neverlander leaned against the gunwale.

"Hey, what happened to that pouch I gave you?" he asked.

"What?"

"The pouch," James repeated, pointing to my throat. "The one you asked for."

I frowned and fumbled at my neck, feeling for the leather pouch full of finger bones that had been there the last time I'd thought to check. But James was right; they were gone. Had they fallen off at some point? Maybe while I was searching the island of the Lotus Eaters? That—I'd realized after returning to James and the ship—was the name of the place Circe had sent me to. In Odysseus' time, the island had been inhabited by what amounted to opium addicts who got stoned daily on the fruit of the island's trademark flower.

"I'm not sure what happened to it," I replied, hesitantly. "I feel like...I gave it to someone. Someone who needed it."

Circe arrived just as James was about to ask a follow-up question. But the young man took one look at the witch up close and immediately clammed up, averting his eyes with all the sophistication of a Catholic schoolboy caught staring at a half-naked cover model. Circe, for her part, seemed to find the Neverlander's modest reaction amusing.

"And who's this one?" Circe asked me.

"His name's—"

"James," the Neverlander replied, clearing his throat. "My name's James."

"It's a pleasure to meet you, James. I'm Circe."

"Careful she doesn't turn ye into a pig," I drawled.

"I only do that to the men I *don't* like," the witch replied, smirking. "The ones I do...well, no one's ever complained."

"Speakin' of complaints," I interjected, looking for a gut reaction, "Morpheus sends his regards."

"I doubt that," Circe said, chuckling. "He's not my biggest fan."

"Why's that? D'ye lie to him too?"

"He resents me, I think." Circe left it at that, craning her head to look inside our boat as though I hadn't just accused her. "Who else have you brought me?"

"Patients. I was hopin' you could help 'em. This is—"

"Tiger Lily. And Tinkerbell. Oh, don't look so surprised. I told you I'd been watching you for some time. I know your crew." Circe licked her lips, eyeing James. "Intimately, in fact."

"And the other two?" I asked. "What about the Greeks? Can ye tell me what happened to Narcissus and Helen?"

"Sorry," Circe replied, looking genuinely apologetic. "Once they joined the enemy, I couldn't track them in the pools. That's the way it is with the Frozen One. His stolen power, the spell that's been woven around him, keeps him hidden from us."

"What about Tiger Lily and Tink?" James interjected. "Can you help them?"

"Yes, my dear mortal, I can. But first we need to get them back to my home. I've already prepared beds and the potions we'll need to stabilize them. Can you carry Tiger Lily? It's not terribly far."

"Yes," James said eagerly, his face filled with more hope than I'd seen since I told him I would save Neverland. "I'll do whatever it takes."

"I can see that," the witch replied, looking thoughtful. She faced me. "Bring the flower and the pixie. You and I have a great deal to discuss, and we're running out of time."

45

*T*he rhythmic clunk of Circe's mortar and pestle filled the room as the witch ground the lotus flower into dust, the muscles of her forearm tensed and bulging like the scooper's at your local ice cream store. She snaked throughout the room as she worked, mumbling some spell under her breath that left the air charged and smelling faintly of oranges. I, meanwhile, lounged on a wicker bench I'd fetched from the garden, at ease despite the plethora of questions I'd yet to have answered.

The reason for that, of course, was simple: for once neither I, nor my crew, were in any immediate danger. Mostly, that was thanks to Circe, who —true to her word—had converted one of her villa's many unoccupied rooms into a veritable clinic complete with a round-the-clock Nurse Barca, who'd not only been overjoyed to see me but to have visitors in general. Mercifully, Tiger Lily and Tinkerbell had already benefited from the draught Circe gave them upon arrival; they'd passed out almost immediately, no longer thrashing, their temperatures and coloring stabilized.

"This won't mend them completely," Circe had warned, addressing James. "They do not belong in this realm and will only grow worse if forced to remain. My potion will sustain them, however, until we can figure out a way to send you home. In the meantime, you are welcome to stay here as my guests, provided you abide by my rules. But we can discuss all that later. For now, I have to borrow Quinn."

That had been about an hour ago. Since then, Circe had barely spoken a word to me other than to ask for the flower, which I'd handed over as per our agreement. In hindsight, I probably should have held onto it as collateral, but—what with my crew safe and relatively sound—I supposed I was feeling generous. You might even say it was one of my virtues.

Sadly, patience was not.

"So, are ye goin' to tell me what you're doin'? Or am I supposed to know?"

Circe flashed me a piqued look, though her mumbling never ceased. In a matter of minutes, the air grew uncomfortably hot, then frigidly cold—all the more freezing for having made me sweat a moment before. The citrusy scent grew stronger until it seemed like I'd pried open an orange and shoved my nose up against its pulpy interior; I fought the urge to sneeze and failed. At last, Circe tipped the pestle's contents into a stone beaker, steam rising off her shoulders like smoke. She bent over her workstation, taking deep breaths. Before I could ask her what she'd just done, however, she threw her hair back in a messy bun and faced me directly.

"Well, that's done," she said, matter-of-factly. "So, questions. Let's have them."

"I—oh, we're doin' this now. Got it." I sat up and gathered my thoughts, then realized I had too many of those to keep straight. Dammit. "So, I have three big ones, and a bunch of little ones."

"I'd say we have time for two big ones."

"Well, now I have four big ones. First question, why do we only have time for two big ones?"

"Ask that one last," Circe replied, amusement tugging at the corner of her lip, though I noticed it never quite reached her tired eyes. "For now, let me take a stab at answering the predictable ones, shall I?" Circe raised her left hand, her fingers spread wide, and began counting them down one at a time. "One. Yes, I could have told you everything from the beginning and helped you without making you get the flower, but there was a reason for that which shall become clear, shortly. Two. I left out the name of the island because I knew you'd be even more guarded and less likely to succumb to Morpheus' power if you knew what the lotus flower was capable of. Three. Yes, there was a reason he put you through what he did, but no, I can't tell you what it is."

"What about—"

"Four. As far as I can tell, your goddess and you have begun merging, which is why you're beginning to sense things you can't explain, and why she's started taking on some of your...finer traits. No, I don't know what that means for you long term, and no, I didn't intend for any of that to happen."

I opened my mouth to say something, closed it, then opened it again.

"Five," Circe said, dropping her last finger so that she stood with a clenched fist. "Yes, I think the Neverlander is yummy. And no, I don't care that I'm thousands of years older than he is."

"Ew," I said, waving my arms, rapidly. "I was so not goin' to ask that!"

"Well, did I miss anything?"

"How am I supposed to know? I'm pretty sure I had others a second ago, but now I've got an image of ye and James stuck in me head, and all I really want to do is be anywhere but here."

"Don't worry, I'll be gentle with him."

"Dear God, please make it stop."

"All kidding aside," Circe said, kneeling so we were eye to eye, her expression far more serious than I was ready for, "on behalf of the Titan realm, I want to thank you, Quinn. For what you did to save the Laestrygonians. For what you've sacrificed. I know I was hard on you. Cruel, even. But now that you know what was—what is—at stake, I hope you can forgive me, one day."

Staring into the witch's surprisingly guileless face, I realized I believed her. That, deep down, I'd found her inconsistent behavior hard to buy from the beginning; short of being mentally unbalanced, no one could be that gentle one moment and that callous the next. And, if there was one thing I *could* say on Circe's behalf, it was that she was exceptionally level-headed.

"Don't mention it," I mumbled, awkwardly.

"I can't promise that. Now, ask the last one."

"The...oh, right. Why are we runnin' out of time?"

"Because Max is dying," Circe replied, rising to her feet and crossing to her counter full of assorted memorabilia as though she hadn't just dropped a nuclear bomb into the middle of our heart to heart. "And, if you want to save him and still intend to stop the Frozen One, then we have until sundown."

"Wait, I thought ye said Max was stable?" I asked, leaping to my feet.

"He was." Circe snatched up a bottle of some strange white liquid that looked suspiciously like melted toothpaste and poured it into a bowl, then tossed a dash of yellow powder in with it. "But over the last few nights he's taken a bad turn. There have been seizures, and they've had to restart his heart. The mortal doctors believe that, if he has even one more night like that, he may not make it."

"How long?" I asked, connecting the dots with a painful realization, my voice laced with suspicion. "How long have ye known?"

"I only realized it the night you left, the night you fought the Frozen One, I swear. I had no idea it would affect him at all, let alone like that." Circe continued bustling about her little laboratory as though she hadn't just admitted that what we'd done to turn me into a goddess was directly linked to what was happening with Max—the reason why he nearly died every night. "That's why I sent Triton. Why I insisted you hurry back."

"But he didn't tell me to hurry back," I countered, angrily. "He told me to go get a goddamned flower! Your goddamned flower!"

"Because without it," Circe replied, her voice even and steady, "there was nothing we could do. Even if we'd sent you back to the mortal realm first thing, there was no guarantee that Max would wake up. In fact, I'm certain now more than ever that he would not have. The lotus flower was—is—your only hope."

"*Me* only hope?" I balled my hands into fists, struggling not to smash everything in sight. "Ye really expect me to believe ye sent me after a flower for me own good?"

"No, I expect you to think the worst of everyone, because that's what you do!" Circe countered, her own anger leaking through for a moment before she composed herself once more. "The plan was to give this to you as a gift. A reward for helping us. But plans change. Because it's not just Max who needs saving, now."

"Wait, what the hell are ye talkin' about?"

"Hell is *exactly* what I'm talking about." Circe took up the stone beaker and began pouring it through a sieve into the bowl she'd been fussing with. "I told you before that the Frozen One can hide from me, yes? Well," she went on before I could answer, "I learned early on that I could track him using those blindspots. I can't see what he's doing, but I do have a good idea where he is, most of the time…"

"Well, where is he?"

"It seems he and Frankenstein have decided the answers they seek won't be found in the Titan realm, after all. Someone has convinced them that the path they're looking for goes through the Underworld, itself. They've already reached the Gates. Soon, I believe they'll breach them."

I shook my head, trying to clear my thoughts, feeling like I'd just been hit with a half-dozen right jabs to the face. Had Helen told them about the Gates, as she'd once told me? Is that why they'd suddenly changed course? And what did any of that have to do with Max, or the lotus flower?

"Part of me hopes they won't survive," Circe went on, shaking her head. "The afterlife can be a brutal place, after all. But I wouldn't have thought they'd have dominated the Eighth Sea, either."

"Hold on, hold on," I insisted. "What does any of this have to do with me? With Max? I'm not seein' the connection."

"That's because I haven't told you what *this* does, yet," Circe replied as she blended the bowl's unappealing mixture with a spoon. "And because I worry that, once I *do* tell you, you'll say yes without thinking about it like you always do. Which will only make me feel guilty if you fail."

That made me hesitate. I took a moment to study the witch's body language, to study her trembling hands and the rigid line of her back. She was afraid, or at the very least nervous. Which meant whatever her solution was, she didn't like it. But that wasn't the question. The question was whether or not hers was the only way.

"That's a lot of hypotheticals," I said, at last. I joined her at the counter, placing my hand on her shoulder. "Why don't ye let me decide for meself what I do and don't need to know?"

So, Circe told me the truth.

The whole truth.

And, of course—like an idiot—I said yes without even thinking about it.

*D*ying sucks.

    Anyone who tells you different, I decided, was either lying or trying to sell you life insurance. But then, I suppose I was just bitter; I'd only discovered I was immortal a short while ago. I hadn't even gotten to cross off any of the exceedingly stupid things on my bucket list, like trying to catch a bullet with my bare hands, or riding a saddled tiger, or headbanging in a German moshpit.

I'd had such big dreams.

"Don't fear the reaper," I sang, pulling my covers up to the bottom of my chin, staring up into the light, waiting for death to come for me.

"Why's she singing?" James whispered sidelong to Circe, who stood leaning in the doorway.

"Because she's an idiot."

"James, James, come close...I can't see that far..." I reached for the Never-lander, waited to feel his hand in mine as Circe's lotus flower potion worked its way through my bloodstream. "Oh, James," I said, sniffling, "promise me somethin'."

"Uh, sure, Quinn. Anything."

"Stay away from that vile harlot, Circe."

James glanced back at the witch, who had a very nasty smile plastered across her face. Pulling a classic Ferris Bueller, I flashed her a bold wink before resuming my deathbed pose.

"And James," I went on, channeling every pathetic bone in my body, "don't forget...to find...and bring back...her pigs."

"Quinn, that's enough," Circe interjected.

"She's comin' for me, James. I can hear her. The witch is comin' for me!"

"You're going to give the boy a complex," Circe said, tapping James on the shoulder and waving him away. "Seriously, the potion should kick in any minute. It should feel like falling asleep. I've already arranged for someone in our camp to meet you on the other side, she—"

"Parting," I interrupted, pressing my hand against Circe's cheek, "is such sweet sorrow."

"Wow, that's really deep, Quinn," James said. "Did you come up with that, yourself?"

"Aye, but don't ye worry, for cowards die many times before their deaths, while the valiant only taste of death but once."

"She did *not* come up with that. You did *not* come up with that, Quinn." Circe glared at me, daring me to contradict her. "Say it, or I'll kill you for real."

I met the witch's gaze.

"Speak me fair in death, Circe. Speak me fair."

From the corner of the room, I could hear Barca laughing. The two Neverlanders in the beds next to mine lay silent, still sleeping even though the sun had begun to fall a while ago. Soon, it'd be nighttime, and I'd be dead—or as good as. That—it turned out—was what Circe's flower was meant to do: put me in a coma so deep that I could bypass the Gates of the Underworld altogether and, once there, find Maximiliano's soul, save him, and stop Ryan once and for all.

"I swear," Circe said, exasperated, "you spend one night with Nate Temple, and now you're completely incorrigible."

"D'ye hear that James? She said I'm courageous."

At this point, even James had caught on to the joke. Which was great because I wasn't in the mood to end things on a sour note; Circe and I both knew that this trip came with a one-way ticket and no return flight scheduled. I wouldn't be dead, but—unless I found my own way out—I wouldn't be leaving the Underworld anytime soon, either.

But then, what was life if not a gamble?

True to Circe's word, when the potion finally did its job, there was no pain. No suffering. I merely drifted, untethered, floating on the surface of a placid lake. I let my last breath out in a long sigh, closed my eyes, and said the most ridiculous thing anyone has ever said. Ever.

"I would have made a good Pope."

Quinn returns in 2020...

*Turn the page to read a sample of **OBSIDIAN SON** - Nate Temple Series Book 1 - or **BUY ONLINE**. Nate Temple is a billionaire wizard from St. Louis. He rides a bloodthirsty unicorn and drinks with the Four Horsemen. He even cow-tipped the Minotaur. Once...*

TRY: OBSIDIAN SON (NATE TEMPLE #1)

*T*here was no room for emotion in a hate crime. I had to be cold. Heartless. This was just another victim. Nothing more. No face, no name.

Frosted blades of grass crunched under my feet, sounding to my ears like the symbolic glass that one would shatter under a napkin at a Jewish wedding. The noise would have threatened to give away my stealthy advance as I stalked through the moonlit field, but I was no novice and had planned accordingly. Being a wizard, I was able to muffle all sensory evidence with a fine cloud of magic—no sounds, and no smells. Nifty. But if I made the spell much stronger, the anomaly would be too obvious to my prey.

I knew the consequences for my dark deed tonight. If caught, jail time or possibly even a gruesome, painful death. But if I succeeded, the look of fear and surprise in my victim's eyes before his world collapsed around him, it was well worth the risk. I simply couldn't help myself; I had to take him down.

I knew the cops had been keeping tabs on my car, but I was confident that they hadn't followed me. I hadn't seen a tail on my way here but seeing as how they frowned on this kind of thing, I had taken a circuitous route just in case. I was safe. I hoped.

Then my phone chirped at me as I received a text.

I practically jumped out of my skin, hissing instinctively. "Motherf—" I cut off abruptly, remembering the whole stealth aspect of my mission. I was off to a stellar start. I had forgotten to silence the damned phone. *Stupid, stupid, stupid!*

My heart felt like it was on the verge of exploding inside my chest with such thunderous violence that I briefly envisioned a mystifying Rorschach blood-blot that would have made coroners and psychologists drool.

My body remained tense as I swept my gaze over the field, fearing that I had been made. Precious seconds ticked by without any change in my surroundings, and my breathing finally began to slow as my pulse returned to normal. Hopefully, my magic had muted the phone and my resulting outburst. I glanced down at the phone to scan the text and then typed back a quick and angry response before I switched the cursed device to vibrate.

Now, where were we?

I continued on, the lining of my coat constricting my breathing. Or maybe it was because I was leaning forward in anticipation. *Breathe*, I chided myself. *He doesn't know you're here*. All this risk for a book. It had better be worth it.

I'm taller than most, and not abnormally handsome, but I knew how to play the genetic cards I had been dealt. I had shaggy, dirty blonde hair—leaning more towards brown with each passing year—and my frame was thick with well-earned muscle, yet I was still lean. I had once been told that my eyes were like twin emeralds pitted against the golden-brown tufts of my hair—a face like a jewelry box. Of course, that was two bottles of wine into a date, so I could have been a little foggy on her quote. Still, I liked to imagine that was how everyone saw me.

But tonight, all that was masked by magic.

I grinned broadly as the outline of the hairy hulk finally came into view. He was blessedly alone—no nearby sentries to give me away. That was always a risk when performing this ancient rite-of-passage. I tried to keep the grin on my face from dissolving into a maniacal cackle.

My skin danced with energy, both natural and unnatural, as I manipulated the threads of magic floating all around me. My victim stood just ahead, oblivious to the world of hurt that I was about to unleash. Even with his millennia of experience, he didn't stand a chance. I had done this so many times that the routine of it was my only enemy. I lost count of how many times I had been told not to do it again; those who knew declared it *cruel, evil, and sadistic.* But what fun wasn't? Regardless, that wasn't enough to stop me from doing it again. And again. And again.

It was an addiction.

The pungent smell of manure filled the air, latching onto my nostril hairs. I took another step, trying to calm my racing pulse. A glint of gold reflected in the silver moonlight, but my victim remained motionless, hopefully unaware or all was lost. I wouldn't make it out alive if he knew I was here. Timing was everything.

I carefully took the last two steps, a lifetime between each, watching the legendary monster's ears, anxious and terrified that I would catch even so much as a twitch in my direction. Seeing nothing, a fierce grin split my unshaven cheeks. My spell had worked! I raised my palms an inch away from their target, firmly planted my feet, and squared my shoulders. I took one silent, calming breath, and then heaved forward with every ounce of physical strength I could muster. As well as a teensy-weensy boost of magic. Enough to goose him good.

"*MOOO!!!*" The sound tore through the cool October night like an unstoppable freight train. *Thud-splat!* The beast collapsed sideways onto the frosted grass; straight into a steaming patty of cow shit, cow dung, or, if you really wanted to church it up, a Meadow Muffin. But to me, shit is, and always will be, shit.

Cow tipping. It doesn't get any better than that in Missouri.

Especially when you're tipping the *Minotaur*. Capital M. I'd tipped plenty of ordinary cows before, but never the legendary variety.

Razor-blade hooves tore at the frozen earth as the beast struggled to stand, his grunts of rage vibrating the air. I raised my arms triumphantly. "Boo-yah! Temple 1, Minotaur 0!" I crowed. Then I very bravely prepared to protect myself. Some people just couldn't take a joke. *Cruel, evil,* and *sadistic* cow tipping may be, but by hell, it was a *rush.* The legendary beast turned his gaze on me after gaining his feet, eyes ablaze as his body...*shifted* from his bull disguise into his notorious, well-known bipedal form. He unfolded to his full height on two tree trunk-thick legs, his hooves having magically transformed into heavily booted feet. The thick, gold ring dangling from his snotty snout quivered as the Minotaur panted, and his dense, corded muscles contracted over his now human-like chest. As I stared up into those brown eyes, I actually felt sorry...for, well, myself.

"I have killed greater men than you for lesser offense," he growled.

His voice sounded like an angry James Earl Jones—like Mufasa talking to Scar.

"You have shit on your shoulder, Asterion." I ignited a roiling ball of fire in my palm in order to see his eyes more clearly. By no means was it a defensive gesture on my part. It was just dark. Under the weight of his glare, I somehow managed to keep my face composed, even though my fraudulent, self-denial had curled up into the fetal position and started whimpering. I hoped using a form of his ancient name would give me brownie points. Or maybe just not-worthy-of-killing points.

The beast grunted, eyes tightening, and I sensed the barest hesitation. "Nate Temple...your name would look splendid on my already long list of slain idiots." Asterion took a threatening step forward, and I thrust out my palm in warning, my roiling flame blue now.

"You lost fair and square, Asterion. Yield or perish." The beast's shoulders sagged slightly. Then he finally nodded to himself in resignation, appraising me with the scrutiny of a worthy adversary. "Your time comes, Temple, but I will grant you this. You've got a pair of stones on you to rival Hercules."

I reflexively glanced in the direction of the myth's own crown jewels before jerking my gaze away. Some things you simply couldn't un-see. "Well, I won't be needing a wheelbarrow any time soon, but overcompensating today keeps future lower-back pain away."

The Minotaur blinked once, and then he bellowed out a deep, contagious, snorting laughter. Realizing I wasn't about to become a murder statistic, I couldn't help but join in. It felt good. It had been a while since I had allowed myself to experience genuine laughter.

In the harsh moonlight, his bulk was even more intimidating as he towered head and shoulders above me. This was the beast that had fed upon human sacrifices for countless years while imprisoned in Daedalus' Labyrinth in Greece. And all that protein had not gone to waste, forming a heavily woven musculature over the beast's body that made even Mr. Olympia look puny.

From the neck up, he was now entirely bull, but the rest of his body more closely resembled a thickly furred man. But, as shown moments ago, he could adapt his form to his environment, never appearing fully human, but able to make his entire form appear as a bull when necessary. For instance, how he had looked just before I tipped him. Maybe he had been scouting the field for heifers before I had so efficiently killed the mood.

His bull face was also covered in thick, coarse hair—he even sported a long, wavy beard of sorts, and his eyes were the deepest brown I had ever seen. Cow-shit brown. His snout jutted out, emphasizing the golden ring dangling from his glistening nostrils, and both glinted in the luminous glow of the moon. The metal was at least an inch thick and etched with runes of a language long forgotten. Wide, aged ivory horns sprouted from each temple, long enough to skewer a wizard with little effort. He was nude except for a massive beaded necklace and a pair of worn leather boots that were big enough to stomp a size twenty-five imprint in my face if he felt so inclined.

I hoped our blossoming friendship wouldn't end that way. I really did.

Because friends didn't let friends wear boots naked...

Get your copy of OBSIDIAN SON online today!
http://www.shaynesilvers.com/l/38474

*If you enjoyed the **BLADE** or **UNDERWORLD** movies, turn the page to read a*

sample of **DEVIL'S DREAM**—*the first book in the new* **SHADE OF DEVIL** *series*
by Shayne Silvers.
Or get the book ONLINE! *http://www.shaynesilvers.com/l/738833*

*Before the now-infamous Count Dracula ever tasted his first drop of blood, Sorin
Ambrogio owned the night. Humanity fearfully called him the Devil...*

TRY: DEVIL'S DREAM (SHADE OF DEVIL #1)

God damned me.

He—in his infinite, omnipotent wisdom—declared for all to hear…

Let there be pain…

In the exact center of this poor bastard's soul.

And that merciless smiting woke me from a dead sleep and thrust me into a body devoid of every sensation but blinding agony.

I tried to scream but my throat felt as dry as dust, only permitting me to emit a rasping, whistling hiss that brought on yet *more* pain. My skin burned and throbbed while my bones creaked and groaned with each full-body tremor. My claws sunk into a hard surface beneath me and I was distantly surprised they hadn't simply shattered upon contact.

My memory was an immolated ruin—each fragment of thought merely an elusive fleck of ash or ember that danced through my fog of despair as I struggled to catch one and hold onto it long enough to recall what had brought me to this bleak existence. How I had become this poor, wretched, shell of a man. I couldn't even remember my own *name*; it was all I could do to simply survive this profound horror.

After what seemed an eternity, the initial pain began to slowly ebb, but I quickly realized that it had only triggered a cascade of smaller, more numerous tortures—like ripples caused by a boulder thrown into a pond.

I couldn't find the strength to even attempt to open my crusted eyes, and my abdomen was a solid knot of gnawing hunger so overwhelming that I felt like I was being pulled down into the earth by a lead weight. My fingers tingled and burned so fiercely that I wondered if the skin had been peeled away while I slept. Since they were twitching involuntarily, at least I knew that the muscles and tendons were still attached.

I held onto that sliver of joy, that beacon of hope.

I stubbornly gritted my teeth, but even that slight movement made the skin over my face stretch tight enough to almost tear. I willed myself to relax as I tried to process *why* I was in so much pain, where I was, how I had gotten here, and...*who* I even was? A singular thought finally struck me like an echo of the faintest of whispers, giving me something to latch onto.

Hunger.

I let out a crackling gasp of relief at finally grasping an independent answer of some kind, but I was unable to draw enough moisture onto my tongue to properly swallow. Understanding that I was hungry had seemed to alleviate a fraction of my pain. The answer to at least one question distracted me long enough to allow me to think. And despite my hunger, I felt something tantalizingly delicious slowly coursing down my throat, desperately attempting to alleviate my starvation.

Even though my memory was still enshrouded in fog, I was entirely certain that it was incredibly dangerous for me to feel this hungry.

This...*thirsty*. Dangerous for both myself and anyone nearby. I tried to remember why it was so dangerous but the reason eluded me. Instead, an answer to a different question emerged from my mind like a specter from the mist—and I felt myself begin to smile as a modicum of strength slowly took root deep within me.

"Sorin..." I croaked. My voice echoed, letting me know that I was in an enclosed space of some kind. "My name is Sorin Ambrogio. And I need..." I trailed off uncertainly, unable to finish my own thought.

"Blood," a man's deep voice answered from only a few paces away. "You need more blood."

I hissed instinctively, snapping my eyes open for the first time since waking. I had completely forgotten to check my surroundings, too consumed with my own pain to bother with my other senses. I had been asleep so long that even the air seemed to burn my eyes like smoke, forcing me to blink rapidly. No, the air *was* filled with pungent, aromatic smoke, but not like the smoke from the fires in my—

I shuddered involuntarily, blocking out the thought for some unknown reason.

Beneath the pungent smoke, the air was musty and damp. Through it all, I smelled the delicious, coppery scent of hot, powerful blood.

I had been resting atop a raised stone plinth—almost like a table—in a depthless, shadowy cavern. I appreciated the darkness because any light would have likely blinded me in my current state. I couldn't see the man who had spoken, but the area was filled with silhouettes of what appeared to be tables, crates, and other shapes that could easily conceal him. I focused on my hearing and almost instantly noticed a seductively familiar, *beating* sound.

A noise as delightful as a child's first belly-laugh...

A beautiful woman's sigh as she locked eyes with you for the first time.

The gentle crackling of a fireplace on a brisk, snowy night.

Thump-thump.

Thump-thump.

Thump-thump.

The sound became *everything* and my vision slowly began to sharpen, the room brightening into shades of gray. My pain didn't disappear, but it was swiftly muted as I tracked the sound.

I inhaled deeply, my eyes riveting on a far wall as my nostrils flared, pinpointing the source of the savory perfume and the seductive beating sound. I didn't recall sitting up, but I realized that I was suddenly leaning forward and that the room was continuing to brighten into paler shades of gray, burning away the last of the remaining shadows—despite the fact that there was no actual light. And it grew clearer as I focused on the seductive sound.

Until I finally spotted a man leaning against the far wall. *Thump-thump. Thump-thump. Thump-thump...* I licked my lips ravenously, setting my hands on the cool stone table as I prepared to set my feet on the ground.

Food...

The man calmly lifted his hand and a sharp *clicking* sound suddenly echoed from the walls. The room abruptly flooded with light so bright and unexpected that it felt like my eyes had exploded. Worse, what seemed like a trio of radiant stars was not more than a span from my face—so close that I could feel the direct heat from their flare. I recoiled with a snarl, momentarily forgetting all about food as I shielded my eyes with a hand and prepared to defend myself. I leaned away from the bright lights, wondering why I couldn't smell smoke from the flickering flames. I squinted, watching the man's feet for any indication of movement.

Half a minute went by as my vision slowly began to adjust, and the man didn't even shift his weight—almost as if he was granting me time enough to grow accustomed to the sudden light. Which...didn't make any sense. Hadn't it been an attack? I hesitantly lowered my hand from my face, reassessing the situation and my surroundings.

I stared in wonder as I realized that the orbs were not made of flame, but rather what seemed to be pure light affixed to polished metal stands. Looking directly at them hurt, so I studied them sidelong, making sure to also keep the man in my peripheral vision. He had to be a sorcerer of some kind. Who else could wield pure light without fire?

"Easy, Sorin," the man murmured in a calming baritone. "I can't see as well as you in the dark, but it looked like you were about to do something unnecessarily stupid. Let me turn them down a little."

He didn't wait for my reply, but the room slowly dimmed after another clicking sound.

I tried to get a better look at the stranger—wondering where he had come from, where he had taken me, and who he was. One thing was obvious—he knew magic. "Where did you learn this sorcery?" I rasped, gesturing at the orbs of light.

"Um. Hobby Lobby."

"I've never heard of him," I hissed, coughing as a result of my parched throat.

"I'm not even remotely surprised by that," he said dryly. He extended his other hand and I gasped to see an impossibility—a transparent bag as clear as new glass. And it was *flexible*, swinging back and forth like a bulging coin purse or a clear water-skin. My momentary wonder at the magical material evaporated as I recognized the crimson liquid *inside* the bag.

Blood.

He lobbed it at me underhanded without a word of warning. I hissed as I desperately—and with exceeding caution—caught it from the air lest it fall and break open. I gasped as the clear bag of blood settled into my palms and, before I consciously realized it, I tore off the corner with my fangs, pressed it to my lips, and squeezed the bag in one explosive, violent gesture. The ruby fluid gushed into my mouth and over my face, dousing my almost forgotten pain as swiftly as a bucket of water thrown on hot coals.

I felt my eyes roll back into my skull and my body shuddered as I lost my balance and fell from the stone table. I landed on my back but I was too overwhelmed to care as I stretched out my arms and legs. I groaned in rapture, licking at my lips like a wild animal. The ruby nectar was a living serpent of molten oil as it slithered down into my stomach, nurturing and healing me almost instantly. It was the most wonderful sensation I could imagine—almost enough to make me weep.

Like a desert rain, my parched tongue and throat absorbed the blood so quickly and completely that I couldn't even savor the heady flavor. This wasn't a joyful feast; this was survival, a necessity. My body guzzled it, instantly using the liquid to repair the damage, pain, and the cloud of fog that had enshrouded me.

I realized that I was laughing. The sound echoed into the vast stone space like rolling thunder.

Because I had remembered something else.

The world's First Vampire was *back*.

And he was still *very* hungry.

Get the full book ONLINE! http://www.shaynesilvers.com/l/738833

Check out Shayne's other books. He's written a few without Cameron helping him. Some of them are marginally decent—easily a 4 out of 10.

MAKE A DIFFERENCE

Reviews are the most powerful tools in our arsenal when it comes to getting attention for our books. Much as we'd like to, we don't have the financial muscle of a New York publisher.

But we do have something much more powerful and effective than that, and it's something that those publishers would kill to get their hands on.

A committed and loyal bunch of readers.

Honest reviews of our books help bring them to the attention of other readers.

If you've enjoyed this book, we would be very grateful if you could spend just five minutes leaving a review on our book's Amazon page.

Thank you very much in advance.

ACKNOWLEDGMENTS

From Cameron:

I'd like to thank Shayne, for paving the way in style. Kori, for an introduction that would change my life. My three wonderful sisters, for showing me what a strong, independent woman looks and sounds like. And, above all, my parents, for—literally—everything.

From Shayne (the self-proclaimed prettiest one):

Team Temple and the Den of Freaks on Facebook have become family to me. I couldn't do it without die-hard readers like them.

I would also like to thank you, the reader. I hope you enjoyed reading *HURRICANE* as much as we enjoyed writing it. Be sure to check out the two crossover series in the TempleVerse: **The Nate Temple Series** and the **Feathers and Fire Series**.

And last, but definitely not least, I thank my wife, Lexy. Without your support, none of this would have been possible.

ABOUT CAMERON O'CONNELL

Cameron O'Connell is a Jack-of-All-Trades and Master of Some.

He writes The Phantom Queen Diaries, a series in The TempleVerse, about Quinn MacKenna, a mouthy black magic arms dealer trading favors in Boston. All she wants? A round-trip ticket to the Fae realm...and maybe a drink on the house.

A former member of the United States military, a professional model, and English teacher, Cameron finds time to write in the mornings after his first cup of coffee...and in the evenings after his thirty-seventh. Follow him, and the TempleVerse founder, Shayne Silvers, online for all sorts of insider tips, giveaways, and new release updates!

Get Down with Cameron Online

facebook.com/Cameron-OConnell-788806397985289

amazon.com/author/cameronoconnell

bookbub.com/authors/cameron-o-connell

twitter.com/thecamoconnell

instagram.com/camoconnellauthor

goodreads.com/cameronoconnell

ABOUT SHAYNE SILVERS

Shayne is a man of mystery and power, whose power is exceeded only by his mystery...

He currently writes the Amazon Bestselling **Nate Temple** Series, which features a foul-mouthed wizard from St. Louis. He rides a bloodthirsty unicorn, drinks with Achilles, and is pals with the Four Horsemen.

He also writes the Amazon Bestselling **Feathers and Fire** Series—a second series in the TempleVerse. The story follows a rookie spell-slinger named Callie Penrose who works for the Vatican in Kansas City. Her problem? Hell seems to know more about her past than she does.

He coauthors **The Phantom Queen Diaries**—a third series set in The TempleVerse—with Cameron O'Connell. The story follows Quinn MacKenna, a mouthy black magic arms dealer in Boston. All she wants? A round-trip ticket to the Fae realm...and maybe a drink on the house.

He also writes the **Shade of Devil Series**, which tells the story of Sorin Ambrogio—the world's FIRST vampire. He was put into a magical slumber by a Native American Medicine Man when the Americas were first discovered by Europeans. Sorin wakes up after five-hundred years to learn that his protege, Dracula, stole his reputation and that no one has ever even heard of Sorin Ambrogio. The streets of New York City will run with blood as Sorin reclaims his legend.

Shayne holds two high-ranking black belts, and can be found writing in a coffee shop, cackling madly into his computer screen while pounding shots of espresso. He's hard at work on the newest books in the TempleVerse—You can find updates on new releases or chronological reading order on the next page, his website, or any of his social media accounts. **Follow him online for all sorts of groovy goodies, giveaways, and new release updates:**

BOOKS BY THE AUTHORS

CHRONOLOGY: *All stories in the TempleVerse are shown in chronological order on the following page*

PHANTOM QUEEN DIARIES

(Set in the TempleVerse)

by Cameron O'Connell & Shayne Silvers

COLLINS (Prequel novella #0 in the 'LAST CALL' anthology)

WHISKEY GINGER

COSMOPOLITAN

OLD FASHIONED

MOTHERLUCKER (Novella #3.5 in the 'LAST CALL' anthology)

DARK AND STORMY

MOSCOW MULE

WITCHES BREW

SALTY DOG

SEA BREEZE

HURRICANE

NATE TEMPLE SERIES

(Main series in the TempleVerse)

by Shayne Silvers

FAIRY TALE - FREE prequel novella #0 for my subscribers

OBSIDIAN SON

BLOOD DEBTS

GRIMM

SILVER TONGUE

BEAST MASTER

BEERLYMPIAN (Novella #5.5 in the 'LAST CALL' anthology)

TINY GODS

DADDY DUTY (Novella #6.5)

WILD SIDE

WAR HAMMER

NINE SOULS

HORSEMAN

LEGEND

KNIGHTMARE

ASCENSION

FEATHERS AND FIRE SERIES

(Also set in the TempleVerse)

by Shayne Silvers

UNCHAINED

RAGE

WHISPERS

ANGEL'S ROAR

MOTHERLUCKER (Novella #4.5 in the 'LAST CALL' anthology)

SINNER

BLACK SHEEP

GODLESS

CHRONOLOGICAL ORDER: TEMPLEVERSE

FAIRY TALE (TEMPLE PREQUEL)

OBSIDIAN SON (TEMPLE 1)

BLOOD DEBTS (TEMPLE 2)

GRIMM (TEMPLE 3)

SILVER TONGUE (TEMPLE 4)

BEAST MASTER (TEMPLE 5)

BEERLYMPIAN (TEMPLE 5.5)

TINY GODS (TEMPLE 6)

SHADE OF DEVIL SERIES

(Not part of the TempleVerse)

by Shayne Silvers

DEVIL'S CRY
DEVIL'S BLOOD

Made in the USA
Coppell, TX
14 January 2022

71638277R10163